Passing the RED LINE

CHICAGO DARK KNIGHTS BOOK 2

JOCELYNE SOTO

Edits by My Brother's Editor

Proofing by My Brother's Editor

2nd Proofing by Becky at Bookcase Media

Cover by Cat @ TRC Designs

CONTENTS

The majority of my life has centered around one thing and one thing only.

Hockey.

Being the daughter of a player, I know the ins and outs of the sport. Including the hurt that can come with it.

I've grown to hate it.

That hate runs so deep that when a player steps into my life in a towel, I do everything I can to hate him too.

After a few summer nights, though, it starts to become impossible.

Especially as the season starts and we spend more time together when I take the position as lead photographer on his team.

The same team my dad coaches.

Now I'm back in the hockey world, falling for a grumpy hockey player I should want nothing to do with and dealing with my dad and his apologies.

Fingers crossed being back in this world doesn't hurt me anymore than it already has.

PLAYLIST

Players - Con Leroy
Here With Me - d4vd
Lipstick Lover - Janelle Monáe
Baby - Eslabon Armado
Alone -Jozzy
bad idea! - girl in red
Falling - Trevor Daniel
Noche De Sexo - Wins & Yandel, Romeo Santos
If I Ruled the World - Nas, Ms. Lauryn Hill
Lost - Frank Ocean
Angel Baby - Troye Sivan
I wanna Be Yours - Sofia Karlberg
Call Out My Name - The Weeknd
Falling for U - Peachy!, mxmtoon
I don't rly like u - Role Model
Baby I'm Yours - Arctic Monkey

Love - Keyshia Cole
Open Arms - SZA, Travis Scott
K-Pop - Travis Scott, Bad Bunny
All of the Girls You Loved Before - Taylor Swift

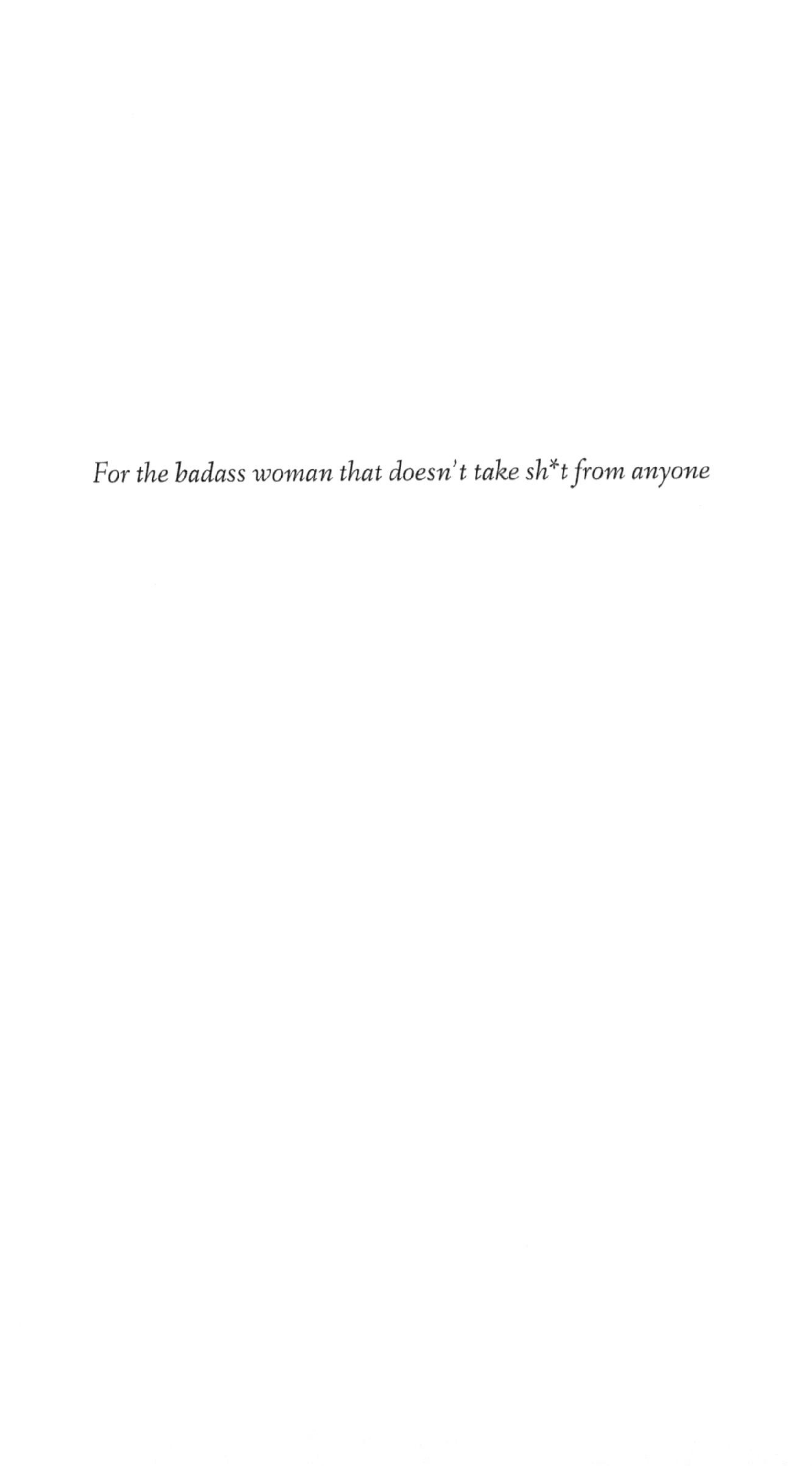

*For the badass woman that doesn't take sh*t from anyone*

PROLOGUE
ELIANA

18 years old

IT'S MY SENIOR YEAR.

The year where I should still be acting like a kid before getting thrown into the grown-up world. I should be out enjoying life before heading off to college. I should be partying and drinking with my friends. Going to football games, all while pretending that I actually care about the sport and having the time of my life. I should be looking for a dress for prom next month and picking out outfits for my European trip this summer.

I should be doing so many fun things and enjoying these last few weeks of freedom, but instead, I'm stuck attending hockey games on a Saturday.

Well, I shouldn't say stuck since I *chose* to be here, but still. I could be spending my time doing something a lot more productive than spending all day in an arena with a bunch of parents who think their kid is the next NHL legend.

Newsflash. There's a ninety-nine-point-nine percent chance that they aren't.

Don't get me wrong, I love hockey, I do, but I learned at a very young age that there is more to life than a stick and a puck. More to living than spending every waking hour on the ice shooting a rubber disc or doing speed drills.

This thinking is something that comes from being the daughter of an NHL player. It's something my mom drilled into my head from the bright age of five. Hockey is not the most important thing in the world. There are other things that make life happy and bright.

That thinking, though, is not something that has been able to make it through the heads of my father or my boyfriend.

My dad I get, since hockey has been a part of his life since he was about two, and it continued well into adulthood with a professional career. And it's going to continue since he just got offered the head coach position with the Chicago Dark Knights.

How he was able to step away from hockey for a bit to get married and have a kid is beyond me. That man made hockey his everything, and it's part of the reason why he and my mom are now divorced, and I see him only once a month.

As for my boyfriend, he has also been playing since he was about two. He's good and according to my dad, has the potential to go places, but the dude can't go ten minutes without mentioning anything not related to the damn sport.

We've been together for close to a year, and at first it was cute how much he talked about the sport he loved, but after a while, it got annoying.

But nonetheless, I'm the supportive girlfriend and attend every single game.

Which is why I'm currently in a random ice rink three hours from home on a lovely Saturday, cheering on my boyfriend, Kalen, in his second game of the day.

I would much rather be shopping with my best friend, but I'm here, sitting next to my boyfriend's parents, surviving on snack bar nachos and room temperature water.

"Peter," Kalen's mom, Liz, says, nudging her husband. "Peter," she says again, trying to get the man's attention.

It takes a full minute for him to acknowledge his wife.

"What, Liz?" he asks, almost annoyed that she would interrupt him while the game is going on.

You're here because of Kalen. You are here because of Kalen.

I tell myself, trying my hardest not to let my dislike for his parents bother me as much as it usually does. They are good people when they want to be.

"Is that a scout over there?" Liz asks, pointing to a man a few rows down.

Both Peter and I look over to where she is pointing, and right away, I can see why she would think he was a scout. The way the man is watching the game and quickly typing on his phone a few seconds later gives it away.

I've been to enough hockey games in my lifetime to be

able to spot one. Hell, I know a few of them because they are buddies with my dad.

The man that Liz is pointing at is in fact a scout. Do I know him? Doubt it.

Peter is not even able to answer before Liz starts talking again.

"I think it is. He has to be here for Kalen," Liz states, practically jumping up and down in her seat.

A part of me wants to burst her bubble and say that if the man is a scout, there's maybe less than a two percent chance he's here for Kalen. There's a higher chance he's here for one of the opponents, but I'm not that cruel.

"Do you think he's here for Kalen, Lia?" she asks me, turning to give me a smile that tells me that I should agree with her or end up on her bad side. A smile that I know well.

I give her a nod and a small smile back. "Yeah, he could be."

She doesn't like my answer because she scoffs and turns back to her husband. "I'm going to go talk to him and introduce myself."

I'm not the only one that thinks that's a bad idea because Peter finally gives his wife more than ten seconds of his attention.

"And why would you do that?" he asks, looking at her like she's crazy.

"Because someone has to put our son's name out there, unlike some people who won't even pull strings with their father."

A direct hit in my direction.

Ever since Kalen and I started becoming more than just friends over a year and a half ago, I've been told by both his parents that I should put in a good word for him with my dad. What they don't know is that from the start of our relationship, I've tried so hard to get my dad to notice him. He's even gone to a few of his games.

And while my dad thinks Kalen is good and has the potential to go places, he doesn't think he's NHL material. This is something that he has told me and something that I've come to realize on my own these last few months.

Kalen isn't a great team player, which is ironic to say the least.

I don't say anything as Peter looks at me with a completely blank stare. I just keep my face as neutral as possible to hide the fact that their words affect me.

It's like they think that I don't give a shit about Kalen or his hockey career.

I care. I'm here every game. I tried talking to my dad. What more can I do?

Peter nods at his wife, and with a huff, she stands up from her seat and starts making her way down to the man who may or may not be a scout.

I don't say anything.

If they want to make things harder for their son, then so be it. I'm just an eighteen-year-old girl. I have no sway in the NHL world, no matter who my dad is.

Ignoring Liz and her determination to get her son's name out there, I turn my attention back to the ice.

It takes me a second to find number ten on the ice, and

when I do, I can't help but smile. I might find it annoying that all he talks about is hockey, but that doesn't mean that I'm not proud of my boyfriend. I am, and I tell him after every single game.

I just hope that he is able to make his dreams come true and not let his ego or his parents get in the way.

Five minutes after she left, Liz comes back to her seat with a not-so -pleased look on her face. Things went badly with the possible scout; I just know it.

Am I a horrible person for wanting to laugh?

"What's up with you?" Peter asks as soon as she sits down.

She goes on this whole tangent about how the man was so rude to her, but halfway through I close my ears to her and try to concentrate on the game.

The operative word being 'try' because my attention is quickly drawn to someone down by the ice.

Ninety-nine percent of the time, I don't think too deeply about the reason why an individual wears something. What they wear is none of my concern.

But seeing what this individual is wearing has so many scenarios running through my head.

Why?

Because this person, this *girl*, is wearing my boyfriend's number on her back. I usually don't give a shit, but this shirt definitely doesn't look like she bought it through the team and most definitely looks like she made it herself.

Interesting.

Have I seen her before? Maybe I have, and I'm just

noticing because she's wearing Kalen's number. Maybe she has a shirt for every player, and I'm reading way too much into it.

She must be someone's sister and is here supporting her brother's team, and today is Kalen's turn in her never-ending rotation of shirts.

That has to be it.

For the next ten minutes or so, that's what I try to convince myself of, and by the end of the third period, I'm almost there, but then it all goes in the trash the second the final buzzer sounds through the arena.

Kalen's team lost, and instead of skating off the ice with teammates after shaking hands with the other team, he skates over to the girl with the number on his back, and he fucking kisses her!

What the actual fuck?!

I'm seeing things. I have to be fucking seeing things because no way in actual hell am I witnessing my boyfriend kiss another girl while I'm only about fifty feet away, sitting next to his parents.

No fucking way!

"Oh, look. Layla is already with Kalen," Liz says as she starts getting up from her seat to head down to ice level.

Layla?

Who the fuck is *Layla?*

And how does Liz know her? Better yet, why the fuck is Liz not freaking out about the fact that her son is kissing another girl in front of me?!

"Who is Layla?" I find myself asking, finally taking my

eyes off Kalen and whoever the fuck this Layla chick is and looking over at Liz.

I think something clicks in Liz when I ask the question because for the first time tonight she is speechless.

She doesn't even have to answer my question, I already know it by the expression on her face.

Layla is Kalen's side piece.

The asshole has been cheating on me.

How the fuck did I not see this?

I go to every single one of his games. I spend almost every single moment outside of school and family activities with him, and yet, and *yet,* the asshole still found a way to fucking cheat?

Did I miss the signs? Has he been acting all dodgy and I missed it completely? I know that my head has been on all things fun this year, but I sure as hell would have noticed something that told me he has someone on the side.

Right?

Right?!

I don't know.

What I do know is that I'm so fucking done.

Not giving a shit, I stand up from my seat and start making my way down to the ice.

"Lia, honey. Please wait," Liz says behind me, trying to be sweet.

I ignore her. If she wanted to be sweet, she should have had my back the second she found out her son was cheating on me. Any ounce of respect I had for the lady is completely gone.

Who the fuck lets her son cheat on someone and is okay with it?

People dodge me as I make my way down to the first row of seats, as they should. Because I'm seeing fucking red watching my boyfriend continue his make-out session with another girl.

They pull apart as soon as I'm about five feet away. Like it makes any fucking difference.

"You shouldn't have come," Kalen says to the redhead in front of him, stroking her cheek.

I don't let her respond. I just chime in.

"Oh, she totally should have. Because if she hadn't, then I wouldn't have found out that you are a two-timing asshat, mommy's boy."

The two individuals in front of me jump and separate from each other before they both turn to look at me with wide eyes.

"Who are you?" Layla says, her voice so small and full of shock.

I almost feel bad for her.

"His girlfriend. Oh, actually scratch that. His *ex-girlfriend.*"

Layla is looking at me like she didn't know that Kalen had a girlfriend. That this is all as much of a surprise to her as it is to me and is about to cry. All the while, her boy toy is looking at me like he can't believe he got caught.

Did he forget I was in the stands?

I come to every fucking game!

Now I'm really done.

"Fuck you!" I say shoving a finger into my so-called boyfriend's chest, before turning to his side piece. "And fuck you, too."

Given the tears in her eyes, she really didn't know that Kalen had a girlfriend, so I shouldn't be mad at her, but I don't really give a shit.

I start walking away, and as I do; I hear my name being called behind me.

"Lia, wait." Kalen says, skating along the boards.

I don't bother turning around.

"Eliana!" he yells, and when there is an opening in the boards, he grabs my arm and pulls me to a stop.

"Tell me, Kal," I say, turning and pulling my arm from his grip. "Why the fuck did you stay with me if you had eyes on someone else? You could have saved yourself a lot of explaining, if you would have called it quits when you met little miss redhead over there."

Kalen looks at me for a long minute before letting out a sigh and letting his head sag to his chest.

"I wanted you to put in a good word for me with your dad."

My worst possible nightmare has come true.

"Is that why you're with me? Because of my *dad?*" Never has a boy made me want to cry until this very moment.

The asshole in front of me doesn't even look up. He just gives me a nod.

I'm a fucking fool.

I should have expected this. I should have known that at

some point in my life someone was going to use me to get to my dad. Never did I think it was going to be Kalen.

Stupid girl.

"Fuck you," I spit out and start walking away again, and like before, Kalen stops me.

"Can you still put in a good word for me, though?" he asks, actually looking sincere.

The audacity, the fucking audacity of this boy. And I do mean boy because even though he's eighteen years old, and technically an adult, there is nothing manly about him.

I slap a smile on my face. "Sure." Kalen's face lights up. "I'll tell him that you broke his little girl's heart by not keeping your dick in your pants. Let's see how he feels about that."

If I was the violent type, I would slap this asshole across the face, but that's not the person that I am. So, without a last look at Kalen, the boy who I thought would be my everything, I walk out of the arena.

As soon as I'm in the parking lot, I pull out my phone and call the only person that I can think of to pick me up.

My dad.

He's a lot closer to me than Mom is, distance-wise. He'll pick me up. I'll tell him what Kalen did, and after he punches the asshole in the face, he will drive me home and lecture me the whole way about not dating pussy-ass bitches who don't deserve me and then buy me ice cream to make me feel better.

He'll be there for me when I need him the most. I know he will.

But as the phone rings and rings, and eventually goes to voicemail, my hope dies down a little. I call him again, and the same thing happens.

Three times I call him and three times he doesn't answer.

On the last call, tears finally escape my eyes.

My dad isn't picking up, and he's not going to come to get me.

At this very moment, I realize something—I fucking hate hockey players.

They disappoint and hurt you every chance they get.

CHAPTER ONE

ELIANA

Present Day - 10 years later

I DON'T KNOW what triggered it.

In all the years since it happened, I haven't let myself think about the time that my dad didn't answer his phone during what I thought was one of the toughest days of my life.

To some people something as simple as not answering the phone and making your daughter wait a total of six hours before picking her up, would be something that they could easily get over. Something that they could possibly laugh about during birthdays and Christmas dinners.

For me, that moment was the turning point in my current relationship with my dad, so the less I think about it, the better.

Even though it was a very short period in my life, but that very short period showed me that there are certain times in this life where I don't matter. Even to my father.

That moment has a hold on me, and I try to bury it as often as I can.

But apparently, I don't bury those memories deep enough because that day pops up when I least expect it.

Take right now for example. I'm in the back of a rideshare on my way to interview for a new job. A permanent job. I shouldn't be thinking about that day.

Yet I am.

Maybe it's being in Chicago.

Maybe it's the job itself.

Who am I kidding? I know exactly what triggered my trip down memory lane. It's the city, the job I'm interviewing for, and my father all wrapped up together in one.

Why I torture myself like this is beyond me.

I'm here, though. I shouldn't be, but I am. No matter the shit relationship I have with my father and his favorite sport, the offer that landed in my email a few weeks ago was way too good for me to ignore. But now, I'm second guessing everything.

Out of all the job assignment emails to land in my inbox, this is one that I should have scrolled past it and let it get lost in the other thousands of unopened emails.

I shouldn't have let my curiosity get the best of me. But I did, and I did indeed open the email that had the words "Dark Knights Team Photographer opening" in the subject line.

At first, I thought it was something that my dad had orchestrated as a way to repair our relationship, like he has been trying to do for the last couple of years. A cruel way to make me spend time with him outside of our quarterly dinners.

For a minute, I was pissed off thinking that he probably made his team fire someone to give me into this position. Then I read the email.

It was an email straight from the assistant to the Dark Knights' marketing and communications director. An email mentioning how they had seen my work for other sports teams and loved it, that they would like for me to come interview for the photographer position that is opening up at the start of the next season.

They praised my work and didn't mention my dad or my connection to the team once.

I read through the email a total of five times to make sure that I was reading it correctly. After the sixth time, it finally clicked, and the second it did, I got excited.

They wanted me for my work, not for my connections. It could be that my dad might have mentioned my name or told the team that he had a daughter that was a photographer. But the way they wrote the email told me otherwise.

So instead of ignoring it, I replied and accepted the invitation to interview.

If I get the job offer and accept it, I will be seeing my dad a lot more often than I do now and work in a sport I vowed to hate for the rest of my life. I think I'll be able to handle it. Fingers crossed.

But first things first.

I have to get out of the car, walk into the arena, and actually get through with the interview.

The driver pulled up to the Dark Knights' arena a whole minute ago, and I have yet to reach for the door handle and push myself out of the car.

From the window, the arena taunts me.

Especially with the big-ass banner hanging down the side with my dad's face on it.

Who puts the face of their head coach on a banner?

Shouldn't that spot be reserved for the players who are going to fill the seats?

If it were up to me, I would put the Knights' top enforcer, Christian Rodriguez, there.

He's killing it this season, and he's definitely a bigger draw than my dad. In my own honest opinion.

If I get this job, the first thing I'm going to do is schedule a photoshoot and get that banner taken down.

I don't know why seeing his face bothers me so much, but it does.

I really need to work on my daddy issues.

"Are you okay?" The driver's voice pulls my attention away from my plan to take my dad's banner down.

I almost forgot I wasn't in the car alone.

"Yeah, all good. Thanks so much for the ride," I say to him and throw him a smile before finally pushing the door open.

The March wind still has a bit of a bite to it, but it's a welcoming bite that serves as a distraction as I make my way over to the main door of the building.

In the years since my dad became the head coach for the team, I've only been here a handful of times. Once or twice for basketball games and a few other times when I was trying to appease my dad, and I telling myself be a better daughter.

Never have I been here in a professional capacity, so I have no sense of direction. Thankfully a security guard is there to guide me.

"You look familiar," the older gentleman tells me as he leads me to the elevator bank.

I turn to look at the security guard, who introduced himself as Gus and playfully narrow my eyes at him.

"Did we go out, and I didn't call you back?" I ask, trying really hard to not let my smile slip.

Gus's cheeks get a little red, and when he realizes that I'm joking, he lets out a chuckle.

"Darling, if we were to go out to dinner, I would be your first call the next day," he throws me a wink, and I can't help but finally let my smile escape. "A young girl like you would have the best night of her life with someone my age."

No doubt about that. The friendly security guard has to be in his seventies. And if I had to guess, he has a long list of stories to tell that could make a night worthwhile.

"Well, maybe if I get this job, we can go to lunch together and see if that is true," I say, throwing a wink at him.

Another hearty chuckle escapes him. "I will hold you to it. What's your name again, darling?" Gus asks as soon as we get into the elevator.

Here I was trying to deflect, but I guess nothing gets by Gus.

"Eliana," I tell him.

Everyone in my life calls me Ellie after I abandoned the

nickname Lia when I was eighteen. Nobody calls me by my full name, not outside of a professional setting that is. Gus says he recognizes me, and maybe he does. For all I know, my dad is friends with the guy and has shown him a picture of me, but one thing I'm sure of. My dad wouldn't call me Eliana. He never has unless he was angry with me.

So, Gus here, won't know that name.

Which is better for me.

I don't need this friendly security guard letting my dad know that I'm within a mile of him, even if I am prepared to see him today.

For a good twenty seconds, Gus's face goes through the whole process of trying to figure out if my name is familiar to him or not. I'm about to give myself a high five for dodging the father bullet, but the second the man in front of me smiles, I know I'm going to have to make a trip down to my dad's office as soon as I'm done here.

Fucking fantastic.

"You're Coach Anderson's daughter, aren't you? He has a picture of you on his desk. I knew your name sounded familiar. I just couldn't pinpoint it," Gus tells me, a belly laugh rolling through the elevator.

My dad has a picture of me on his desk? I didn't know that.

It has to be one from when I was a kid because I can't remember my dad taking a picture of me the last few years that would be worthy of his desk.

I'm going to need to stop by his office after this to see it for myself.

Nodding, I answer Gus's question. "I am, and here I thought nobody would know he even had a daughter."

I thought the Knight's captain, Liam Crawford, was the only one who knew about my father having a daughter. Mostly because me and daddy dearest had an okay relationship during Liam's rookie year, so I was around a bit more, and over the years, the captain and I have become friends.

"Coach Anderson is quiet about a lot of things, but on the occasion, he'll mention his daughter and how good her photography work is," Gus says to me, his smile growing like a proud grandpa.

Huh.

First the picture on his desk, and now he talks about me? And tells people he's proud of me? What the actual fuck?

Is this some sort of sign from the universe that I have to try to repair my relationship with my dad?

Maybe.

Am I going to listen to said signs?

Maybe.

I need to concentrate on this interview first. Once that's done, I will think about fixing my parental relationship for what feels like the hundredth time.

"Well, I'm glad my dad has told you about me," I tell Gus, as the elevator doors slide open with a little more honesty in my words than I expected.

"If I see him, I'll let him know that you are here," He answers, throwing me a wave as I walk out of the steel box.

Great.

"Thanks, Gus," I say, thanking him for guiding me up to

where I needed to go, not for him wanting to tell my father that I'm here.

"Of course. Have a great interview, Miss Eliana." My new friend throws a wave in my direction before the elevator doors close, and he's gone.

With Gus gone, I'm left standing in a hallway facing two big glass doors that have a huge Dark Knights logo right in the center.

As an artist, the Knights logo is my absolute favorite in all of sports. There's something about it that just fits so perfectly with the team and the city. There is no other logo like it. And maybe it's just me, but it has almost a vigilante-of-the-night kind of feel to it.

Like whoever named the team really liked he caped crusader himself and thought it was the best idea in the world to name a hockey team after him. And honestly, it works.

You're distracting yourself.

I am.

For years, I told myself that I was happy traveling and it being just me and my camera. When it came to settling down in one place, I thought it would be in my forties and I'd take it one day at a time.

But when the email from the Knights landed in my inbox, a part of me relaxed because if I was able to get the job, I wouldn't have to think about where or when my next assignment would be. I would have a steady paycheck and not have to worry about whether I can afford a roof over my head for the next two months.

It was like a wave of relief washed over me that I wasn't

expecting. Especially given that if I were to end up doing it, I would be working for the same team as my dad.

Now here I am, about to walk into an interview that could let me settle down, sweating through my blouse.

"I can do this. I can *do* this." I square my shoulders and push open the glass door to walk into the madness that is an NHL team's front office.

I guess this is what it's like when your team is on a hot streak and has a high chance of making it to the playoffs. Madness, madness anywhere.

"Are you Eliana?" A female voice says from my right as soon as the door closes behind me.

Turning, I find a woman who looks about my age standing a few feet away from me with a smile on her face.

"I am," I say, walking over to her and extending my hand.

"It's nice to meet you. I'm Heather, and I'll be the person you are meeting with today. I'm so glad you were able to make it."

"Me, too," I say to her, really meaning it.

"Should we get started? Your email said that you were just finishing up an assignment down in Puerto Rico, and I want to hear all about it." Heather guides me to a conference room, and for the next two hours we talk about everything.

What the position entails. A handful of my assignments and if I have any knowledge about hockey or the hockey world. When I told her just how extensive my knowledge of the sport really is, I knew I had the job in the bag.

The team's photographer is retiring at the end of the season, so I would start the position at the beginning of the next season. I have a summer gig lined up in California and nothing after that so if I get the job, it would all work out perfectly.

"So, I think I have everything that we need. The team loves your work," Heather tells me, giving me a big smile that I can't help but return.

"I'm glad." My words may not project it, but I'm bursting at the seams to jump from my seat and start giggling like a madwoman.

"Is there anything you want to add to the interview before I go and draw up the official offer letter?"

This whole interview has been about my work and how I would be perfect for this position. The whole time, there has been no mention of my family background.

As much as I want to keep who my dad is a secret, I have to tell her. I can't start a job with secrets.

"Actually, yes." I start, squaring my shoulders again like I did when I first walked in here. "You should know that the name Eliana Solis is what I use professionally. My legal name is Eliana Solis-Anderson, as in Dark Knights' head coach Shawn Anderson. I'm his daughter."

"Oh," Heather answers, surprised, but she quickly fixes her expression. "I didn't even know that Coach Anderson had a daughter. Maybe if I had, this whole process would have been a whole lot easier."

I let out a laugh with her, but it's a little strained. "So, me being his daughter isn't a problem?"

Heather shakes her head. "Of course not. The Knights

are a family blood or otherwise, and your work speaks for itself. We would have hired you without Shawn either way."

I let out a fist pump in my head.

"Great," I say, my smile stretching so big, it's hurting my cheeks.

"Great. Well, Eliana, I would love to welcome you to the Dark Knight family."

Never did I ever think I was going to walk willingly back into the hockey world, especially after it has hurt me countless of times. Yet here I am.

I'm officially a Knight, even though I still hate hockey and some of its players.

Maybe with time, that hate will go away.

Fingers crossed because I can't do my new job with a resting bitch face.

CHAPTER TWO

ELIANA

Four Months Later

I WAS WRONG.

If my hate for the hockey world hadn't dwindled in the ten years since it first betrayed me, why did I think that three months would make the difference? No idea.

It's been four months since I accepted the position with the Knights, and while I'm excited to start working in a few weeks, I can't help but to second guess accepting the position.

And it has nothing to do with my dad like I thought it would.

Coach Anderson was surprisingly happy that the team offered me the position and that I took it.

The way he smiled and hugged me when I told him threw me off, but I hugged him back and for the first time in years, I thought about what it would feel like to have a decent relationship with my dad. Me taking this job might be a step in the right direction for us, a direction that I know my mom would be happy about.

Taking this job might be good for me and my dad, *but* there are other aspects of this sport that made me hate this world, and the number one aspect on the list is my ex-boyfriend.

Kalen Bradford.

The cheating asshole was the first tipping point of my hatred for my favorite sport. The second was everything that came after our breakup. All the torture he put me through.

For almost nine years, I hadn't talk to him, seen him, or even thought about him. He hurt me too much to want anything to do with him. Yet a month after I take a job in Chicago, the bastard decides to send me a message on social media asking me how I've been. There is no such thing as a coincidence with this man.

I should have ignored the message, and for a few weeks I did, but then he sent another congratulating me on the new job, and I gave in and responded. It was a moment of weakness. One that I regretted instantly, and one that I'm still kicking myself in the ass for.

How he found out about my new job is beyond me, since the team hasn't even announced anything, and won't, not until at least August, and I only told a handful of people. But he knows and now is trying to use that bit of news to get on my good side. Not going to happen. Not in a million years.

My guess is that Kalen wants to play for the Knights, and

he thinks the way to do that is to go through me. That we would get friendly again, and I would talk to my dad about possibly trading for him.

Well sucks for him because it didn't work ten years ago and it sure as hell won't work now. Especially after everything that he put me through. If things had been different when we had broken up, I might have considered it, but they weren't. He can kiss my ass.

Since we broke up, I've been keeping minimal tabs on my asshole ex. Mostly because I never wanted to be in the same state as him.

He made it to the NHL after being drafted at twenty and signed with Vancouver after graduating from Buffalo State.

He's an okay player, spending most of his time on the second line, in the penalty box or even suspended, and has a lot of growing to do. But he can be beneficial player if or when someone gets hurt, and he knows that. And that opinion comes strictly from a former hockey fan. As his ex-girlfriend, he is horrible and would not benefit a team in any way.

Since the Dark Knights just won the Stanley Cup, and I'm now working for them, I can see why he would be contacting me.

But I'm putting my foot down. I'm not going to let the cheating bastard make me regret taking this job.

I'm doing this for me, and even if I don't get back something that he took away from me all those years ago, I will be okay.

God, thinking about that asshole puts me in a sour mood.

I need to get my head back on straight.

"For the rest of summer, no more thoughts of Kalen the cheater," I say to myself as I drive down the coastal highway.

Before taking the job with the Knights, I had planned on spending the entire summer in California working as a freelance photographer for one of the soccer teams.

The job started about three weeks ago, and I'm loving being under the California sun.

There's something calming about hearing the waves of the ocean crashing against land.

In all the traveling that I've done throughout my adult life, that one sound has always found a way to ground me and make me stop and think about the direction I want things to go in. It's not a sound that I hear very often, so when I do have it in my vicinity, I try to take it in as much as I possibly can.

As someone who grew up in Minnesota, the closest thing we had to an actual beach was a lake. I had never understood why people loved the beaches that the west coast had to offer so much. Now I do.

Days like today make me so damn happy I chose to become a photographer. I can travel anywhere, whenever I want, and get to explore the beauty that the world has to offer.

The photo session I had today with the soccer team ended a lot earlier than I thought it would, so I decided to spend the rest of my day at the beach and relax as much as I can. Take in as much sun as I can because Chicago has brutal winters, and I've got to keep my tan up as much as possible.

A pale and pasty Eliana is not a happy Eliana.

I've been waiting for a day like today since I landed in San Francisco. Thankfully, I planned ahead and went to the store as soon as I got here and bought all the beach essentials I needed to keep in the trunk of my rental. I even got a little cooler that I fill up every morning with food and drinks. I wanted to keep things handy just in case the craziness hit me, and I wanted to hear the waves crash.

Today, I'm thanking myself for thinking ahead.

I drove for a good thirty minutes before I found the perfect beach hidden by a residential area. After I find parking, I grab my stuff from the trunk, and I make my way down to the shore, settling myself close to an old lifeguard shack.

The second that I slide off my shorts and my butt hits the chair, I start to relax.

The beach is almost deserted, with only a few people along the length of the shore. The sun is out and shining perfectly, and the sound and smell of the ocean take me to a happy place. A place where I don't have to think about work, my ex, or even the text messages from my dad that are waiting to be answered.

Just me, the sun, the waves, and the sand between my toes. Pure serenity.

Well, at least for about twenty minutes it's pure serenity. My sweet peace and quiet is quickly ruined when music starts to blare from somewhere close by.

Everything was so damn peaceful with the occasional

word being spoken by a stranger walking by or dog barking while they were playing catch. I was able to handle those sounds. I was able to handle mild interruptions.

What I can't handle is nineties rap filling the silence and getting louder by the minute.

Don't get me wrong, I love nineties rap, but not when I'm trying to have a peaceful afternoon to myself.

Shaking my head, I reach for my bag, and start looking for my noise canceling headphones. I take nearly everything out and come up empty.

I know I put them in there this morning, I even used them at the soccer field.

A sigh escapes my lips. I must have either left them at the field or left them in the car. I could go check, but I'm way too comfortable to walk all the way back to where I parked right now. Great.

Just ignore it.

Right.

Just ignore it.

I can do that. I can totally pretend that there isn't any music blaring and just close my eyes and continue to take in the sun.

I try to repeat the whole "just ignore it" mantra as I close my eyes, lean my head back and try to concentrate solely on the waves.

I try but fail when the music gets even louder.

"Seriously? What the actual fuck?" I say, my eyes popping open and looking around the beach to find the culprit. Whoever it is, they're going to get a good kick in the ass.

I look around for a good minute and to try to find whoever it is that has an industrial size speaker, but I come up empty. There's nobody close by.

The closest person to me is about a hundred feet away, and they are walking in the opposite direction with their dog. There is a group of kids on the other side by the water, but the music is not coming from their direction.

It's coming from behind me.

Turning, I look up at the cliff and see a line of houses at the very top of the rocky hillside. Each one has a small porch facing the beach and a set of stairs that lead down to the sand.

Standing up from my chair, I try to get a better look at all the porches that I can see. From where I'm standing, most of the houses have their sliding doors closed—all of them except for one.

I try to concentrate on the music, and sure enough it's coming from the house that has the door wide open.

Two things can happen.

One, I can be a calm, and collected person and not do a single thing about the music and move on with my day.

Or two, I can be a total bitch, go up to the house and demand whoever lives there to turn their shit down so I can get back to my self-care for the day.

The music continues to get louder and louder, so I make the choice without a second thought.

Option two it is.

The people that live there are going to think that I'm a complete bitch, but I don't give a fuck.

I walk over to the stairs, and thankfully, the gate that separates the private property from the beach is unlocked, so it doesn't take much for me to push it open and head up to the covered balcony.

Whoever lives here has money. The house looks absolutely beautiful from where I'm standing. A perfect beach house. The covered porch is spacious with a barbeque pit and a hot tub in the corner, and it looks like the perfect place to relax and enjoy the view.

From the looks of things, it has recently been used for entertaining. There are wine glasses, wine bottles, and beer bottles around the fire pit and... a pair of panties on the table?

"Gross," I mutter to myself, making sure not to touch anything. Whoever used this porch last, had fun, and I don't want to catch anything that they may have.

"Hello?" I call out, hoping that someone will come out, so I don't walk into the house and have the cops called on me.

But my call goes unanswered. The only thing that I can hear is the music that sounds like it is coming from the TV, just inside the porch sliding door.

I call out again and again with no answer.

Rolling my eyes, I walk into the house like I own the damn place, stepping over a bra that matches the panties outside and start looking for the TV remote.

Thankfully, I don't have to look long because the remote is exactly where it should be on the coffee table.

Hopefully, whoever lives here believes in ghosts and

won't think anything about the volume of their music magically lowering.

"There. That's better," I say to myself once the music is at a decent volume, and it doesn't sound like I'm at a concert.

Feeling good about not getting caught, I place the remote back where I found it and start heading back the way I came.

I make it halfway past the couch, about to celebrate my—

"Who the fuck are you, and what the fuck are you doing in my house?" A male voice rolls through the room, and I automatically go stiff, and all thoughts of celebration seize.

Great. I might get arrested.

I should have let it go. A little music wasn't going to hurt me. Or I should have waited until someone heard me and turned the music down themselves. There was no need to trespass.

Of course, I think that now that I've gotten caught.

Awesome job, Eliana.

Conceding, I turn to face the owner of the house, and the second that my eyes meet his face, my mouth drops to the ground.

No freaking way.

He owns this house?

Out of all the people in the world whose house I could have walked into, it had to be one of the hockey players from the team that I just signed onto. A grumpy hockey player at that.

Christian Rodriguez, the Dark Knights' starting left wing, stands a few feet away from me looking like it's taking everything in him to not walk over to where I am, grab me by the hair, and drag me off his property. Not only that, but the man is only wearing a towel, with his whole body glistening from just stepping out of the shower.

My hate for hockey and its players may run deep, but I'm not going to deny it when I see a gorgeous man, and Christian Rodriguez is definitely a gorgeous, mouthwatering man. His dark hair is still wet and flopping all over the place, and his bone structure is definitely not what you would expect from a hockey player.

Like I said, the man is mouthwateringly gorgeous.

Even when he looks seriously pissed off. And I mean, I would be, too, if I caught someone in my house. If it was me and I saw it was my coach's daughter, I would just brush it off. Maybe once he gets over the shock of finding a stranger in the house, he will do just that, and we can laugh about it once the season starts.

"I'm going to ask one more time before I call the cops. Who the fuck are you, and what the fuck are you doing in my fucking house?"

I look at the man in front of me and study his facial expression, and it takes me a second to put it all together.

He has no idea who I am. He's not like Gus who looked at me like I was familiar to him.

There is no familiarity in Christian's eyes. He truly doesn't know that I'm his coach's daughter. To him, I'm just a strange woman standing in the middle of his house. A half-naked woman at that, since I didn't put on my shorts before coming up here. So, I'm just standing there in bikini bottoms and a tank top, in a stranger's house! Well, no stranger, I know who the grumpy asshole is, but he doesn't know me, that's for sure.

Fuck.

There's no doubt in my mind about it now. I'm one hundred percent going to get arrested today.

CHAPTER THREE

CHRISTIAN

I THOUGHT I heard something when I got out of the shower.

For a second, I thought that it was Leslie, the girl from last night, talking to me from the bedroom, but when I walked out of the bathroom and saw her asleep, I brushed it off.

But then the music started to lower, and instantly the hairs on the back of my neck started to stand up.

I had put the music up that loud for a reason and the only way to control it was through the remote in the living room. And given that my guest was still sound asleep in my bed, there could only be two explanations.

My house was suddenly haunted, or someone was here. My money was on the second one.

Grabbing a towel, I quickly made my way out to the living room. For a quick second, I thought it was my brother who had come over without telling me, which is something he always does, but of course I'm wrong, and it's not him.

Instead, it's a woman who looks like she was spending some time down by the water, in her barely-there bikini bottoms and decided to make herself comfortable in my home.

The home that outside of my family, only four other people know about. Well, five now, if you count the woman who is currently in my bed.

Nobody knows I own this house, so nobody, and I mean nobody, should be walking in like they own the damn place and turn down my music.

No matter how good their ass looks in that bikini. Yes, I looked at this strange woman's ass. She bent down, for fuck's sake, and if I wasn't pissed that someone had broken into my sacred space, I would have continued to look.

"Don't make me ask again," I say through my teeth, the grip on my towel so tight that my fingers might rip through the fabric.

"Your music was too loud," she answers, crossing her arms across her chest and popping her hip out.

She's going to give me attitude? In my house? Really?

"So? It's my music," I say, almost yelling, but I rein it in.

"It may be your music, but some people are trying to relax down there," she says, pointing down to the shore, "and your music was messing with my peace and quiet."

"So, because I was messing with your peace and quiet, you decided to break into my house?"

The chick rolls her eyes at me like I'm the one inconveniencing her and not the other way around. I don't know why, but my dick decides to jerk at the gesture, and I have to remind it, that this is not the time and this woman for all we know, is the enemy.

"I didn't break in. The door was open."

The door was open.

I'm one hundred percent sure I closed that door last night before going to bed and still had it closed this morning. Which means my guest must have gotten up at some point between breakfast and now and left it open.

One more reason to get her out of my house. She is jeopardizing my safety.

"You could have waited outside for someone to come out," I say to the strange woman.

I don't know why I'm standing here arguing with her. If it was anyone else, I would have kicked them out already and called the cops. For all I know this chick is a puck bunny who has been stalking me and waiting for her chance to catch me off guard to make her move. All so that she can get a picture and tell her friends that we're together.

It's happened before and I'm sure it will happen again.

I'm not buying the whole music thing.

Was it loud? Yes, extremely, but I had ulterior motives for having it that way.

"I did. I even called out. And guess what? Nobody responded, so since the door was open, I took it upon myself to walk in and turn the music down. You have neighbors, you know. They don't want to hear your concert at two o'clock in the afternoon."

If only she knew that the houses next to me are empty during the week, and there won't be a neighbor in sight until Saturday. People and their vacation homes.

Hell, this house sits empty most of the year, too, and the only time I use it during the off season or we have a game in San Jose, and I want to sleep in my own bed instead of in a hotel.

But, of course, I don't tell her that. She's a stranger. I don't need her coming back and squatting when I'm not around.

"They don't give a shit. Now, take that pretty ass of yours and get out of my house before I call the cops and tell them that a crazy jersey chaser broke in," I threaten, wanting to be done with this conversation. I have already wasted most of my day entertaining one woman, I don't have time for another one. I have shit to do.

"Jersey chaser? I am not a fucking jersey chaser!" The bikini-clad woman screams out, like I insulted her.

I shrug. "I don't know that. For all I know you're a puck bunny who wants to get a piece of any hockey player she spots from a mile away."

A laugh wants to escape at the way she gasps. "You think so highly of yourself, don't you?" I give her a shrug. "Besides, what makes you think I even know who you are?"

I raise an eyebrow at her. This girl is a spitfire, but her facial expressions are shit. I saw recognition the second she turned around. "You don't?"

That gets me another eye roll. "Fine. I know who you are, but just because I do, doesn't mean I give two flying fucks about you being a hockey player or the fact that your team won the Cup a month ago. Trust me, finding out you live here was just as much of a shock to me as it was for you finding me here."

"Doubt it. Now get the fuck out," I say, pointing toward the back door.

"Are you always so damn difficult? I just lowered your music. Chill," she says with more sass than I have time for. If this woman was somebody who didn't get on my damn nerves, this would be excellent foreplay. My dick twitching tells me that my body agrees.

"You broke into my house. I won't chill," I say, a little annoyed that I'm finding this woman attractive in any way.

"The door was freaking open!" she yells back.

Having had enough of this, I turn to head back to the bedroom to grab my phone. This woman isn't going to leave on her own accord, so I might as well call the cops.

I'm stopped short, though, when Leslie steps out of the room wearing absolutely nothing.

"What's going on?" my overnight guest asks, rubbing the sleep out of her eyes.

Fuck. Finally.

I've been trying to get this girl to wake up ever since she fell asleep after our post-breakfast activities. I have tried everything to wake her up, including turning the music all the way up so that she wouldn't be able to sleep through it, but she didn't budge. I missed a workout because I didn't want to leave her alone in my house, and I was close to missing dinner at my mom's if I didn't do something.

Who would have thought that all I had to do to wake her up was argue with someone breaking into my house?

Leslie stops rubbing her eyes and looks up. It takes her a second to realize there is someone else here, but she doesn't move to cover herself up. She just smiles at me and at my intruder.

"Oh, you invited someone to join in on our fun?" she asks, coming closer to me and sliding a hand up my bare chest.

Is she serious right now?

"Gross," the intruder says, making a gagging sound like the actual thought of a threesome makes her sick.

"You don't have to join. You can just watch," Leslie tells the other woman before turning back to me to roll her eyes.

"Fuck that. I'm out," the intruder announces, causing me to turn back and watch as she walks out. "Have fun with your little sexcapades. I want no part in them. Keep the music down so I can relax and get my much-needed sun. Good luck with the real jersey chaser in the room," she tells me before flipping me off, and walking out the back door and heading down the stairs toward the beach.

Jesus.

I should be the one flipping her off, not the other way around.

Thank fuck she's gone.

If I see her again, it will be too soon.

Now that one headache is gone, it's time to deal with the other.

"We don't need her anyway," Leslie says, closing the

distance between us and pressing her naked body against mine. "What do you say you lose this towel and go for another round?"

Tempting.

But I already broke a handful of my rules by having her here for this long. I don't want her to think that whatever this is between us is going to go past today. Because it's not.

I need my alone time, and I can't have it with Leslie here.

"As much as I would love to take you up on that offer," I say, placing my hand over hers and sliding it off my body. "I have a few things I have to take care of later today, so I have to cut this short."

I should have cut it short before breakfast, but this girl enticed me with maple syrup and her nipples, and I couldn't find it in me to say no.

"Oh, okay," Leslie lets out, sounding disappointed. "Maybe we can meet up later in the week and have a repeat."

There is hope in her voice, something that I'm used to hearing when it comes to women.

"I don't think that is going to work. Like I said last night, this would only be for one night, nothing more would come from it, and I would really like to keep it that way."

Don't get me wrong, Leslie is a beautiful girl, but the intruder was right. The girl I spent last night with is in fact a puck bunny, something that I very much knew when I brought her home last night and was okay with. I needed to de-stress, and she offered to help me out.

But one night is one night.

I could say that I don't do relationships, and I just fuck

whenever and wherever, but that would be a complete lie. I do have relationships, and I'm all for them, but where my life is at the moment, there's no time for one, and it wouldn't be fair to any woman.

My team just won the Stanley Cup, and if we keep our heads out of our asses, we can work toward another one. I should, and need, to concentrate on that.

But, of course, I am a man with needs. So, fucking around for one night here and there isn't going to hurt anyone.

Unless you're like your best friend and get a girl pregnant after one night, then live happily ever after.

Nope, I'm good.

Leslie looks up at me like she wants to argue, but after a few seconds, she gives me a nod. "That's fine. Do you mind if I jump in the shower really quick? I have a shift later today, and I would rather not smell like sex."

She doesn't have a shower at her place?

I'm about to tell her no, but then my mom's voice sounds through my mind telling me how she raised me better than to tell a woman to leave when she needs something.

I can already hear a lecture coming my way when I go over to her house for dinner tonight. Not that I will tell my mom about my sexual activities, but I swear she's going to know somehow.

So, I give Leslie a nod. "Go right ahead.

"Yay. You are awesome. Thank you." She slaps a kiss on my lips and then runs back to the bedroom.

The fact that I don't check her out as she walks away tells

me that I'm very much done with our night together, and by next week I will probably forget about it.

Does that make me an asshole? Very much.

Without disrupting Leslie as she uses my shower, I quickly toss my towel in the hamper and pull on some clothes before heading to the kitchen and making myself a sandwich from the minimal stuff I have in my fridge.

I really need to make a trip to the grocery store; I just haven't had the time.

After winning the Cup about a month ago, everything has been go, go go. First it was a three-day celebration bender that some of the guys and I went on followed by another bender at the celebration parade.

We were not only celebrating our win but also the fact that our captain and my best friend, Liam Crawford, had become a dad to a beautiful little girl. It was a double celebration. So, we went all out.

From there, it was interviews and podcasts, movie premieres in Los Angeles, and photoshoots in Costa Rica. The whole month was jam-packed with shit that my agent and manager had lined up for me, because apparently after the season was done with, I was one of the top NHL players who people wanted to get to know.

I'm not made for that type of shit, but I did it anyway.

Three weeks later, I was finally able to find a window where I was able to come home. And by home, I don't mean Chicago.

Home for me is in California. Home is along the central coast, in the middle of the ocean and the crop fields and the redwoods. Home is where my parents and brother are. I love Chicago, don't get me wrong. It's one of my favorite places in the world, but this place holds a special spot in my heart. It's the one place where I can be who I truly am and not hide from a single person.

I was itching to get home, and when I walked into this house three days ago, I was finally able to relax after a whole month of putting on a face.

These past three days have been spent with my family, getting workouts in, and catching up on some much-needed sleep, so groceries haven't been a priority. I've been surviving on food I took from my mom's fridge, but from the looks of things I need to take a trip to the store really soon.

The shower is still running as I make my sandwich and head outside to the back balcony to eat it. When I'm done with my lunch and clean up the mess from last night, the water finally shuts off, but by that time, I'm not even thinking about getting Leslie out of my space.

No, my attention is drawn down by the water on my bikini-clad intruder taking pictures of the waves crashing into the sand.

I figured she would leave since I ruined her relaxation time, but she surprised me when she appeared again about five minutes ago. My guess is that she has a spot by the life-guard shack stationed close to the cliff, so I wouldn't be able to see her from here.

But now that she's by the water, I have the perfect view.

Somewhere between her leaving my house and now, she

has ditched the tank top that covered most of her body, so now I get to see all of her.

She has curves for days, and that bikini she has on does nothing to hide just how fucking delicious she looks. I have no doubt in my mind that she would feel amazing in my hands. The shit I would do to her if she gave me attitude again.

Fuck.

This woman broke into my house and was a pain in the ass, and here I am thinking about what I want to do with her body. All the while, I have another woman in my house.

I really am an asshole.

Thankfully, Leslie comes out of the bedroom, dressed in the clothes she had on last night and walks over to me while picking up her bra and panties from where she threw them on the floor last night.

She tells me that she is all set and ready to go, so I give her a nod and try to forget about the woman down on the beach who broke into my house and has my dick twitching in her direction.

Wanting to get her off my mind for good and get on her nerves one last time, since I'll never see this woman again, I decided to turn up the music to the absolutely loudest it will go before leaving the house and taking Leslie back to her car.

I missed seeing her reaction in person, but that didn't stop me from watching it over and over again from the camera I have out on the back balcony.

The girl was absolutely fuming as she climbed back up

the stairs to my house and even more so when she tried the door and found it locked.

I could hear her yells through the music, and it was absolutely hilarious. She called me every single name in the book, but I don't give a shit.

She broke into my house; she touched my stuff.

This was my payback, and I enjoyed every single damn second of it.

CHAPTER FOUR

GLUTTON FOR PUNISHMENT.

That's what I am. I am a damn glutton for punishment and don't give a shit about getting on people's bad side. That has to be it.

Because no way in hell would any sane person go back to the place where her day of relaxation was ruined. A sane person would steer clear of the beach where the grumpy hockey player lives and not want to interact with him again just to provoke him and get payback. A sane person would find another beach and not see said grumpy hockey player until the season starts up.

That's what a sane person would do, but apparently, I'm not a sane person. I'm voluntarily going back to the beach that puts me in the vicinity of Christian Rodriguez and his damn grumpiness. And I'm doing it for no other reason than to see if I can get under the man's skin some more and possibly get revenge on him for cutting my beach day short.

Like I said, I'm a glutton for punishment.

I should have let it go the first day. I should have ignored the music blasting the second time around and just moved down the beach where it wouldn't bother me and continued on with my day. But I didn't.

I stomped back up to his house with the mindset of breaking in again and turning the music off. When I found the door locked, I yelled at the door for a good five minutes before realizing that the asshole had left. To top it off, I didn't decide to leave until I saw a camera at a top corner of the house pointing straight at the door which meant that the bastard was witnessing me go crazy on his door and was probably laughing.

It pissed me off, so I flipped off the camera and decided it was best to head home before I embarrassed myself some more. When I got home, I couldn't believe I let a stupid hockey player ruin my day, so I started thinking of ways to get payback.

So here I am, three days later, at the same beach, in a different location with hopes of seeing the gorgeous, grumpy asshat so I can annoy him beyond belief like he annoyed me.

Only seems fair.

Is there a point to all of this? No, but if anything, it tells him not to mess with me when the season starts.

There was no photo session with the soccer team for me today, so I was able to make it to the beach this morning after stopping by the grocery store to get food for the day. I had no idea if or when I was going to see my target, so if I was going to spend all day at the ocean shore, I wanted to be prepared for anything.

There is a high chance that I won't be able to follow through with my plan today, and that's okay. I have the rest of summer to make it happen.

After settling in my chair, with my whole body lathered in sunscreen and a hat covering most of my face, I grab my kindle from my bag and start to feel my shoulders deflate into a pool of calmness.

I wouldn't say what I do is stressful particularly, but there are some good days and some bad days. Sometimes getting the perfect picture can be a total headache or the easiest thing in the world.

Right now, things are a cakewalk compared to what they will be once I officially start with the Knights, but even then, I will have a team behind me that will make things a whole lot easier.

That's something that I will have to learn, though. I'm so used to working on my own and taking care of things myself, that having a team behind me where I can delegate things is going to be a hard thing to get used to.

I'm sure with time, I will get used to it and learn how to work with a team. I just have to get there and not get freaked out by it and quit. This is a job of a lifetime, and I don't want to fuck it up.

Putting the stress of starting a new job to the side, I continue to read my book for the next hour or so with the occasional people watching session.

It's Saturday, so there are more people here than there

were earlier in the week, but only a handful. People are out and enjoying the summer sun with their kids and dogs and having fun in the water.

As I watch people jump in and out of the water, I have my ears open for any sounds that may come from behind me. At first, I was listening for music, but when that didn't start, I started to listen for anything else.

Footsteps or voices.

The voices don't come, which is fine, I don't need to hear him and his bunny going at it in the living room. The footsteps do come about two hours into my beach day, though.

Even through the voices of the families having fun and the waves crashing, I'm able to make out the faintest movement on the porch above me. When I hear footsteps coming down the stairs, I can't help but smile at my plan coming alive.

I keep my eyes down on my kindle to make whoever is coming down the stairs believe that I'm so enthralled in my book, I don't notice a single thing.

The smile on my face grows even more when what sounds like an annoyed growl rumbles through my ears.

"Excuse me. You're blocking my beach access," the grumpy hockey player says from behind me.

"Am I? I didn't even notice. You can go around," I answer, not even looking up to see his face.

"First you break into my house and now you're denying me access to a public beach?" he asks.

I guess he recognized me right away. And here I thought that he was going to forget all about me.

"First, I didn't break into your house." I finally look up from my kindle and turn in my chair to face the man towering over me. "Your door was wide open. It's not my fault that you don't take your security seriously and keep the doors closed. Second, like you said, this is a public beach, so I can sit anywhere I want. And I want to sit right here, in front of this cute little gate. Besides, I like this spot, it gives me the perfect amount of sun."

I turn back from him and go back to reading. I make it through a whole sentence before I feel something leaning against the back of my chair and get a whiff of his scent a little too close to me.

Is that his cologne, or his aftershave or just his natural scent?

Who cares? It's not like I like it or anything.

"Move," Christian growls into my ear, his single word traveling down my neck and through my body like a shiver.

"Or what?" I say, not turning to face him. His face is too close for comfort, and if I turn, I will no doubt be able to look into his eyes. I bet they are filled with evil.

"Or I'll pick you up, chair and all, and throw you in the fucking ocean."

"You wouldn't fucking dare," I say through my teeth, turning slightly to narrow my eyes at him. The asshole is bluffing. I know he is.

"Try me, hermosa. I'll pick your ass up right now and throw you into the cold water. Move. Out. Of. The. Way."

I roll my eyes at him calling me hermosa. The bastard is trying to sweet talk me so that I can do what he wants. That's not going to happen. No matter how much my body likes being called hermosa, I'm staying put.

I give the asshole a shrug and toss my hair back so that it hits him in the face. "I'm good. Like I said, you can go around, or...hey, here's an idea, you can jump over me. You're a professional athlete, you can jump that high and not get hurt."

I'm acting like a complete brat and not the twenty-nine-year-old woman that I am, I know that, but the man threatened to call the cops on me and ruined my peace and quiet.

He deserves this shit.

For a solid second, I think my hockey player friend here is going to listen to me and go around, but when I feel my chair move, I start to panic.

No way in hell is he actually going to pick me and throw me in the ocean!

He is not that strong, no matter how many ab muscles he may have.

Of course, the asshole proves me wrong and moves the chair enough from the other side of the gate for me to face him and when I'm about to ask him what the hell he's doing, I get disoriented. Somehow, he was able to not only move the chair, but to also slide one of his arms under my legs and throw me over his shoulder.

It takes me a minute to find my bearings. The asshole has my upper body against his back, and my legs over his shoulders. I'm literally staring at his ass right now where a minute ago I wasn't even looking at him.

"What the hell are you doing?! Put me down!" I slap him against his thigh, but Christian doesn't even react.

He just pushes my chair and all of my things to the side with the gate before kicking them away for good measure and starts walking toward the water.

I slap his leg again, trying to push myself away enough for him to put me down, but all he does is tighten his hold on me.

"I told you what would happen if you didn't move," he growls, not drifting from his path to the water.

"I swear to God, Rodriguez, if you don't put me down right now, you're dead. I'm going to break into your house in the middle of the night and use one of your skates on you!" Okay, so I'm being dramatic, but I really don't want to be thrown into the ocean.

"Hermosa, what makes you think you will get that far? I'll have you arrested before you even reach the backdoor."

"Don't call me hermosa. I'm not your hermosa. Save that name for your puck bunnies," I say, closing my eyes to keep myself from getting dizzy from all the movement. I swear I can feel all the blood rushing to my ears.

"I'll call you whatever I want. Seems only fair since you know my name, but I don't know yours," he says right before slapping his hand against my thigh to hold me still.

"I hate you so much." Now I'm the one growling.

"The feeling is mutual, babe," he says, another slap landing on my leg.

As we continue to walk toward the water, I catch a glimpse of more than a few families staring at us and given Christian's celebrity status, I can already hear the people on social media going off with their theories about what's going on between us.

"Great. People are staring at us. If someone takes a picture of us and blasts all over the place, and I lose my job, I'm going to blame you," I say, slapping him against his back this time.

"You're a pain in the ass, you know that?" he says, and even though it was supposed to be a rhetorical question, it gives me an idea.

Not thinking twice about it, I close the distance between me and Christian's boardshorts-covered ass and bite down.

"What the fuck?!" he yells out, releasing his hold on my legs enough that I can slide out of his grip and throw myself on the ground.

The sand is soft enough to not knock the wind out of me, but I'm still going to hurt tomorrow morning.

How the actual fuck did me trying to annoy Christian go this far? We're acting like children.

"Did you just bite me?" he asks, looking down at me like he can't believe that the top of his right ass cheek has a bite mark on it.

"I told you to put me down. You didn't listen, so I had to think of something. You're lucky it was just a bite on your ass. I could have bitten something else." I push myself up and brush off as much of the sand off my body as I can. I would rather deal with sand than the cold-ass Pacific Ocean water.

"What the fuck is your problem?" he asks, closing the distance between us.

"I don't have a problem." I say dismissively.

"Sure, you do because you are making it your mission to annoy the shit out of me, and you have been since day one," he says, and I look up just in time to see mischief in his brown eyes.

Have his eyes always been that shade of brown, almost like caramel in color? I've seen pictures of him before and seen him on TV, but I've never really paid attention to his eyes. The color suits him. It gives a sense of warmth to his tough and hard exterior. I like it.

Stop thinking about his eyes. At least it's his eyes, and not his bare chest, that is currently staring back at me. Does this man even own a shirt?

"I can say the same thing about you. You could have ignored me just now but no you had to go all caveman and throw me over your shoulder."

"You call it caveman; I call it payback for breaking into my house," he says, giving me a smirk that I'm sure is expected to make me melt.

Not going to happen.

I roll my eyes. "This is why I hate hockey players. You're pompous assholes."

"Ah, so that's it. Someone hurt you in the past, and you decided to take that anger out on every single player you come across. News flash, hermosa, not all hockey players are the same.

I look at the man in front of me. Really look at him. I know nothing about him. What I do know is solely based on what I've read online or seen on social media or TV. He may be right in saying not all hockey players are the same—I know from first-hand experience that Liam isn't—but I don't know if that is true of Christian.

At least, not yet.

"From my experience, they are," I say the words without even thinking.

I don't talk about my hatred toward hockey players. I keep that close to the heart. Hell, my dad, who's at the center of it all, doesn't even know the root cause of it. He just thinks that I hate hockey because of Kalen, and while that is part of it, it's not the whole story. And I'm not about to tell Christian Rodriguez.

He was about to throw me in the ocean, for crying out loud.

"I could stand here and tell you that you are wrong, but I have a feeling that you won't listen to me. So, I'm going to go and get in the workout that you so rudely interrupted. Have a nice life, hermosa. I hope I never get to see you again."

"Gee, you say the sweetest things," I say, giving him another eye roll, letting the whole interruption thing go.

"I try," he says, giving me another one of those smirks again. "Stay out of my way, will you?"

"Gladly." I turn and walk back to where my stuff is, not giving Christian a second look.

This day has definitely turned into something that I wasn't expecting. At the very least, I got under Christian's skin like I wanted to.

Now, I just have to hope that the asshole doesn't retaliate in some way. I'll find another beach to spend any down time I may have over these next few weeks, but once the season starts and he finds out we are working for the same team, all hell could break loose.

I just have to hope that he keeps the ass biting to himself.

I don't need a lecture from my dad about how I can't go around biting his players on the ass.

That would be absolutely mortifying.

CHAPTER FIVE

CHRISTIAN

I'M NOT GOING to lie.

I'm a little disappointed that I haven't seen the pain-in-my-ass-bikini-wearing intruder in a whole week.

Whenever I went down to the beach for a run, I looked for her, waiting to find her at the bottom of my stairs just like before, but every day I went down, and she wasn't there.

After four or five days, I concluded she had finally backed down after the whole almost throwing her in the water thing, and I was never going to see her again.

Which works out for me. I don't need our little game getting out of hand and one of us actually calling the cops because one of us crossed an unspoken line.

I do miss sparring with her, though, and if I knew her name, I might have looked her up and possibly continued it just to pass the time a little faster. But I don't know her name, and I see that as a good thing because it saves me from the inevitable headache she would cause.

While I see it as a good thing, my body and mind, on the other hand, don't. Apparently, my brain thinks it's appropriate to think about the woman when I least expect it.

These last few days have been filled with thoughts of the strange woman who made my blood boil. Thoughts of her soft skin. Thoughts of my hands on her ass and taking a bite just like she took one of me. Images of her in nothing but that string bikini of hers, all wet and ready for me to explore. Scenarios where her spitfire personality had me so damn sexually frustrated that the only way I can get her to stop talking is by having her drop to her knees and take me in her mouth.

Too many things came to mind. Things that I shouldn't be thinking about whatsoever, but I am and to say I didn't have blue balls the whole week because of it, would be a complete lie.

But I'm putting my spitfire intruder behind me. Thinking about her isn't going to make her materialize out of thin air, so it's best not to think about her.

Besides, this is one less annoying pain in the ass to deal with. Now that she's gone, I get to enjoy my alone time and concentrate on getting my body and mind ready for the next season.

I will start doing that tomorrow.

Right now, though, all I want to do is grab a drink with some friends.

Every year when I come home for the offseason, I try to hang out with some of my friends from high school at least once or twice. We all took different paths in life and have busy schedules, but we at least try to get together to grab a drink and catch up.

We're not as close as we were when we were teenagers, but we're okay with that. We're still there for each other when we need to be and that's all that matters.

I pull up to the bar in downtown San Jose, a few blocks away from the arena hockey fans call the Shark Tank, and walk over to the bar that my buddy texted me earlier in the day.

As soon as I walk in, I don't feel as overwhelmed as I usually do walking into a bar. It might have something to do with the fact the place isn't as packed as I thought it would be on a Friday night.

I was mentally preparing myself to deal with drunk people all night as they danced around the small space. But from the looks of things, this place is a dive bar that sells pizza with a few pool tables and an area for people to hang out in the back. Not a place I would picture in a downtown area, but it works.

"Here I thought that I was going to have to drag you out of your fortress on the beach," A familiar voice sounds through on my left, and when I turn toward it, I do something that I rarely do when I'm in public. Smile.

"If I remember correctly, I did offer up the house for this," I say to my friend Miguel, clapping him on the back as we close the distance between each other.

"You did, but where is the fun in that? It's good to get out and mingle with the public every once in a while."

I roll my eyes. I like to stay home and to be in my own

space. There's nothing wrong with that. And I do go out when I have the time, just not as often as other people my age do.

"I hope you don't mind, but I invited one of the team's photographers to come along with us. They told me that they were going to go home and just watch a movie, but I thought this would be more fun."

Miguel and his fun.

My friend and I couldn't be any more different. While he is the going out and extroverted type, I have always been the quiet, introverted type. In all the years that I've known him, he has always been the life of the party while I was always hoping for the cops to arrive to shut said party down. The only way we are similar is the fact that we are both professional athletes. Miguel signed with the Major League Soccer team here in San Jose a few years ago, and I went to Chicago to play for the Knights after getting traded.

Even though we have our different personalities, we still work as friends. We were that way when we were kids, and we are still that way today. He invites everyone and anyone to a party or even a get-together with his friends. So, I'm used to random people joining in when we get together.

I give him a nod. "Fine by me."

"Cool," he says, guiding me over to the table where all our other friends are at.

Apparently, I was the last one to arrive.

I take inventory of the table before approaching it, and when I see our addition for the night, I can't help but let out a small snort.

Of course, it's her. Who else would it be? My luck absolutely hates me.

"Christian, this is Eliana. She's working with the Quakes for a few months. Eliana, this is Christian, our grumpy best friend," Miguel says, waving a hand over to the brunette sitting at a table filled with our friends.

Eliana.

I guess my intruder officially has a name.

For some reason, though, the name sounds familiar, but I can't pinpoint where I've heard it. Maybe online somewhere.

"We've met," I say to my friend, not taking my eyes off the feisty brunette sitting a few feet away.

"You have?" Miguel asks, giving me a confused look. Silently asking how.

Eliana rolls her eyes but doesn't say anything.

"Yup, she broke into my house," I say, feeling a smirk forming on my face.

"For the hundredth time, I didn't break in. Your door was wide open. You were the one who was about to throw me in the ocean," Eliana finally says, throwing another eye roll in my direction.

I would bet everything in my wallet right now that if we were still in elementary school, she would have stuck her tongue out at me.

"Because you were in my way," I argue, and I can see the fire in her eyes. I noticed how gorgeous this woman was the first day I met her, but seeing that fire in her eyes, that anger, puts her on a whole new level. A level that makes my dick twitch.

"Whatever," she says, flipping me off as she takes a drink of her beer.

Is she drinking beer because she likes it or because she feels like she has to because everyone else at the table is?

Why do I even care?

"Damn. And here I thought about setting you two up. I'm thinking twice about it now. You two would eat each other alive," Miguel says through a chuckle as he takes a seat a few stools away from Eliana.

Leaving the only one open being the one in front of her. Great. I'm either leaving tonight with blue balls or a headache. I don't know which one I prefer.

Miguel is right, though, Eliana and I would without a doubt eat each other alive, especially with that attitude of hers. The sex would probably be fucking fantastic but neither one of us would make it out alive.

"Your friend is lucky I swore off hockey players a long time ago because he wouldn't be able to handle me," Eliana tells the table, and they all laugh like it is the funniest shit in the world.

They're my friends, so they should be on my side, not hers.

"That sounds like a challenge to me, hermosa," I say, taking a seat and reaching for the empty beer glass in the middle of the table and filling it from the pitcher.

"In your dreams, Rodriguez," she tells me, and even though she gives me a death glare, the way the corner of her mouth twitches, I know she wants to smile.

I guess I'm not the only one that has taken a small liking to our back-and-forth sparring.

"Solis is feisty. I like it," Miguel lets out, and the whole table agrees.

While everyone starts talking and catching up, I can't get the fact that her name sounds familiar out of my head. I've never met an Eliana Solis before. I know that for a fact, but it's her first name that has me scratching my head.

Pulling out my phone, I shoot off a message to Liam, the team captain and my best friend.

CHRISTIAN

Do we know someone named Eliana?

I sent off the message not even caring about the time difference between here and Chicago. The bastard must have been up with his daughter Emma because he quickly responds.

LIAM

Coach's daughter is named Eliana. Why?

CHRISTIAN

Is she a photographer?

LIAM

Yes. She's the one who took those pictures of me and Chloe. I told you this.

Coach's daughter and this Eliana can't be the same person, right? Maybe it's just a coincidence that Coach Anderson has a daughter who is named Eliana who is also a photographer.

CHRISTIAN

Any chance you know if Coach's daughter is in California?

LIAM

She is. During the photo shoot she told us she was taking an assignment with the Quakes this summer. Why??????

If Liam was any other person, I would disown him as a friend for the number of question marks he uses.

CHRISTIAN

Dark brown hair, light brown eyes, and curves for days?

LIAM

(eye-roll emoji) Yeah. WHY????

Seriously, he has to stop with the question marks.

CHRISTIAN

Because she's sitting right in front of me.

I put my phone face down on the table and try to pay attention to the conversations that are happening around me.

I knew there was something familiar about her, but I couldn't pinpoint it. Now that I know, and really think about it, I think I've seen her picture in Anderson's office. He's mentioned her name once or twice, so that's where I know it from. If she is Coach's daughter, then that would explain how she knew who I was and knew my name right away.

But why not just come out and say it? If I had known she was Anderson's kid, I wouldn't have said or done half the shit that I did.

My phone vibrates on the table, which catches the attention of Eliana.

"One of your bunnies trying to get a booty call?" she asks, raising an eyebrow in my direction. Her facial expression is somewhere between pissed off and curious.

Interesting.

I know she's Coach's daughter so I shouldn't mess with her, but it's too hard not to.

"Would you be jealous if I said yes?"

Eliana lets out a snort that most girls would feel embarrassed about. I've come to learn that she's not like most girls. "I feel a lot of shit toward you, Rodriguez. Jealousy is not one of them. It's not even in the top one hundred." She drinks down the rest of her beer and slides her stool back. "I'm going to play pool. Anyone want to join?"

A few of my friends stand up and follow her to the back to where the pool tables are at.

I take the time to check my phone and see Liam sent another message.

LIAM

Don't get on her bad side.

CHRISTIAN

And why wouldn't I want to do that?

. . .

The guy surprises me again by responding. It's close to midnight in Chicago. Emma must not be sleeping through the night yet. She is only just over a month old. I read over his message, and I have to read it at least three times to get over the surprise.

LIAM

> Because not only is she Anderson's daughter. She's also a Knights employee come the start of the season. She's our new team photog.

Well damn, this woman keeps surprising me left and right.

CHRISTIAN

> So... it's too late to say that she bit me on the ass a week ago?

LIAM

> I don't even want to fucking know.

I let out a laugh at my friend's discomfort and go back to catching up with my friends. I have a lot of questions for Eliana, and who knows if I will ever get to ask them. For now, I'm putting them on the back burner and just enjoying the night.

For the next hour or so, it's questions about hockey and life in Chicago for me, and since I'm not in a formal setting, I feel comfortable answering them. The conversation isn't only about me, though. Miguel tells us what it's like to play soccer at the highest level, and a few of the other guys tell us all about what it's like to have kids and how their wives and girlfriends are doing.

The night is turning out to be a great one with laughs and memories.

Eventually, those of us who stayed at the table decided to join the rest of the group at the pool tables.

From the looks of things, it appears Eliana is hustling each one of my friends, and she's good at it, too. Anderson must have trained her to know the ins and outs of all things competitive.

I watch her as she moves around the table. She may be a big pain in my ass, but there is something about her that has me invested in everything that she does.

Her laugh is sweet, and her eyes have a hint of mischief in them that I wouldn't mind having pointed at me occasionally. Her beauty is also something that has my eyes staying on her for a good chunk of time.

She's not wearing a whole lot of makeup tonight, or maybe she is, and she just made it look as natural as possible, and her dark hair is in waves down her back like that's it's natural form.

My eyes run up and down her body, taking every inch of her in. I've only seen her in bikini bottoms and an oversized tank top, so seeing her in everyday clothes is throwing me off. But only for a second because I catch sight of her ass in the jeans that she is wearing, and all I want to do is call whoever sells them and buy every pair so that she can wear them every single day and gift me with that fantastic view.

I'm an ass man, what can I say?

Sometime around eleven-thirty, my group of friends starts to get smaller, and by midnight, it's just me, Miguel and Eliana left standing.

"You guys have a good set of friends behind you," Eliana says as she bends down to take her next shot on the pool table.

I think that is the nicest thing that she said to me in all our banter.

Miguel gives her a nod. "Yeah, and it's good that we've stayed in touch all these years. Most people can't say that. We may not see each other often, but we all know that we're there for each other when we need it the most."

"That's a good thing to have," she says before taking her shot and landing one of her stripes in the left corner pocket.

Miguel and her talk some more about the night, all the while I just watch them play and nurse the beer I got over an hour ago.

I watch every single one of Eliana's movements, not giving a shit if she notices or not.

At one in the morning, Miguel puts down his cue stick and lets out a huge yawn.

"I'm going to head out. Early morning practice and all that," he says, coming over to me and giving me a bro-pat on the back. "It was good seeing you, man. Maybe we can meet up again before you head off to Chicago for the season."

"Yeah. Whenever you want."

He turns to face Eliana and throws her a nod. "Do you want me to give you a ride home?" he asks.

I don't know why, but this territorial feeling starts to grow in my chest at the thought of them riding together tonight. I had asked her if she would be jealous if I was messaging a girl, but now I wonder if I have to ask myself that same question when it comes to Eliana grabbing a ride from my friend.

She's a pain in my ass. She annoys me. She shouldn't be making me feel territorial. Yet she is.

Which is why I speak up before she even gets to answer his question.

"I can take her home," I say, dumping the remainder of my beer into one of the glasses on the table and stacking them up.

Turning back to face them, I find both Miguel and Eliana staring at me with wide eyes— Miguel with wide eyes of confusion and Eliana with wide eyes telling me that she thinks I'm crazy.

"That way she can finish her game. It's not like I have anything to do in the morning," I add as if to explain. Because why else would I want to give the girl that I've been bickering with all night a ride? It's not like I want to explore her naked body or anything.

Sarcasm, my brain is filled with sarcasm.

"Wouldn't that be out of your way?" Miguel asks, raising a dark eyebrow at me. Why does he care what I do with my gas? He's not paying for it.

Does he have a thing for Eliana? Is that why he's so eager to take her home?

I never wanted to beat up my friend, not when we were kids or when we were teenagers, but I suddenly have a strange urge to do just that right this very moment.

Calm down. They work together. They are friends. There is nothing more. You have no reason to get jealous.

I'm not jealous.

I clear my throat, and my headspace, and finally answer Miguel's question.

"No, not at all," I say, keeping my voice even as possible.

My friend gives me a head nod before turning back to face the woman who I should be letting him take home. "Are you okay with Chris taking you home?"

Eliana looks from my friend to me, narrowing her eyes for a split second before she answers him. "As long as he promises to not chop me up into little pieces and throw me into a dumpster."

This woman has a dark sense of humor. I would never tell her, but I'm liking it.

"Why would I throw you in a dumpster? It would be better to spread you all over the mountains. That way nobody will ever find you." The smirk I throw her way only causes her eyes to narrow even more.

We stare down for a minute or so, neither one of us wanting to back down. Eventually, though, she's the one that breaks it.

"Fine, but at least dump one of my hands in the ocean. That way my body will never be fully discovered, and I can still haunt you every time you step into your beach house," she says with so much sass in her voice that my dick starts to twitch.

Eliana is affecting my dick way more than I want it to.

"As long as you don't touch anything below the belt in your ghost form, we'll be fine," I throw back at her, crossing my arms across my chest.

"I guess I can keep myself from cutting off your precious penis in your sleep."

"Jesus, you two are weird as fuck," Miguel says, taking us away from our back-and-forth banter. "I'm going to head out. Try not to kill each other on the way home."

Miguel waves to Eliana and I and starts making his way out of the bar. We both watch him until we can't see him anymore. As soon as my friend is out of sight, I turn to the woman who will no doubt try and murder me in my sleep if I say the wrong thing.

"Color me surprised," I say, closing the distance between us.

"And why is that?" she says, popping her hip a bit and crossing her arms. As much as I try not to, my eyes travel to her chest for a split second. Even through her shirt, I can see that her tits would feel heavy in my hands.

Fuck. I need to stop checking her out on top of thinking anything sexual.

"You told me you hated me a time or two. I for sure thought you were going to tell me to go fuck myself for even offering to give you a ride, yet, you accepted." I raise an eyebrow at her, my hand itching to touch her.

"It's not like I had a choice," she throws at me.

I can't smile at her lie. "You had a choice, hermosa. You could have left with our mutual friend. He was eager to take you home, yet you chose to stay behind with me. Are you planning on choking me to death on the drive home?" A grin forms on my lips as I tease her.

My teasing earns me an eye roll. "Maybe I didn't like my other choice."

"Is that so? And why is that?" I close the remaining distance between us, leaving not even an inch of space between my body and hers. All I need to do is place my hand against her hip, and I'd be able to feel her curves against my body, but I don't. I'll keep my hands to myself. For now.

"I don't have to explain anything to you," she says, looking up at me with an expression that she wants to come off as annoyed, but it's anything but.

"Okay, then. Have fun walking home," I tell her, about to walk around her to leave, but she stops me.

Her right hand lands on my chest, and she pushes me back ever so slightly. She looks up at me from under her eyelashes, and I could be wrong, but from what I can tell, she has lust swimming in her eyes.

Never did I think I was going to see Eliana throw that emotion at me, yet here I am, experiencing it, and it's causing my body to buzz.

Maybe one night together will get her out of my system. Maybe we can have one night, and tomorrow we can go back to hating each other. Hating each other would definitely make working together a whole lot easier.

Eliana flexes her fingers against my chest, caressing the fabric of my shirt like she is contemplating whether she should rip it to shreds or not.

"Maybe I didn't like my other choice because I had a bad day, and I was hoping that my actual choice would help me forget it."

Help her forget.

I can do that, but before I agree to anything, I have to ask her a question that might make her knee me in the groin.

"And if I hadn't shown up, would you have gone home with him?"

If Miguel wasn't my friend, and she had gone out tonight, and I had stayed home, would she be in his car right now, heading to his place with the hopes that he would make her forget her bad day?

Eliana shakes her head and doesn't hesitate in answering. "Before you showed up, I had planned on getting a car and heading to your house, or at least to the beach. I was going to sit by the water and wait to see if you would have come out. That or maybe I would have knocked on your balcony door."

She was going to seek me out.

The last two times we've been within five feet of each other we were at each other's throats. We both spewed words of hate. Yet, somehow with all that we've said to each other, she was still going to come to me to comfort her.

She doesn't know me. She hates me, hates what I do for a living, and yet she was still going to come to me.

Knowing that does something to me.

I place my hand on top of hers and keep her from pulling away.

Her hand is soft, and I know without a doubt that every other part of her will be, too.

"I thought you hated me."

She nods. "I do, but that doesn't stop me from wanting you to fuck me." Her hand slides from under mine, and she slides it up my neck until I feel her fingers in my hair. "What do you say, Rodriguez? Can you put our differences aside and make today a whole lot better for me?"

Who am I to deny her when she asked so nicely?

"Let's go, and I will fuck this day out of existence."

CHAPTER SIX

ELIANA

EVERY SINGLE RULE that I have set for myself when it comes to men, more specifically to hockey players, went out the window the second that Christian told Miguel that he was going to take me home.

I don't know what it was about that specific moment, but seeing him act like that was enough to get every single nerve inside my body to wake up.

That was exactly what I had been hoping for from the second that I saw him walk into the bar earlier in the night. Up until that point, I was trying to convince myself that I shouldn't go to Christian's house after leaving the bar. I was going to do everything I could to talk myself out of the idea had sprung into my head after seeing an Instagram message during my lunch hour. I hated the guy, hated his profession, and he hated me. There was absolutely no reason for me to head down to his beach house and seek him out all because I wanted to forget a few messages.

I tried to figure out why I would even want to turn to Christian in the first place, and the only thing that I could come up with was that even though he is a hockey player, he is the complete opposite of the one who hurt me last. Even though he hated me, he would care enough to make me feel good and possibly make me feel worthy of having my body worshipped. It was a bad idea, but I still wanted to do it.

At least, I did for most of the day and for part of the evening.

When I got to the bar, after Miguel had invited me when he saw I was down earlier in the day, I tried to talk myself out of executing my plan. I was so close pulling the plug and not heading down to the beach when I was done at the bar. So damn close, but of course that all went to shit when I looked up and saw Christian walking in, heading toward the little group I was with.

It was as if life decided to play a dirty trick on me for wanting to throw my plan in the trash. Even more dirty when life decided to leave only one stool open right in front of me.

I tried to act as if him being there didn't affect me. I tried not to stare at him as much as I wanted to, and for the most part, I succeeded.

Then he called me hermosa, and all that started to go out the window. Even more so when I saw him texting someone, and he accused me of being jealous.

Was I?

Maybe a little, but I wasn't going to announce that to him.

The fact that I was even jealous is a bit mind blowing to

me. I have no reason to feel that way toward the man. I hate him. I shouldn't be jealous. Hell, I've only spoken to him twice, and neither time had flirting of any kind. Yet my mind and body wanted his attention on me and me alone.

Which is probably why I got bold and told him exactly what I wanted, and now I'm in his car, on the way to his house.

"We could have gone to my apartment, you know." I throw out as he drives down the winding mountain highway. It should be a crime to be a passenger in a car going down this road after a night of drinking. It's a surefire way to make you puke.

"I like my house better," Christian answers, taking another turn, and I have to make sure I remember to breathe. No way am I going to cover his car in vomit.

"If we would have gone to my place, you could be getting a blow job right about now. Instead, you're taking so many curves that I'm getting dizzy," I say, pouting in my seat.

Christian lets out a chuckle and I think that is the first time I've heard him laugh that didn't have a sarcastic tone following it.

"Nothing is stopping you from leaning over and taking me in your mouth," he says, quickly turning to throw me a wink.

The man starts to shift, and it takes me a second to realize what he's doing. He's starting to unbuckle his belt.

"Maybe if you weren't driving on this highway I would," I throw back at him, my mouth watering against my own will at the thought of having him in my mouth. Is he big? Would he hit the back of my throat and make me lose every single thought as I work him? "If I blow you right now, there might be a chance of me biting your dick off."

Christian gives me a shrug. "I wouldn't mind a few teeth grazes."

Why do I find that hot?

"Another time," I answer. I really don't want to get sick on him.

"So, this is going to happen more than once?" he asks, making one more turn through the trees until he eventually comes out on the historical Highway One.

Now I'm the one shrugging. "We'll see how tonight goes."

The man next to me lets out a snort and shifts one of his arms until it's on my lap, massaging my thigh. "Think I'm not going to be able to satisfy you?"

"You are a hockey player after all, for all I know, your ego isn't the only thing that needs a little help getting inflated."

He lets out a hum, and just continues to drive toward his house. All the while his hand is still on my thigh and moving up.

I hadn't regretted my outfit choice until right now.

"Baby, my ego isn't big, but I can tell you right now that my dick is and you will be begging for more before breakfast tomorrow morning," he tells me, but I can't concentrate on his words. My mind is on his fingers as they make their way between my thighs, opening up my legs just a bit and caressing me through the material of my pants ever so gently.

"Who is saying anything about breakfast?" I ask, trying to keep my voice even to not let him hear how he is affecting me.

"I am," he says, applying more pressure to his caresses. "You're not leaving my house until you have breakfast and at least six orgasms."

"Is that why the girl from a few weeks ago was still at your house well into the afternoon? Because you couldn't get her to at least six orgasms?"

A stupid question, I know, but I'm about to get into this man's bed. I should have a right to know about his sexual adventures.

Christian lets out a howl of laughter that I wasn't expecting. "She was still there because she wouldn't leave. Why do you think I had the music on so loud? I was trying to wake her up, but she wouldn't budge."

Damn. If he would have told me that the first day we met, I might have been nicer to him.

"And did you get tested after her? Have you at the very least changed your sheets? I'm not about to catch something from your extracurricular activities," I say to him. I don't know how I'm able to even use full sentences with him touching me the way that he is, but I am.

"I got tested, and I'm clean," he says, adding a little bit more pressure as he merges to the next lane. "And I changed my sheets weekly." I feel a sweet drag of his finger against the seam of my pants. "Can you say the same?"

He's torturing me.

I nod. "I'm clean, and I get tested every three months."

My body wants to squirm at his touch, but I'm trying to control it. He's affecting me, he's been affecting me for two weeks now, and I'm so close to giving in. I should just let all my urges take over, but I want him to sweat it out.

"Good. Now that that is settled," he says, merging again to pass up a small pickup truck, and in the process taking his hand off me. "Let's start making your day all the better. As much as I loved seeing your ass in those jeans, I'm going to need you to slide them off."

"Why would I do that?" I ask, but still start to push my seat back without waiting for his answer.

"Because I want to play with your pretty pussy and make you come before we get to the house. So, do as I say."

"I always thought you were grumpy, not bossy," I say, rolling my eyes at him, but I still do what he says.

"Hermosa, I can be both," he says as I push my hips up and wiggle myself out of my jeans.

As soon as they are off, I sit there, looking over at Christian, trying to figure out how we got here. Last week, he was threatening to throw me into the ocean. Now, he's seconds away from making me come with just his fingers.

"You think that you can do what you promised and drive at the same time?" I ask, grabbing the hand that is resting on the gearshift and placing it back on my thigh.

The second his hand meets my bare skin a shiver runs through my body. A shiver of the best kind.

Christian maneuvers the car through the lonely highway, only a few cars passing by this late at night, and starts moving his hand from the middle of my thigh up to my core like before. My legs open for him, like they have a mind of their own and are excited for what's about to happen.

His fingers graze my skin ever so gently, something that I wouldn't have expected from an NHL enforcer, before the tips of his fingers run along the lace that covers the most sensitive part of my body.

With each pass his fingers make, I can feel myself getting that much wetter.

"Who knew all I had to do to get you to be quiet was to play with your pussy?" Christian muses as he pats my inner thigh for my legs to open wider. I follow the silent order, and as soon as I do, he moves my panties to the side and starts to tease me some more.

I let out a moan when he starts circling my clit and get so lost in how good it feels that it takes me a second to give him a rebuttal.

"Who knew that all you needed to do is play with my pussy for me to actually like you and not want to rip your head off?" The words come out almost breathless, quickly followed by a moan.

This man has magic fingers.

A slap lands against my core, and instead of yelling out in pain, I'm letting out yet another moan in pleasure. The slap felt so damn good.

"Given how wet you are for me, I think what you feel toward me is a lot more than like."

The words that I want to respond with stay in my throat because before I can even open my mouth, he slides a finger into my entrance, and everything that I was about to tell him is forgotten.

"Fuck, you feel so slick. I'm getting hard just thinking

how you're going to feel wrapped around my cock."

All I can think about is how now I wish that it was his cock sliding in and out of me instead of his fingers.

He quickly slides his finger out and slides two back in, but his two fingers don't fill me. I need more.

"Drive faster, and we will get to that stage a whole lot sooner," I breathe out.

I throw my head back, feeling so close to a release yet so far away. I'm a minute or two away from begging him to make me come, to telling him to pull over and just fuck me, but I hold my words in.

I won't beg. At the very least, not yet.

"Impatient, aren't we?" Christian asks as his thumb sweeps against my clit, causing my right leg to spasm a bit at the pleasure.

"Make me come, or I swear the second that we get to your house, you dick won't be getting touched," I groan out, bucking my hips to get what I want.

Christian just chuckles when all of the sudden his fingers slide out of me, and is no longer touching me.

"What the hell are you doing?" I ask, sexually frustrated. "I was so close."

I'm about to whine some more and tell him that I don't need his hand, that I could do it on my own, when the car comes to a stop.

I was so damn lost in the pleasure that he was giving me, that I didn't notice that we had gotten off the highway and started making our way through the small coastal town to get it to his house.

This man has me losing my mind.

I'm about to suggest that we hurry up to the house to finish what we've started, when Christian leans over the center console and leans over my body and pulls the lever to make the seat go back.

A question is on the tip of my tongue when Christian surprises me again and slams his mouth against mine.

Like his fingers, his mouth is magic. He makes me forget every single thought of getting out of the car, and I let him have his way with my body right here.

As his tongue slides against my bottom lip, I let him in and get a small taste of him.

I'm enjoying his mouth molding perfectly to mine and how deliciously good his hand feels in my hair so much, that I almost miss his hand landing back on my pussy. He circles my clit with his fingertips ever so gently before moving his hand down and teasing my entrance.

He slowly slides one finger in and then another. I'm thinking he is about to go nice and slow when he slides his fingers out again only to slam back into me.

"Oh my god," I pant out, breaking our kiss in the process.

"You want to come, hermosa?" Christian asks, his lips moving down to my neck, all while his fingers continue to slam into me.

"Yes," I moan out, throwing my head getting thrown back, arching my whole body to give him better access to everything.

"Say the magic words," he says into my ear, working me to what feels like the edge of the world.

"Let me come," I say, my legs shaking trying to get my body to the release that it so desperately needs.

"Tsk tsk, hermosa." He slides his fingers out and slaps his hand against my pussy lips, spreading my arousal. Such delicious pain. "You know exactly what you need to say. So say it, and you'll get to come."

I hate him, but I'm starting to really like his bossy side.

Giving in, I reach for his face and bring it up until I'm able to look into his eyes. There is so much lust swimming in them that for a second, I forget what I was about to say.

With my hand on his cheek and me looking him straight in the eye, I give him what he's looking for.

"Please, Christian. Make me come, please."

He wants me to beg. Well, I'm begging.

"My name sounds so fucking hot coming from between your lips like that," he tells me right before he slams his mouth back onto mine.

This time his kiss doesn't distract me. I'm more than fully aware of what his hand and fingers are doing to me. I can feel absolutely everything. It feels like as I get closer and closer to my release, everything that Christian is doing is getting heightened with every passing second.

My legs are shaking uncontrollably, and I have to break our kiss yet again to be able to catch my breath. I'm panting so much that the windows are fogging up even if the weather outside is in the midfifties.

"I'm right there. Christian, please," I beg, needing this release more than I need air right now.

"Come all over my hand, Eliana. Coat it. Do it, and the

second that we get into the house, I will clean you and dirty you up all over again."

A moan fills the car and as he starts rubbing his thumb against my clit, I can't take it anymore. I coat Christian's hand just like he told me to do, and in the process, I let out a moan so loud that I'm sure if there were people walking the beach at this time of night, they would have heard me.

The hockey player who just gave me the most amazing orgasm with just his fingers lets out a small chuckle and kisses me on my neck and slowly moves down to my chest.

I can't believe that I just let this man finger bang me. What I can't wrap my head around even more is the fact that I'm ready to start round two with him.

"Take me inside," I say, my turn to give orders.

Christian hums against the tops of my breast, nipping at the cleavage that is showing.

"Whatever you want, hermosa."

CHAPTER SEVEN

CHRISTIAN

HOW THE NIGHT went from a night out with some of my childhood and high school friends to me bringing Eliana home and pleasuring her, is beyond me.

But weirder things have happened in my lifetime. If life decided to put Eliana in my path tonight, I wasn't going to tell it no. Do I find it crazy that the last two times I was within ten feet of this woman, we were biting each other's heads off, and now we are about to fuck like two bunnies in heat? Of course, I do, but again, life and all that.

Maybe fucking like bunnies will actually make us friends or at least friendly toward each other. Who knows?

As Eliana came down from her orgasm-induced high, I continued to touch her, to kiss her. I didn't know how long this thing between us was going to last, so I was going to enjoy myself and take my time. You know, so she doesn't hate me as much. I know my hate for her started to wither the second she told me that she was having a bad day. I wasn't seeing her as an annoying pain in the ass anymore at that moment. Instead, I was seeing her as a woman who hides a lot of what she is feeling and at times gets tired of hiding and wants to let those feelings go free but doesn't.

She only showed me this side of her for a few seconds, but I saw it. It was in her eyes and in the way her body stiffened just a bit.

It was quick but enough to make me want to give her what she wants.

After making out in the car for almost half an hour, I get out of the car and go to her side to open the door.

"Look at you actually being a gentleman," she says, reaching down to grab her discarded jeans before getting out of the car.

"My mom would have my head if I wasn't," I say, taking a step back and giving her some room, but still covering her enough so nobody else can see her in her lace panties.

It's dark and well after two in the morning, but there still could be someone out on the beach. I don't want anyone to catch a glimpse of her.

She gives me an appreciated smile before sliding on her pants.

"Would your mom also have your head if she knew you almost threw me in the ocean?" she says, pulling her jeans up after sliding both her legs in.

I'm starting to like this woman's mouth a little too much, and I haven't even felt it wrapped around my dick.

I give her a shrug marveling at her body a bit. "She might, but she will never find out."

"Maybe someone should grab her number from your phone and tell her," she tells me, a smirk forming on her face.

Grabbing someone's phone is something that I would do.

I've done it a few times to Liam and our other teammate Blake, and changed their ringtones when they aren't looking.

I wonder if we ignore all the dislike and all the banter, if we are actually a lot more similar than we'd want to admit.

"You'd never get past my passcode," I tell her, giving her a smirk of my own.

"Give me a few days, and I will have it figured out," she says, jumping up to situate her pants. I don't know why she's bothering, since they are going to be off again in a few minutes.

"There it is again. First you tell me you'll suck me off in the car another time, and now you are telling me that in a few days you'll have my passcode. Sounds to me like someone definitely wants to continue whatever it is we are about to do for a lot longer than just tonight."

Eliana's face shifts a bit under the moonlight. Like she's even surprised that she is talking about taking this further than tonight. She hadn't realized it until I pointed it out.

Quickly though, she composes herself.

"I don't, but like I told you earlier, we'll see how tonight goes, then I'll decide."

"You'll decide, huh? I don't get a say?" I pop an eyebrow at her, stepping closer to leave little room between.

She rolls her eyes at me. "Of course, you have a say. I'm not going to force myself on you."

I let out a small chuckle, silently telling her that I'm only teasing. "What if I do want you to force yourself on me? You won't hear me complain if you push me down right this second and make me eat your pussy." I close the distance between us even more if that is even possible and lower my mouth so it's right next to her ear. "I bet you are still wet from your release. I can lick you until you are all nice and clean and are about to come again."

Eliana shivers, and I feel it against my body. I should just pick her up and throw her over my shoulder and just put my mouth where my words say. There is no reason for us to still be talking. I should have my mouth on her pussy right about now.

"So, get on your knees," she orders, pushing me back slightly and starts to push me down.

I chuckle. "I'm not much into voyeurism. Everything nowadays lands on the internet. You want me on my knees, I'll gladly get on them, once we're inside."

She looks up at me through her lashes, and the way she is biting down on her lip, has me thinking so many dirty things.

Her lips are plump and so fucking full. They are so fucking perfect and suit her so well. Right now, next to her ass, her lips are my favorite thing about her. That might change once I have all of her.

Her arms make their way around my neck, and now she's the one whispering in my ear. "What are you waiting for then? Take me inside."

She doesn't have to tell me twice.

I don't hesitate in sliding my hands all over this woman's body until her ass is in my hands, and I have a good grip on her. She is a handful in all the best ways, and I'm not talking about her attitude and that mouth of hers.

Eliana lets out a yell, followed by a quick giggle, as soon as her feet are off the ground and I throw her over my shoulder.

"What's with you and throwing me over your damn shoulder?" she asks, slapping my ass.

"Maybe I want you to bite me again," I say, making my way from the car that is parked in my short driveway to the front of the house.

"If you don't put me down soon, I might," she grunts, and I don't have to see her to know that she is pouting.

I let out a growl at the thought of her teeth on me again. There is something about feeling a little pain during sex that is music to my ears.

It takes me two seconds to enter in my passcode to get into my house and quickly make my way to the living room. The bedroom should be my first choice, but I have plans for Eliana, and the couch gives me a lot more liberty for what I have in mind.

The whole way to the couch, Eliana is grumbling about how she should really stay away from men who can throw her around like a rag doll, and how she is a big girl and I'm just showing off, and how there is no chance in hell she is going to let me ruin her for all other men.

I don't say anything. I just keep the smirk on my face and close the last five feet between me and the couch.

There is no doubt in my mind that I will ruin her for all

other men. That's a fucking guarantee, and I'm going to make sure she knows it.

The second I can, I bend down and deposit Eliana on the couch. She crosses her arms and purses her lips as soon as she hits the cushion, but I don't let her pout her long.

"Strip," I order.

I'm surprised when she raises a perfectly sculpted eyebrow at me but follows through with my directions.

My eyes stay on her as she gets rid of the black V neck she is wearing, revealing a dark green lace bra underneath that just barely covers her nipples. My mouth waters at the sight, and it waters some more as she lifts up her hips, unbuttons her jeans and starts sliding them off her legs. All without getting up off the couch.

The second that she kicks off her pants, she leans back on the couch and looks me over like I'm her next meal and not the other way around.

I pause a few more seconds to take her body in, noticing that her panties are also a dark green. The color stands out against her skin, and it suits her perfectly. The color would also suit my floor.

"Are you going to strip? Or is this going to be a one-person show?" Eliana asks, spreading her legs just a tiny bit and letting one of her hands travel along her torso, leaving behind soft caresses.

Something that sounds like a growl leaves my lips as I watch her touch herself so softly. My hand needs to replace hers quickly.

She moves her hands off her body for a second and

reaches up to take the hair clip that she has in her hair out. The dark brown locks cascade down past her shoulders and frame her face and her chest perfectly.

If her coming on my fingers in the car earlier didn't make me fall on my knees for her, this sight definitely will.

The dark green and the dark brown complement her so well, add the fullness of her body and I'm a weak ass man.

I quickly pull my shirt off, not missing the groan that leaves Eliana's lips. I throw her a wink and keep my eyes on hers as I rid myself of the rest of my clothes. It only takes a few seconds, but as soon as I'm standing there in just my boxer briefs, something in her gaze and in the room changes.

There's more hunger, more lust. More yearning for each other and for what is about to happen. That feeling becomes even more apparent as I slide my briefs down and my cock springs out, already asking for Eliana's attention.

Not being able to resist her anymore, I close the distance between us, moving myself between her legs and reaching out to caress her face as gently as I possibly can. The lust in her eyes doubles as she looks my body up and down. The smirk she gives me as I bend down to take her mouth, tells me that she is excited about what I'm about to do to her.

My lips land on hers, all the while her hand lands on my cock. While our tongues slide against one another's, her hand strokes me, getting me harder than I already was.

Wanting to make her feel as good as she's making me feel, I slide the hand that is resting on the back of the couch down her body.

I cup her covered breast and rub the green lace against

her nipples to give her a bit of friction. The way she moans into my mouth tells me she likes it.

"You like a little discomfort, don't you?" I ask her, breaking our kiss ever so slightly to let her answer.

"Yes," she says through another groan as I rub the green lace against her nipple again.

I hum against her, my mind filling up with ideas. "Then let's give you more."

Now she lets out a hum and that hum continues as I rub the lace against her other nipple, and I slide my hand down her curves until I'm palming her pussy.

I can feel the stickiness from earlier through the lace, and that drives me even more crazy as I rub against her slit. She's sticky because I made her that way.

I slide my hand against her panties, and her hand continues to work me. My cock is pulsating in her hand, and I know that if she continues to do that, I might be coming on her chest instead of in her pussy like I would like. I pull back slightly, but she doesn't like that, and she tells me so by taking my other hand and placing it on her thigh and bringing me closer to her.

"Why are you pulling away?" she asks between kisses.

I move the hand that's on her face down to her breast before answering. "Because your hand feels too good, and I'm trying to prolong this."

She lets out another hum as my tongue slides against hers. "And what if I say fuck prolonging and tell you to get on the couch so I can take you in my mouth?"

Fuck, this woman.

I break our kiss and look down at her. "And here I was about to fall to my knees and make you come on my tongue."

The woman purrs. Even though she is a pain in my ass and hates me because I'm a hockey player, she just might be made for me.

"You can fuck me with your tongue in a little bit. Right now, I want you to get on this couch and slide into my mouth."

"Is that an order?" I ask, circling my fingers against her clit.

She bites down on her bottom lip and gives me a nod. "It is."

"Then who am I to deny such a request?" I say, giving her a grin that she reciprocates.

Following orders, I place one foot on the couch and then the other, until I'm standing on the furniture, and Eliana is under me.

The way she is looking up at me is something that will be engraved in my mind for a very long time.

I step closer to Eliana's mouth until the tip of my cock is so close that all she needs to do is lean forward a little bit and take me. And that's what she does.

With one last sensual look and a flutter of her eyelashes, the gorgeous woman under me leans forward and wraps her lips around my cock.

"Fuck," I grunt out as she slides her tongue against the tip and pulls me deeper into the warmness of her mouth.

I try my hardest not to buck my hips and cause my dick to slide in deeper into her mouth, but it's becoming near damn impossible. I place my hands on either side of her head and try to keep myself together.

But Eliana doesn't want that. No, she wants to drive me fucking wild because she hums around me and slides her hands up my thighs until one of them is cupping me and the other is sliding along my member with her mouth.

"Look at you taking my cock," I say, looking down at her and letting out a groan as I watch her. "This image is going to stay in my head for a long time, hermosa. Every time I jerk off, I'm going to picture you in this very position, taking care of me."

She nods as she takes me in deeper, and I as much as I want to pull back, she doesn't let me.

"You want to take more of me?" I ask her, watching her breasts bounce a bit as I slide in and out of her mouth. I get a nod from her and a tap on the thigh telling me yes.

Giving her a smile, I thrust into her mouth a little more.

"You have such a perfect mouth. Fuck, baby, I don't know how much more I can take. I want to come down your throat." I grunt out, feeling my legs wanting to give out a bit.

Her mouth feels so good that all I want to do is come with her lips wrapped around me and mark her in that way. But I have other plans for her, and coming in her mouth will have to be saved for later.

I thrust into her mouth two more times before I pull back and out of the warmness and throw myself on the couch next to her.

Eliana has a smirk on her face and saliva all down her chin, and the woman hasn't looked hotter.

With a growl, I pull her up and make her stand in front of me. Every single inch of her is on display for me and all it does is make me, all the more hungry for her.

I pull her body toward me, my hands automatically going to her bra to take it off and then to her panties to slide them off her thick thighs.

The second that she is completely naked, I waste no time peppering her skin with hungry kisses. My hands grab at her body, bringing her even closer to me.

"Christian," she pants out as I place a kiss on the top of her pussy, and her hands land in my hair.

There is something about the way she says my name like that that makes me so fucking desperate for her.

I give her pussy a lick, tasting her for the first time and instantly needing more.

"What do you need, Eliana?" I ask, sliding a finger along her folds and finding her wet.

My tongue continues to slide against her pussy, circling her clit and getting her closer to the edge of where I want her to be. I let my hands travel to her ass and grab her cheeks, needing my hands to be filled with her as much as my mouth is.

"I need you inside of me, please. I want to feel you fill me up."

The fact that she is telling me what she wants has pre-cum leaking out even more than it already when she was blowing me.

I give her pussy one last lick and pull her onto my lap.

She lets out a giggle, something that I'm not used to

hearing come out of her, and she settles on top of me with her legs caging me in.

"Ride me, hermosa. Slide me into your tight pussy, and take all that you want," I say, dropping my head into her chest and getting lost in it as if her tits are my own personal toys.

Eliana slides against me. Her pussy coating my cock with her arousal. The way her hips move is desperate, and I'm seconds away from taking over and giving her what she wants. But I don't. I'm going to let Eliana have all the control here. Tonight, is her show. She gives the orders; she tells me everything that she wants me to do. I'm simply her toy to do what she wants with, something that I'm more than okay with.

"No condom?" she asks, moving my face away from her chest and bringing it up so that she can place a hungry kiss against my lips.

"I can go get one," I tell her, taking her bottom lip between my teeth.

She shakes her head. "We're both clean, right?" I give her a nod. "I haven't been with anyone since I last got tested, and I have an IUD, so we are covered in that front. We can go without one."

I let out a small laugh. "And here I thought you hated me."

She rolls her eyes. "I do," she says, moving her hips again, causing my tip to slide closer to her entrance. "But right now, I hate you a little less." She slides some more. "I'm okay with it if you are."

"As long as you agree to not be with anybody else for however long we are doing this," I say against her mouth.

"The same thing goes for you. No other women in your bed as long as I am there. I don't share whatsoever. So, if you plan on bringing someone else home tomorrow, go get that condom."

I shake my head. "I'm all yours, hermosa, until you say otherwise."

Eliana hums and lifts up her hips. "I like the sound of that."

Her hand wraps around my cock and she brings my tip to her pussy, coating me in her arousal before sliding me in and taking all of me.

A sweet gasp sounds through the room as she slides down on me and settles on my lap.

Fuck. I thought her mouth was perfection, but now that her pussy is wrapped around me, I know that I'm wrong.

"You feel so good," she pants out, placing her hands on my shoulders and starts to bounce up and down. "*Jódeme*, Christian. Fuck me until I scream."

The way she says *jódeme* is what does me in.

Everything goes out the window, and I give her every single inch of what she wants. I fuck her until my name is the only thing that she can remember, and both our releases are mingled inside of her and dripping down her thighs.

CHAPTER EIGHT

I'M SEEING STARS.

My eyes opened not even five minutes ago from a deep sleep, and I'm already seeing stars.

Why am I seeing stars so early in the morning? Because I currently have a dark-haired, muscled-filled hockey player with magic fingers and a magic tongue between my legs licking every single inch of my core.

When I decided to go out last night, I did not think I would wake up the next morning like this. With a man that I keep saying that I hated and wanted nothing to do with between my legs after spending countless hours engaged in sex-filled activities, yet here I am, and I'm loving every single damn second of it.

A moan escapes my mouth, and I slide my hand into his hair and give him a hard tug.

"Christian," I breathe out, pulling some more, not sure if

I want him off me or to bring him closer. Five minutes, and this man already has me so close to an orgasm.

As if all the ones that he gave me last night weren't enough.

If I had my camera with me right now, I would be taking a picture of him eating me out as if I'm his last meal.

He hums against me; his fingers digging into my thighs, and continues lapping me up as if I were an ice cream cone, and he is trying to lick up all the ice cream before it melts.

"You saying my name does things to me," he says, moving his mouth from where it was on my clit to my inner thigh. I try to pull his face back to where it was, but the bastard doesn't budge.

"Put your face back where it was, and I will say it again," I say, using the sweetest voice that I can muster.

Christian lets out a chuckle as he kisses his way up my body to my chest. "What if I want to take my time making you come?"

He's crazy. Absolutely crazy.

"How would you feel if I took my time with you?" I throw back, wrapping my legs around his waist and trying to push him down, but the man is too big for me to move even an inch.

"I wouldn't mind." He shrugs right before taking one of my nipples between his teeth.

He's torturing me. He's crazy and torturing me.

"You would be okay with me licking your dick as slowly as possible, giving you feather-like touches, torturing you, and getting you to the edge, not following through and not letting you come and then kissing my way up your body? All while your balls are turning a nice shade of blue?" I say, trying to squirm under him to get a little bit of friction where I need it the most.

"Are you trying to tell me that you are going to get blue balls if I don't make you come with my mouth?" he asks, moving his mouth up to my neck all the while his hands grab onto my breasts, and he gives me a hardy grip that makes me moan.

"That's exactly what I'm saying," I whimper.

"You will be okay," he tells me right before nipping at the skin behind my ear.

"Christian, I swear," I whine, giving him more access to my neck.

"Ask nicely," he says, giving me another nip.

"I did!"

"I didn't hear the word please." Another nip lands on my neck.

"And here I thought I was in charge," I say, remembering last night on the couch when he handed all the control over to me. God, the image of me riding him is going to be in my mind forever. A guy has never made me feel so damn powerful before. Everything that I wanted and told him to do, he did, and it was so damn hot.

"You were last night. Now it's my turn, and I want to hear you say please. I want you to beg for it." A growl sounds out through his bedroom.

This man growls. A lot. Who growls that much? I find it so damn sexy, though.

If I want to get what I want, I have to give him what he wants.

"I said please last night." I argue, the please already on the tip of my tongue.

"I want to hear you say it this morning," he says, dragging his tongue along the length of my neck and moving back down to my chest. At least he's moving down.

A grin forms on my face, loving this game between us. "Fine," I say through a smile. "Please, Christian. Make me come, please. I'm begging you. I need it."

A hum vibrates through his body. "Was that so hard?" he asks, moving his body lower to where I want him.

"No," I breathe out as I feel his tongue at the edge of my mound.

The second that his tongue makes contact with my clit, I'm seeing stars again.

Christian sucks my clit into his mouth, and I feel his fingers at my entrance, teasing me and bringing me to the edge even more.

One finger and then two, slide into me, and I can't help but to arch my body to get more of what he is offering.

"Such a needy pussy," Christian says against me as his fingers slide in and out of my core. "So tight, and so damn warm. Look at you taking my fingers so well it makes me wish it was my cock instead."

I let out a moan. "Me, too."

"Come on my tongue, and I'll slide my cock into this pretty pussy of yours."

His tongue starts to move more aggressively, and his

fingers follow the motions he was giving me last night in the car. Christian is doing so much that my body doesn't know whether to cheer in excitement or to weep in despair with its need for more.

As he moves his fingers in and out of me, I feel closer and closer to the edge of the cliff.

"Christian, please. I'm so close," I pant out, my hands grabbing onto his hair as if it were my lifeline.

"Grind against my face, baby," he says against my folds. "Take anything you want."

I do what he says. I take what I want. I grind against his face and marvel at how good it feels to have his tongue on me and his fingers in me. It's everything.

It doesn't take much. Christian does a come-hither motion with his fingers, and I'm exploding around them.

"Oh my god. Oh my god. Oh my *god*," I yell out, feeling my whole body convulse with the orgasm.

"That's my girl, so damn perfect." Christian makes his way up my body again after licking me clean. "Are you ready for your reward?" he asks before kissing me and giving me a taste of myself.

I nod my head, because that feels like the only body part that I'm able to move. "Yes, please. I need you to fill me up."

"Your wish is my command," he says, shifting a bit to give him the perfect angle to slide into home base.

The second that he is fully in me, I forget about the orgasm I just had and feel as if I can fly again. Christian was telling the truth when he said he was big and he fills me perfectly.

If this man wasn't a hockey player and wasn't a pain in my ass, he would be my perfect man.

"Fuck, you feel fucking perfect," he grunts out as he starts to move in and out of me.

I want to tell him that he feels perfect, too, but I don't want to inflate his ego, so I keep the words to myself. Instead, I wrap my arms around his neck and my legs around his waist and bring his body even closer to me than it already is.

His weight is on me, and it feels amazing.

"You take my cock so damn well," he tells me, pressing his forehead against mine.

All I can do is nod because it feels like he is fucking me into a stupor.

"Did I finally find a way to quiet down that mouth of yours?" he asks, a smirk forming on his face.

I dig my heels into his ass as hard as I can. "If you want to have this mouth of mine wrapped around your dick again, I would shut up and continue to fuck me."

"You say the sweetest things to me." His mouth lands on mine. The kiss is just as hungry as every other kiss that we've had, and I like it too much to pull away.

As Christian slides his tongue against mine, I realize something. I have never felt this much hunger for someone. I've been with a handful of people in my lifetime, and Christian Rodriguez is the only one who has made me this hungry for them. This crazy. This desperate. He is the first man who has made me want more than just one night or even more than just a weekend or week.

Is this what hate sex is? Are we even having hate sex?

I don't know, but I don't ever want to give it up if it's going to feel this good every single time.

"I need you to get there, Eliana. I'm so fucking close," he says, breaking our kiss and slamming into me, like he needs this release just as much as I do.

Giving him a nod, I slide my hand between our bodies and start circling my clit, getting me as close to the edge as he is.

"Shit," Christian lets out as he pulls back and watches my hand between us. "Keep touching yourself, baby. Get yourself there. I need you to get there before I do."

I feel my walls constrict and my legs starting to shake as they rest around his waist. He slams into me, and I'm about to set off.

He continues to slam into me, over and over again, and each time he brings me closer to where he wants me to be.

"Right there. Keep going," I pant out, bringing his face back to mine. "You feel so good inside me. So, so good." I close my eyes, losing myself in everything that he is making me feel. "Oh my god, Christian!"

I explode around him, and not even a minute later, Christian is slamming his face into my neck and getting lost in his own release.

"Fucking hell," he murmurs into my neck, sounds as breathless as I feel.

"Fucking hell is right," I'm able to get out, feeling absolutely sedated.

The second that Christian slides out of me and moves his body off mine and onto the bed next to me, I miss him.

That feeling quickly disappears when he wraps his arm around me and brings me closer to his body. I'm not much of a cuddler, but for this man, I might want to be.

"Let's get you cleaned up. I owe you breakfast." He places a kiss against my hair and starts to get up from the bed.

"If you can make pancakes, I might hate you a little less." I throw out as he walks over to his bathroom.

"I'll see what I can do."

CHAPTER NINE

CHRISTIAN

"I HAVE TO CONFESS SOMETHING," I say to Eliana as I place a plate of pancakes in front of her.

After our orgasm-filled morning, and I cleaned up the mess that we made, I made good on my word and cooked her breakfast. Thank God I had some package mix in my pantry from a family breakfast a few weeks ago, because otherwise I wouldn't be able to see that happy sparkle on Eliana's face.

Breakfast and six orgasms is what I promised her, and she got more than six orgasms and now it's time for breakfast.

"Oh yeah? And what is that?" she asks, stuffing a few pieces of her pancake into her mouth. "This isn't really your house?"

I chuckle. "I'll show you the deed if you want me to," I answer, taking a sip from my coffee.

"Nah, that would just make me hate you even more," she says with a shrug. "So, what do you have to confess?"

I take a bite of my eggs before answering. "I know who you are."

"And who am I?" she asks, going a little stiff and keeping her eyes on her food.

"Shawn Anderson's daughter. And I should I also say the Dark Knights' new team photographer," I answer, getting straight to the point.

The point causes Eliana to put her fork down and look up at me. I try to read her expression, but I can't get a clear read on her.

"Have you known this whole time?" she asks, wiping the corners of her mouth with a napkin.

I shake my head. "I found out last night. Your name sounded familiar, and I couldn't pinpoint where I heard it from. So I asked someone."

She gives me a nod as she reaches for her own coffee mug. "Let me guess. Liam? Because if you would have asked my dad, he would have called me right away."

Now I'm the one nodding. "Yeah, he told me to not get on your bad side. You know since you now control all the pictures that the public sees of me in my uniform."

"And are you going to listen to him?" She raises an eyebrow at me, challenging me.

I give her a shrug. "I think I will continue to take my chances."

"Ha!" she lets out before going back to her food.

I follow suit but only for a minute or two before I'm back to asking questions. "Why didn't you mention anything?" I ask around a mouth full of eggs.

"Why would I?"

"Oh, I don't know. I could have been nicer to you? You're my coach's daughter for Christ's sake." God, if he finds out the shit I have done to his little girl, some of the shit I have said, he will have my ass. I can say bye to the first line.

"What if I didn't want that? What if I didn't want you to be nicer to me? People have been treating me differently because of my dad all of my life. You shouldn't treat me differently just because of who my dad is."

The way she's being defensive about it tells me that people do a lot more than treat her differently because of who her dad is. I want to ask, but I don't know if we are there yet. Hell, up until twenty-four hours ago, I thought I hated this woman. Now that hate has turned into something completely different.

"Is your dad why you hate hockey players?" I ask, not letting the real question that is floating in my mind out.

Eliana lets out a sigh. "Maybe like ten percent of it."

"And the other ninety percent?" The question slips out without me even thinking about it.

Light-brown eyes meet my caramel ones. "Not something that I am willing to talk about over pancakes. Maybe with a whole bottle of wine in my system, but not right now."

Someone hurt her.

She doesn't have to say the words. I can see it in her eyes and in the way her shoulders tense up. Someone hurt her badly, and because of that, she decided to lump all hockey players together, so that she doesn't have the possibility of getting hurt again.

I wouldn't do that.

Jeez. One night with this woman, and I'm already thinking past this morning.

I give her a nod and don't push her. "Well, since we are going to be working together come September, if you ever find yourself with a whole bottle of wine, then my ears are open."

That shouldn't be something I offer. We're not friends. I have no idea what we are, but whatever it is, I want to be there for her if she ever needs it.

"What would be in it for you?" she asks, a small bite to her tone.

"Nothing. Me listening to whatever made you hate hockey players isn't a ploy to get something from you or from your dad. I'm already on his team. What else would I ask for?"

She gives me a shrug. "A brand spanking new contract with a whole lot more money."

I let out a snort. "Your dad has power, but not that much power. If I wanted a new contract, your dad isn't who I would go to. I wouldn't go to you either."

Eliana doesn't say anything. She just looks at me without any expression on her face. Not hearing her say anything at all makes me realize just how much I like it when she doesn't shut up and she's full of sass and attitude.

"Then maybe I will take you up on that offer," she says, moving her food around her plate. "If the time ever comes."

I give her a nod. "If the time comes, you know where I will be."

She nods and goes back to her food and so do I.

We eat in silence for a few minutes, and after she is done with her food, Eliana breaks the silence.

"I have to ask, did my dad tell you he had a daughter?"

Her question throws me.

I take my last bite and answer her question. "He's told everyone. He doesn't mention you often, but he does mention you. He has a picture of you when you were a kid in his office."

"Yeah, apparently I'm the only one who didn't know about that picture," she grumbles under her breath, but I ignore the comment and ask her a question instead.

"Is he supposed to keep you a secret or something?"

"No, I just never expected him to talk about me."

Like that isn't cryptic as shit. Because I'm nosy as hell, as Liam likes to call it, I keep pressing. "Why?"

Eliana looks up at me like she is trying to decide if she wants to have this conversation with me or not. Thankfully by the look on her face, she decides to go ahead.

"My relationship with my dad is complicated. Has been for years. More so since my mom died five years ago. Up until I got hired by the Knights, we didn't really talk or see each other. Maybe once or twice a year. When we did, it always ended in a fight, or one of us got angry about something stupid, and we wouldn't talk to each other for six months or more. When we lost my mom, I threw myself into traveling and work, and he threw himself into the team even more than he already had. I always thought that my dad didn't care about what I did or if he even told people about having a daughter because then they would ask where she was, and he wouldn't know."

Her voice breaks a little. I can see it in her face and hear it in her voice that there is more to the story, but I'm not going to push her to tell me.

"Is that why you have a different last name than him? Because it was complicated?" I ask, something that I've been curious about since last night.

"And here I thought you weren't paying attention to me last night," she says, throwing me a smirk.

"You were the only thing that I paid attention to last night," I tell her the truth.

A small blush creeps up her cheeks, but she tries to hide it and gets back to the topic we were just talking about.

She gives me a head shake. "No. My full name is Eliana Solis-Anderson. My mom is Puerto Rican, so I got her last name, too. My dad filled out my birth certificate wrong, and instead of making it Anderson Solis, he put my mom's last name first. In the end, it worked out. I use Solis in a professional setting, and my whole last name everywhere else."

Puerto Rican.

That explains how she knows Spanish.

"So do you know how to make mofongo?" I say, wiggling my eyebrows at her, trying to lighten the mood a bit.

I knew that our head coach didn't have a good relationship with his daughter. I've heard things with my own ears, and Liam has told me a thing or two.

Never did I think that I wanted to know more than what I already did, but I do. And I have so many questions I want to ask, but I don't want Eliana to run away from whatever this is between us.

She hasn't told me she wants to stab me to death today, so I see that as progress.

"Is that your way of asking me to make it for you?" she asks, a small smile spreading on her lips.

I give her a curt nod. "It is."

"Well, I guess you're in luck because I do know how to make it."

"How about we make a trade then? You make me mofongo, and I make you whatever Mexican dish your little heart desires?" I throw out, planning ahead to be able to see this woman again.

Something has shifted between us between since the last time we saw each other and last night. Maybe it was me threatening to throw her in the ocean. Maybe it was a better understanding of who each other are. Whatever the case may be, I know for a fact that I don't want this to be the last time that I see Eliana this summer before reporting to training camp.

As much as I thought that this woman annoyed me, I've grown to enjoy our conversations.

"And you said that I was the one who was planning on this extending past one night," she throws in my direction, a laugh following right behind it.

I'm starting to really like her laugh, and I want to hear it some more.

Fuck. I think I'm developing a crush on the woman who was a pain in my ass a week ago. Who knew guys can have crushes past the age of sixteen?

"What can I say? I have somehow become attached to you sometime between the orgasm in the car and that lovely wakeup call this morning. Even if you are an annoying pain in the ass sixty percent of the time."

Another blush creeps up her cheeks, and her smile becomes slightly bigger.

"If anyone is a pain in the ass, I would say that it's you, and not me," she throws out, picking up her coffee mug, hiding that pretty blush behind the porcelain.

"Agree to disagree," I say, throwing her a wink.

She takes a sip of her coffee before putting the mug back down on the kitchen table and facing me straight on. "I may have gotten attached to you, too."

If there wasn't a table between us, I would be dragging her onto my lap and having my way with her yet again. She's only wearing one of my T-shirts, so it wouldn't take much to get her naked.

"I knew you found me charming." I throw her another wink.

Eliana lets out a snort. "Please. If anything, I got attached to your body and the magic it performs. It has nothing to do with your charming personality."

"Keep telling yourself that. I'm a catch, and you know it. No matter the power of my dick."

Her laugh sounds out, and for the next two hours, I do everything that I can to hear it as much as I can.

After cleaning up our dishes and then cleaning up the

kitchen, we head out to the back porch to spend the remainder of our time together watching the waves crash against the shore. We talk about the different foods that we have tasted from different Latin American countries and some of the places we've both traveled to. We don't touch on childhoods or hockey whatsoever.

I was right thinking we are both similar even though there are certain aspects that say we shouldn't be.

After the previous two interactions we had before last night, you would think that we would have spent those two hours spewing out insults at one another, but that wasn't the case. I enjoyed my time with Eliana more than I expected, and from the way she laughs and smiles, I might be able to guess that she feels the same way.

"I should get going," Eliana states after checking her phone. "I have an early shoot tomorrow that I have to prepare for."

We're currently sitting on the couch I have on the balcony. Well, I'm sitting, and Eliana is spread out, with her legs on my lap and her upper body still covered by my T-shirt.

She says that she has to go, but she doesn't make a move to get up.

My hand continues to caress her calf just like it has been doing for the last hour or so. Definitely didn't expect to be this comfortable with the woman who broke into my house a few weeks ago.

"Let me change really quick, and I'll take you home," I offer, not wanting to end our time together.

"It's okay. I can call a car," she says, finally sitting up causing my hand to fall from her calf.

"Eliana." I try to argue.

"Christian," she throws back, raising an eyebrow at me, telling me to challenge her.

I will never win against this woman.

"Fine, but at least give me your number so I can call you when you get home."

"You mean *you* give me *your* number, so *I* can call *you*. Not the other way around."

"No, I meant give me your number so I can call you," I say to her, a grin spreading across my face.

"You're weird as hell, but whatever. Give me your phone." She holds out a hand, and I let out a laugh as I reach over to the table in front of us and hand over my phone. "You better not use it at two in the morning for a booty call," she grumbles.

"No promises on that one," I joke.

She grumbles under her breath as she types in her phone number and hands it back to me.

I instantly call her and notice that she has a generic ringtone, and I promise myself that the next time I see her, I will change it. Generic ringtones are fucking boring.

We silently walk back into the house, and Eliana gets dressed while I call her a car. I would much rather drive her home, but I may get attacked somehow, so I will save myself.

When the car arrives, Eliana is all ready to go, so I walk her out, even though she told me not to.

"I'll call you when you get home," I say, opening up the back door of the waiting car for her.

"A little stalkerish, but whatever floats your boat."

"See you later, pain in my ass," I say, leaning in and giving her a chaste kiss. Something that takes both of us by surprise, but the smile she wears quickly has the surprise evaporating.

"See you later, grumpy. Don't brood too much."

I shake my head at her and watch as she gets into the car. I stay outside until the car starts to drive off, and when it's out of sight, I start to head back in.

I'm not even inside two seconds when my phone rings. I grab it from where it is on the kitchen counter and check who it is.

I snort as I answer. "You just left. Let me guess you miss me and my magic dick already?"

"God, no. I called because I forgot to tell you something," Eliana's voice comes through the other end.

"Oh yeah? And what is that?"

"I still hate you, Rodriguez," she says, followed by a quick giggle.

"Don't worry, Solis. I still hate you, too."

CHAPTER TEN

CHRISTIAN

ONE OF THE disadvantages of spending the offseason several states away from your home rink is the fact that you can't just drive to your team's facility and get in some ice time whenever you want. Well, at least to me, it's a disadvantage.

While a large number of the players in the league have access to an ice rink wherever they land for the offseason. Be it be a team-affiliated rink, a rink that is close to home with no NHL affiliation, or even the rink that they built in their own house, I don't have any of that in my part of California.

Sure, there are ice rinks within a fifty-mile drive from me, but a large number of them are in enemy territory or have very limited hours. And while I don't mind stepping into enemy territory and stepping into their team-affiliated rinks, I try not to do it very often. I don't want them to get the wrong idea.

And as much as I want to build a rink in my own house, no way was I going to spend over ten million dollars on a house in the Bay Area that would give me enough property to do that. Especially since I don't need more than two rooms.

I have to get creative with how I get some skating time. Workouts are not a problem; skating, on the other hand, can be.

As much as I would like to feel the ice under my blades every single day, inline skating gets me through when I need it the most.

Especially when my off season is a lot shorter than it usually is, with the Dark Knights winning the Cup and all.

Ever since I signed with the Knights almost five years ago, I've had at least four months to gradually get ready for the season. What with our team always choking when we were close to playoff time. But this is different. We have the Cup, and we have to work twice as hard to get ready for the season to come.

Something that me and every single one of my teammates are more than happy to do. Usually, our offseasons are filled with family time, golf, and fishing, but this summer is different. If we are going to keep the Cup where we want it, we have to put in twice the work to show everybody that the Knights winning the Cup wasn't a one-time thing.

Which is why I'm currently under the hot July sun, sweating my ass off, shooting pucks into a net that I've had since I was a kid.

I could have done this in my garage where I have an air conditioner, or even at my parents' house where it's a lot cooler, but no, I decided to come to the park near the house to get a quick workout in. Days like today are when I should really think about my choices.

At least there aren't a bunch of kids around right now. There usually are since it's summer vacation and all that. But somehow, I got lucky with only a few moms and kids over at the playground. Nobody around who will come and mess with my concentration.

I skate around the asphalt, losing myself in the music coming in through my earbuds, and shooting the pucks that I strategically placed throughout the small court.

I've been at it for about two hours, and I should call it a day, but my concentration is on point, and I want to get in as much work as I can.

For the next forty minutes or so, I'm so deep in the zone that I don't notice there is someone at the entrance to the court taking pictures of me with their camera. Most of the time, I would be bothered by people taking my picture without my permission, but given who it is, I'm more than okay with it.

"How long have you been standing there?" I ask, taking out my earbud and skating over to where the intruding photographer is standing.

Eliana gives me a shrug, not moving from her spot where she is leaning against the chain link fence. "About fifteen minutes. Quake practice ended early, so I decided to come this way."

Since our night together almost a month ago, Eliana and I have been spending a lot more time together. Both in bed and out of it. We definitely don't hate each other as much as we did when we first met. We don't see or talk to each other every single day, but there is still constant communication going on between us that definitely puts us in the more than a friend and less than a couple category. Is that something we should talk about? Maybe, but neither of us feel inclined to do so.

Last night she had texted me about possibly grabbing lunch today after she was done with her morning practice with the Quakes. I told her yes, and this morning I sent her the address of the court so that she could meet me here.

"Why didn't you interrupt me?" I say, wiping the sweat off my face with the shirt I took off when I got here and tucked into my shorts.

"I was told a long time ago that you don't interrupt a hockey player while he's in the zone. Besides, I was able to get some pictures you can use for your socials if you want."

Her hockey player comment sticks in my brain. Is that something that she heard from her dad or someone else? She said that her dad was only a small part of why she hates hockey players, and I've come to learn that her hate sprinkles into the sport itself, but that's all. She hasn't voiced what or who is to blame for most of her hate for the game and its players.

Its' comments like the one she just made that make me want to ask, but I hold it in. She'll tell me when and if she wants to.

I ignore the intruding comment and turn the conversation to her pictures.

"I don't post on social media, but if you took the pictures, then I'm willing to break my rule for you."

"How sweet of you," she says, sending an eye roll my way, all the while a smirk forms on her lips. "You tagging me in a picture will make my career."

Her being sarcastic is like music to my heart.

"Hey, I can get you places."

She lets out a snort. "If I didn't use my dad's name to get to where I am, what makes you think I'm going to use yours?"

I give her a shrug. "You like me more."

Another snort. "That's debatable, but okay. Are you almost done? I'm hungry, and the sandwich that I ate on the way is not cutting it."

I nod. "Let me pack up, and we can go."

She gives me a smile, and I go do what I have to do.

This has been our routine for the last few weeks. We meet somewhere, either my house, the gym, the Quakes practice facility, or their stadium, or somewhere random and go grab a bite to eat and then spend the rest of the day together either at my place or at her rental.

Ninety percent of the time it's at my place because, according to Eliana, the beach and hearing the waves is calming to her. Because I feel the same way, and it's the very reason I bought the house, I was more than okay with spending almost all of our time together there. Is she in the one place that I like to be alone? Sure, but having her there isn't as bad as I had expected. It feels nice to share that house with someone who enjoys it as much as I do.

Never thought I would even think, that but here we are. So much for me hating this woman. A part of me still wants to throw her in the ocean just to see what she will do. I'm an ass, I know.

The next five minutes are spent taking off my skates and picking up the pucks that are all over the court. After putting everything in my hockey bag including my gloves and the sweat-covered shirt, I grab the net and my stick before heading back to where Eliana is still standing.

"Does this place have a shower?" she asks, wrinkling her nose as I close the distance between us.

I shrug. "It's got a two-stall restroom that doesn't get cleaned as often as it should. Why?"

She looks me up and down like I have a disease or something, and I completely miss the point. "Because I don't know if I can sit through lunch with you smelling like that. You stink."

I'm sweating, but no way I stink. For good measure, I check by lifting my arm and smell my armpits and then my hands. My hand definitely smells from my gloves, but that's normal. Just a quick hand wash, and it will be gone. It's not like I was working out in full gear. Now that smell is bad. I have to get a new hockey bag every year because of it.

"I don't stink," I tell her.

"Yeah, you do," she argues. "You smell like an old hockey bag that was never cleaned out."

I wonder if this is what Liam was talking about when his girlfriend Chloe told him he smelled like rotten cooked cheese. By the end of last season, he made it his mission to shower before he went home. Pretty sure he will continue doing it for the rest of his career.

"It's called sweat."

"It's called disgusting, and you need a shower," Eliana throws back, gagging a little for effect.

I can either concede and go home to take a shower, or I can skip the shower altogether and just go to lunch and make her suffer with the smell.

The second one can lead to a few things, one of them would possibly knee to the balls as payback for making her smell my supposed stench.

I like my balls a little too much to make them go through that.

So conceding it is.

"Fine," I say, giving up on the argument. "How about we head to my house so that I can shower, and you can order food, and have it delivered there? Would that make you happy?"

"I'm always happy being close to the ocean. Not smelling you and your nasty sweat would be an added bonus."

"Then let's go, princess."

"How did you end up playing hockey?" Eliana asks hours later as we sit on the back balcony, looking at the sun setting over the ocean.

She's sprawled out on the patio sofa again with her legs on my lap. The only difference between when we first did this and now is that she's still in her clothes and is not wearing one of my T-shirts like I would have wanted her to. Which is fine, I'll have her wearing just my shirt in no time.

"Why do you want to know?" I ask, sliding a hand over her covered leg.

She gives me the best shrug she can in her current position. "Don't take this the wrong way, but hockey is very much a white-man-dominated sport. It's not often you see an individual of color on the ice at the professional level."

She's right.

Across the NHL, fewer than ten percent of the players identify as something other than Caucasian. It's more than it was a few years ago, but it could be a lot better.

Me choosing hockey as my sport instead of soccer or baseball was definitely surprising to most people in my life. More so when I decided I wanted to go pro and actually succeeded.

"When I was about five or six, my dad got tickets to a Sharks' game as a gift from his work. We didn't know much about it other than what we'd seen on TV, so my dad was going to give the tickets away."

No me gusta. ¿Para qué voy a ir? The memory rings clear in my ear.

"My dad didn't want to go. I still remember him telling my mom that he didn't even like hockey, and he had no reason to go. But my mom told him it would be fun for me and my brother, to keep the tickets, and to take us. He finally agreed, so we went. I was small, but I still remember what it was like walking into the arena. We were a baseball family and walking into Candlestick Park the few times we went never felt the same way to me as walking into that arena did. It was the second I walked in there, there was electricity running through my veins. And then the game started, and it was so different from anything else. From any other sport. I fell in love with it right away. When we got home that night, as soon as I walked in the door, I told my mom that I wanted to play hockey. At first, she told me no, that it was too dangerous, but I asked every single day until she said yes."

"Did you annoy your mom? Is that why she said yes?" Eliana asks through a chuckle.

I can't help but laugh with her. "Probably. I can be very determined when I want to be."

"I know a thing or two about that," she tells me, nudging me with her heel.

"What are you talking about?"

"Um, hello. You were determined to throw me in the ocean."

"That was a different type of determination" I throw a wink at her.

While I throw her a wink, she rolls her eyes at me. "Whatever. Answer the question. Did your mom only say yes because you annoyed the hell out of her?"

I let out a small laugh. "You would think, but no. At least that's what she told me when I asked her years ago. She said that she let me play because she saw how excited I was talking about it. She wanted to see if that excitement was real or if it was all talk. So, she and my dad looked into the few youth hockey leagues this part of the state has to offer. They found out the Sharks have a youth program where they offered skating classes and hockey lessons. They signed me up, and in no time, I was a Junior Shark.

"I stayed in the program all through high school, won a NorCal Championship, and when I was eighteen decided to try my hand at the draft. Like you said the league is dominated by white players, no way was anyone going to draft the brown kid from an agricultural town who hasn't been living and breathing hockey since he was in diapers. But I took the chance, and to my surprise, the team that built me into the player I was decided I was good enough to take a chance on. I was surprised as fuck, but I was thankful. My parents were, too."

Eliana shifts until she is sitting up, and her legs are no longer on my lap. She surprises me, though. I thought that she was going to just sit next to me, but instead she brings her body closer to mine until there is no space between us and leans her head against my shoulder.

"I looked you up once. I was watching TV and flipping through the channels when I came across a Knights game. You guys were playing the Sharks a few weeks after you got traded, and the commentators were talking about how they wished you had stayed with the Sharks. They wanted their hometown player back."

I lean my head to rest on top of hers. "Yeah, my first year in Chicago, I wanted to go back, too. I loved being a Shark. They'd been my favorite team since I was six. I thought I was going to wear pacific teal all of my career. I was so damn close to asking your dad and our GM at the time to trade me."

"Why didn't you?" she asks, her voice filled with curiosity.

"Because I realized that I wasn't made to be the hometown player everyone wanted me to be. With the Sharks, I would have always had the title. Everyone was going to know my name, would want a piece of me. I would always have to be the perfect player, when I knew for a fact that I wasn't. I didn't want that, and it took me a whole season with the Knights to realize just how good I had it there. I missed my old team, sure, but I was good where I was. The Knights never have wanted me to be anything but who I am, grumpy and all and they've stood behind me when shit got tough."

"So, you're planning to be a Dark Knight for life?" Eliana asks, nudging my arm with her head to be able to lift it and place it around her shoulders. I don't hesitate in bringing her body closer to mine.

"If I have a choice, yeah, that's the goal, but who knows?. I might end up in Arizona or something."

"Ew. Arizona is way too hot. At least go to Seattle or New York." I'm not looking at her, but I know that she is wrinkling her nose, like she does when she doesn't like something.

"Why? Are you planning on visiting?"

"Please. You'll be an afterthought if you ever leave the Knights," she says through a laugh.

Why is it that I wanted her to say the opposite?

Fuck, am I getting attached to this woman?

Maybe I am.

"What about you? Why photography?" I ask, trying to shift my thoughts in a different direction than me developing feelings for this woman. We're sleeping together, that's it.

Then why is she in your arms right now as if you two were a couple?

Because it's cold outside.

Eliana is silent for a minute or two. For a second, I start thinking that she didn't hear me, when she finally says something.

"I wasn't as young as you when I discovered my love for taking pictures," she starts off, cuddling deeper into my side. "It was actually something I discovered when I was eighteen. The summer I graduated high school, I went to Europe with a group. Before I left, my mom gave me a camera, and she told me to look at this trip through the lens of a camera and not through the lens of my phone. I had brushed it off as something she probably saw on an inspirational sign or something, but I still grabbed the camera, and I took it with me.

"As we went through France and Spain, I started taking more and more pictures with the camera than with my phone. It was when we were in Greece, I think, when I realized that I loved looking at things through the lens of a camera. I fell in love with taking pictures on that trip, and I couldn't wait to get home and get them developed. After that I started taking photography classes wherever I could and saved up for almost a year for a professional grade camera. I was going through a tough time with a few personal things, so taking pictures started to become my escape. I even started planning a trip around the world with my mom to thank her for giving me the chance to explore this new passion, but of course things didn't work out."

"Why not?" I find myself asking, enthralled in her by life story.

"My mom died before we were able to go anywhere. Lupus."

Fuck.

I knew that Coach Anderson was married before and that he was now divorced, but I never thought about what had happened to his wife. Eliana had mentioned that her mom wasn't here anymore a time or two before, but I never thought to ask. It might have been years ago, but I can hear it in her voice that losing her mom still affects her.

"So, you never went on that trip?" I ask, feeling my own voice wanting to crack.

"No, I did. I just had to lose my mind a bit before I was able to convince myself to go. To be able to pick up the camera again. I ended up going about a year after she died. I took that trip for her. At first, it was about capturing everything that I wanted her to see. At the beginning the trip was for her, but it ended up being for me. If I hadn't gone on that trip, I never would have picked up a camera again. But I did, for my mom. At eighteen, I never thought that I would love photography so much, and now I can't live without it. I may have lost my mom, but she gave me something that gives me so much back in return."

Not being able to resist myself, I turn so that I can place a finger under Eliana's chin and make her look up at me.

There are tears in her eyes that she is trying so hard not to let fall.

The small smile she gives me tells me that she is trying to be strong at this very moment, but the emotions running through her are too strong, and they could take over any minute.

It may not be my place, but I shift my hand from her chin up to her cheek and try to comfort her in the best way I can.

"Your mom would be proud of you. Hell, she is proud of you," I say, leaning forward just a bit and placing a small kiss against her lips.

"You don't know that," she says when I pull away.

"I do. You made a name for yourself, without your dad's help. Not only that, but you're also the team photographer for a professional hockey team at twenty-eight. Only a handful of people can say that. She would be proud of you, Eliana."

Her light brown eyes look up at me, as if she is trying to decide if I'm being honest with her, or if I'm just spewing out bullshit.

It's not bullshit. It's the absolute truth, and if we were in a different type of relationship than what we are now, I would tell her that I'm proud of her, too.

Because I am. I've known this woman for six weeks, and I'm proud of all that she's accomplished, and I don't even know half of it.

Instead of saying words, Eliana leans up to place a kiss on my lips just like I did to her a minute earlier.

"Thank you, Christian."

"You're welcome." I say, giving her another kiss, wishing I could do so much more.

CHAPTER ELEVEN

ELIANA

"WHAT?" I yell out, trying to be heard over the shower in Christian's master bathroom.

The water pressure here is so much better than at my rental. I freaking love it so much.

"I said," Christian says, opening up the shower door and getting in, "that I might not make it back home tonight, but you're free to stay here if you want."

I hear his words, but I'm not paying attention to what he's actually saying. The only thing that I can concentrate on is that the man just walked in here like he owes the damn place and legit moves me out of the way so that he can start washing his hair.

"Excuse me, I was busy," I say, narrowing my eyes at him.

"I have to get to the airport. Did you even hear what I just said?" he asks, looking down at me as he lathers shampoo in his hair.

"Yes, I heard you." I cross my arms at him.

134

"What did I say then?" he asks, turning to face me, and I try really hard not to look at him below the waist.

"That you might not be home," I answer, grabbing the shampoo bottle from his hand and squirting some into my hand.

Who does this man think he is ruining my shower?

"And?" he asks, reaching over me to grab the conditioner.

I finally met a man that actually uses conditioner and not that two in one shit.

"And what?" I say, pushing him out of the way so that I can get under the water.

If this is going to be a daily occurrence, he's going to have to install two shower heads in here. A girl needs her own space sometimes and he's taking up most of it. Damn huge-ass hockey players.

"What else did I say?" he asks, and I turn just in time for him to give me an eye roll.

"That I can stay here if I want to," I answer, sighing as the water from the shower head hits my scalp so perfectly.

"And you're just going to ignore that?"

"No," I say, turning to face him. Christian is currently washing his body and seeing him all wet and lathered up is doing something to me between the legs. But like he said, he has to get to the airport, so there is no time for anything fun. But how I wish I could get a little relief. "I heard you loud and clear. You're not going to be here, so I'll sleep at my rental. Like I have been doing."

I watch as Christian comes closer to me, pushing me

further under the shower head until he is under it, too, and his body is pressed against mine.

"You haven't been sleeping at your rental though," he says, washing his body off, throwing a smirk at me.

It's too early for him to be smirking at me like that.

"Yes, I have. I slept there the other night," I threw back, remembering going to the small apartment I have in San Jose and putting on my sleep clothes and getting to bed.

"You mean the night that you called me at eleven o'clock at night because you wanted ramen, and instead of you ordering it yourself and having it delivered to your rental, you made me get out of bed to meet you at a dingy food truck and then we came here afterward? That night?"

Crap.

Have I really not slept at my rental?

I go there, that's where I do most of my work in the morning before going to the soccer arena, but have I really not slept there? I try to think, but the last time I can honestly remember spending the night there was before the balcony when Christian and I had a heart to heart about how we got into our careers.

That was almost three weeks ago.

"Have I really spent every single night here for the last three weeks?" I ask out loud, not able to believe it.

Christian nods, coming closer to me and pushing me against the wall until his body is completely pressed against mine, and his face is able to go directly to my neck.

The way he kisses my neck makes me weak in the knees.

"You have," he says, taking my earlobe between his teeth and letting his hand roam down my naked body.

As much as I would love to get lost in him right now, I can't. I'm having an existential crisis.

"Wait," I say, pushing him back a bit. Just enough for me to see his face but still have his body mushed up against mine. "If I'm spending every night here, does that mean that we're dating? Are we in a *relationship?*"

I know that we said that we weren't going to be with other people however long that we do this for, but did I unknowingly step into a relationship with a hockey player? A hockey player who is technically my coworker at that?

"I mean, we fuck," Christian says, leaning down again, this time bending down further so that he can pepper kisses, nips, and sucks against my breast. "But we also go to dinner." Suck. "We eat breakfast together." Kiss. "And we meet up to have lunch." Nip. "We sleep in the same bed. We see each other every single day, text each other all the time." He takes my nipple in his mouth. "I think our hate turned into lust and then turned into like, which has blossomed into something."

"Something?" I ask, half moaning at the way he's taking care of me.

"Something," he says, giving my nipple one final tug before he stands back up to full height. "Is it a full-blown relationship? I don't know. I do know that I don't find you as annoying as I did when you broke into my house. I also know that I like having you here and spending time with you. Maybe it's not a full-blown relationship, but it has the possibility of getting there. For me at least. You may not feel the same."

It's not even a question. I do feel the same.

Christian is right.

Our hate and annoyance for one another turned to lust, and it quickly became something more. I've been more open with him and being around him has made me feel something that I've only felt through photography. And that is feeling little bit freer. He makes me laugh and doesn't judge me or get mad when I bring out the sarcasm or the attitude. He matches it just as much. And we have a lot more in common than I thought we would when I first walked into his house.

I don't even hate the fact that he's a hockey player. I mean, I do, but not as much as I did when he first stepped into my life. My hate for him being a hockey player is more about what I've experienced with other players, and I'm projecting it onto him. I'm used to people wanting to be with me or spending time with me because of my dad and what he can bring to the table. Christian doesn't need that from me. He's already at the highest level, he's already playing for the team my dad coaches. He doesn't need me in the way that others have, and like he told me himself, *his* name could get me places. Do I want it to? Absolutely not, but I'm not used to it being that way.

I'm not used to men, especially those in this profession, to not need me in that way.

There's this feeling deep inside of me that tells me that if Christian and I do become more, with time, he will make my hate for his profession and for his sport completely go away.

That being with him will make me fall in love with the sport that was once a big part of my life again. Not only that, but he is also capable of giving me something that I have yearned for for a very long time.

True companionship.

God, how did this all happen so fast? Two months ago, I was trying to get under his skin to see if he would break, and now, I'm in his shower thinking about jumping into a relationship with him.

I've been so in my head that I didn't realize he was waiting for me to say something until I look up and find him staring at me all while the water is hitting his face.

Time to be honest with him.

"I feel the same," I say, sliding my arms around his neck.

"Thank fuck, because if you didn't, I was going to start questioning my own sanity for imagining shit."

"I may have to question your sanity either way. I would have thrown my ass in the ocean and been done with it, yet you still put up with it." I lean up and place a kiss against his jaw.

"You're dealing with my grumpy ass, so I guess we're even." He grabs at my ass for effect.

I will never tell him this, but I love it when he does that. I'm not a small girl, haven't fit into jeans that were smaller than a size ten since high school. So, every time he grabs my ass, or any part of me for that matter, like he is hungry for me and possibly his last meal, it makes my body soar.

"You're not as grumpy as I thought you were," I muse,

sliding my hands into his hair and starting to massage his scalp.

The way he closes his eyes is all I need to get me through the day.

"That's because it's summer. The second the season starts, the grump will be out fully. Some players on other teams are just assholes and get on my nerves."

"Then I guess I have something to look forward to." I place a kiss on his lips before pulling away again. "Are we really deciding if we are going to turn this relationship into more than what it already is in the shower?"

He shrugs. "We can talk about it more when I get home, just as long as you are here."

"I'll be here."

"Then we will make it official then. For now, though, I'm going to need you to turn around and place your hands against the wall so I can take you from behind," he orders, making the tingle between my legs a lot more prominent.

"I thought that you had to get to the airport," I say, but still follow orders. As soon as my hands are against the wall, I wiggle my ass a bit against Christian's groin. He lets out a moan that drives me crazy.

"I do, but I have a pressing issue to take care of," he tells me right before a slap lands against my ass cheek.

"What pressing issue is that?"

"Making you all dirty again with my tongue and leaving you wanting more," he tells me, letting his hands slide down my body, until I hear something hit the floor.

I look back and see Christian on his knees.

"I do like a man on his knees doing dirty things to me."

"Great, now shut up and only speak to scream out my name."

Christian and his magic tongue make me come and yell out his name just in time for him to make his flight.

CHAPTER TWELVE

CHRISTIAN

IF I DIDN'T HAVE to go to Chicago to sign my new lease, I wouldn't have come. I would have stayed in California, spending the rest of my morning between Eliana's legs and making her scream as much as I could. But of course, I had to fly out on the first flight to sign two sheets of paper.

Those two signatures could have been done through email but of course my building likes to do everything in person.

It's done, though, and I have a brand new lease for the next two years, which is what I have left in my Dark Knights contract.

I should buy a place; it would be nice to own a place in Chicago, but I have to think about the fact that I might not be here in five years. As much as I like to think that I'm going to be playing for Chicago forever and hate the idea of playing for another team, I have to be realistic. Shit could happen, and for all I know I can be in Florida in three years.

It would be a good investment, though. Whether I stay in the city or not. And it's definitely something I should think about, but right now all I want to concentrate on is spending time with some of my teammates and getting on my flight home later today to get back to my girl.

My girl?

Is she even my girl if we technically haven't made anything official?

According to my brain she is.

I guess my mind is getting a few hours ahead of itself.

"I think Rodriguez is broken," Blake, my teammate and friend, says, breaking me out of my headspace.

When I found out I was coming to Chicago for the day, I sent a message out to Liam, Blake, and our teammate Logan so we could grab a bite to eat before I headed back to California for the next three weeks. I didn't need to. I could have just flown in and out of Chicago without them noticing, but they've been hounding me about spending the summer so far away from them so I decided to shut them up and to not be a shit friend and take them to lunch.

Liam and Blake said yes, and Logan said he was in New York for his brother's wedding.

Now here we are at a sandwich shop by the river, taking in some of this muggy Chicago heat, joined by Sophia, Blake's supposed best friend forever.

If you ask me, the dude has feelings for her, but he is too scared to admit it.

"What makes you say that?" Liam asks him right before he takes a bite of the sandwich in front of him.

"Because he's smiling. I've never seen the man smile," Blake answers him, eyeing me like he is trying to figure out if I've been replaced by a robot or something.

"That's not true. He smiled when you guys won the Cup," Sophia adds, shoving her best friend.

"He also smiled the first time he held Emma," Liam throws out, mentioning his two-month-old daughter. Which reminds me. I still have a bet to pay off.

Last December while Liam's girlfriend Chloe was pregnant with their daughter Emma, Blake and I had a little race during one of our practices. The loser had to change Emma's diaper for a whole day once she was born. Because I had decided to let Blake win, I got stuck on diaper duty. As much as I love the kid, I don't want to change dirty diapers.

So, I will refrain from reminding Liam and Blake that the bet hasn't been paid yet.

"Those times are different," Blake says, almost yelling out the words. "Those were smiles of enjoyment. What's so enjoyable about eating a deli sandwich with three of your friends?"

Jeez, a guy has a good morning eating his girl out in the shower and then taking her from behind, and he gets judged for smiling a little bit.

"Aww Jacobi has his panties in a bunch. If you don't enjoy our company, Blakie, you can just say so," I tell him, finally saying something and adding to the back and forth.

"Your company is sometimes debatable," he says, giving me a shrug.

"Blake!" Sophia reprimands him with a slap on the arm

before turning to me. "Don't listen to him. It's nice to see you smile. Whatever the reason may be."

"I know the reason," Liam answers from where he sits next to me at our four top.

"You don't know shit." And he doesn't. Other than the night at the bar, I haven't mentioned Eliana to him. He doesn't know that I started sleeping with her that night, or that she's been in my bed ever since.

"Oh, really? So that smile on your fucking face has nothing to do with that picture on your phone?" My best friend asks, nodding to the device on the table between us.

"What picture?" I think he's been hit in the head too many times.

"The one on your lock screen. You know, the one of a sunset overlooking the beach where you have a woman's legs on your lap. That picture."

No way he had seen the picture on my lock screen that closely and was able to pick out Eliana. There's like an inch of her showing.

"It could be a stock photo," I say to him, trying to throw him off.

"Or it could be the same picture that someone posted on their Instagram page a couple days ago."

Fuck, I forgot that she was going to do that.

Every night after eating dinner, Eliana and I go out to the balcony and watch as the sun goes down. It has become our little nightly routine.

Earlier in the week, after we had finished dinner, we went out to the balcony and sat on the couch like we usually do. For some reason this time around, I felt inclined to take a picture of the sun setting. There isn't much to the picture, just the ocean, the sun, and a fraction of Eliana's legs.

Nothing special. It was just a nice way for me to capture some of my favorite things in one click.

Eliana liked my photography skills so much that she had me send the picture to her so that she could post it. Since I don't check any of my social media accounts, I didn't know she actually did it. I don't even know if I'm following her, but apparently Liam is, and as soon as he saw the picture on my lock screen, he put two and two together.

"She posted the picture?" I scratch my head.

Liam nods. "I saw it a few days ago. The view looked familiar, but I didn't put it together until I saw you check your phone when we got here."

"Has she posted anything else?" I ask, curious if I'm all over her page. Or if she's declared me as hers for nobody else to touch. Would that bother me? Nope, the opposite actually.

My best friend shrugs. "There are pictures from what I know now is your balcony, but nothing that screams that she's with you."

Why do I wish she had?

"Who is this *she* we're talking about?" Blake asks, trying to get into the middle of our conversation. The dude is like a puppy.

I roll my eyes while Liam answers him. "Remember how I told you we're getting a new team photographer?"

He nods. "Yeah, you said not to get on her bad side."

"Well, it looks like our friend here is on her good side."

"Oh, shit. Rodriguez has a girlfriend?" Blake asks excitedly.

"She's not my girlfriend," I throw out, because she's not.

"Dude, you have a picture of her on your lock screen. She's definitely your girlfriend," Blake argues and now I'm the one rolling my eyes.

"You have a picture of Sophia on your lock screen and she's not your girlfriend," I say right before I flip him off. Not going to lie that my relationship with Blake is a lot of mindless banter, and in a way, it reminds me of all the shit Eliana, and I throw at each other.

"Oh, I put that there, you know to, scare away the jersey chasers," Sophia chimes in. "Blakie here is trying to concentrate on hockey this year and not on who's in his bed."

I know for a fact that is not the real reason, but I don't argue with her. Instead, I just razz Blake some more.

"Damn, I never thought I'd see the day when Jacobi would be going celibate," I say, and it's the truth. Blake goes through women like I go through socks. It's scary and impressive all at the same time.

"I'm not going celibate. I'm just taking a break," he says, giving Sophia a shove for giving me information about him that I can use to torment him later. "Anyway, this isn't about me. This is about you and the girl that you have on your lock screen. So, what's her name?"

Damn hockey players and their love for gossip.

"None of your—"

"Eliana Anderson," Liam tells him.

This fucker. I'm revoking the best friend card. I'll give it to Logan; he doesn't get all up in my business.

"Anderson? As in Coach Anderson? As in our head coach? That Anderson?" Blake asks, his eyes going wide.

"The very one," Liam confirms.

"Dude, you're dating Coach's daughter?"

"I'm not dating Coach's daughter." I mean, I technically am, but I'm not going to tell them that. Eliana and I have to officially talk about it first before I go telling my nosy friends.

"You're sleeping with her, taking pictures with her, and putting them on the lock screen on your phone. Dude, you're dating her. Does Coach know?"

His question stumps me.

Does he know? I know Anderson's relationship with his daughter is not great, but Eliana has told me that they've been trying to work things out ever since she got hired by the Knights. He texts her and calls her occasionally, but I don't know if the fact that she is spending time with me is even a topic of conversation.

I doubt that she has told him anything. If she had, she would have either told me or Anderson would have my head already for defiling his little girl.

"I doubt it. Eliana hasn't said anything," I answer, giving him a shrug. "And don't go telling him either," I say, kicking Blake in the shin. "I don't need him chewing my ass out at practice because he didn't hear it from his daughter first."

"I get it. Damn. Did you seriously have to kick me?" he complains, leaning under the table to rub at his leg.

"Can I ask a question without getting kicked?" Sophia asks, raising her hand like we were still in school.

I give her a nod. She knows I would never kick her. Her best friend, on the other hand, is a different story. "Go for it."

"What are you going to do when the season starts up in three weeks? Doesn't the team have a no fraternization rule? Wouldn't that extend to her, too?"

More questions that I don't know the answer to and most definitely something that Eliana and I have to talk about.

I know about the no fraternization rule the team has. Hell, I know it by heart because when Eliana started spending more time at my house, I pulled out my contract to read it through. All because I had a feeling that whatever we were doing might extend past the summer. I didn't know for sure, but a part of me did hope. Back then I was okay with possibly saying goodbye to her once the end of August came rolling around.

Now that it's here, and we're three weeks away from training camp, goodbye is the furthest thing on my mind.

Fuck.

My feelings for this woman are a lot bigger than I thought.

"Honestly, I have no idea. We haven't talked about what will happen in three weeks."

We haven't even mentioned that training camp is going to be here before we know it. We're just living life as if nothing between us is going to change in a few weeks' time.

"Are you going to?" Liam asks after quickly checking his

phone. He's probably checking to see if Chloe and Emma are okay.

I take a drink from my water before answering. "If you would have asked me yesterday, I would have said probably not. But things shifted this morning before I left, so now I think having that conversation is one that we have to have soon."

"So, it's serious with her?" Blake asks.

Is it? I didn't think it was. Hell I just talked about moving what's going on between us to the next stage his morning, but things could quickly shift.

Right now, Eliana and I are just enjoying our summer. Enjoying the companionship we offer each other and taking in the warm days with shared meals and laughs and finishing the days off in bed together. There is no seriousness, no hard-ship, just ease.

Never did I think I would want more than that. I have never been much of a relationship type of guy, but with Eliana, I want to be. I want to move past the summer days and ease and step into everyday life with her where things aren't always as easy and understanding. I want to possibly build a future with this woman or at the very least, see where things between us could go.

I answer him as truthfully as I can. "It could very much be heading in that direction."

"Damn," Blake says, leaning back in his chair as if we just had the deepest conversation in the world, and it took a toll on him.

"Yup." I say, falling silent.

We sit in the quietly for a few seconds before Sophia breaks our silence when she reaches over and places a hand on my arm.

"You two will figure it out," she says, giving me a reassuring pat. "I don't know her, but I know you. Well sort of. This is the most I've heard you talk that wasn't throwing insults at Blake, but that's beside the point. What I'm trying to say is that I know you enough to know that when you want something, you will do what you can to make it work. You two will figure out what to do when the season starts. No doubt you will."

"I damn sure hope so."

CHAPTER THIRTEEN

ELIANA

THIS DAY ENDED up being a lot longer than I thought it would be.

After Christian left at the butt crack of dawn to head to the airport, after having an orgasm-filled shower of course, I started my morning by editing a few pictures, jumping on a call with the Knights marketing team to start preparing for the upcoming season, and then heading to the stadium for a Quakes game against Los Angeles.

It's currently ten at night, and my day still isn't over.

The Quakes game went into overtime and eventually a penalty shot shootout. The game ended a whole hour after it was supposed to. As soon as it was done, I started editing pictures so that the social media team could start posting them.

Now two hours later, I'm still at the stadium trying to finish up the edits so that I can go home and sleep.

Even though it's been a long day, and all I want to do is

shut my computer and never see it again, I did think of a few things that would be more efficient. Things that I can hopefully implement with the Knights when the season starts in a few weeks to make the job a whole lot easier for everyone involved.

I honestly don't know how the start of hockey season is almost here. It feels like I just signed my contract with the team last month, and then it turned into June, and then all of a sudden September starts next week.

My plan was to finish up August with the Quakes before handing the job to someone else and then head to Chicago sometime around the first of the month to get situated. In my plan, I was going to hold in my feelings and stay with my dad for a week while I looked for a place to live for the season. No way would I survive living in a hotel or even with my dad long term. I thought by now I would have a list of places to check out, but I have nothing. I haven't even talked to my dad about me staying at his house for a few days.

Then there is the whole Christian thing.

Are we going to be together during the season? Are we not?

If we make it official like we talked about this morning, would we have to tell my dad and the team, or would we keep it a secret?

If we don't make it official, do we go back to hating each other, all the while throwing sex eyes whenever we see each other?

So many questions to figure out the answer to.

One thing I know for sure, my assignment with the

Quakes ends in three days. After that I will have more time to think about life in Chicago, and everything that comes with it.

I spend the next half hour finishing up editing the pictures I took tonight, and some time after eleven, I call it a night.

There are still a few people still in the team offices as I grab my stuff and start heading out. I wave bye to a few of them and head to my car debating if I should just head to my rental or to Christian's.

As much as I love the beach house, my rental is my best bet. I don't want to go over the mountain when I'm this tired. That road has too many curves in it as it is, I don't need to be half asleep going down it.

I'll just text Christian to head to the rental when he arrives in San Francisco. He'll probably be too tired to drive all the way home.

God, if someone would have told me at the start of the summer that I was going to be this involved with a hockey player, I would have laughed in their face. Yet here I am, very involved with one and thinking about being more involved.

The world has a cruel way of telling me that I was wrong to put all hockey players in the same bubble. Because one bad seed doesn't make them all the same.

I'm about to get into my car when my phone starts to ring. Given how late it is it has to be Christian. His flight probably got in early, and he's calling to see if I decided to go stay at his house or not.

I fish my phone out of my bag and answer it without looking.

"Hey, I was about to text you. I'm just leaving the arena, and I'm too tired to head down to your house, want to use my rental for once?" I ask, throwing my gear into the back seat, feeling dead on my feet.

"About to text me, huh? And here I thought you would never speak to me again," a male voice that is very much not Christian says from the other side.

It takes me a second, but I recognize the voice. I haven't heard it in ten years, but I still know who that voice belongs to.

I pull the phone back from my ear and check the phone number. It's a Vancouver number. I should have checked before answering.

"How did you get my number?" I ask my high school boyfriend, a severe bite to my tone.

When he first started contacting me a few months ago, I responded to a few messages and then told him to fuck off.

The messages I had sent before I sent him a middle finger emoji weren't anything special. Just me asking what he wanted and why he was contacting me. When he didn't give me a clear answer, I stopped it and blocked him.

In none of those messages did I give him my number.

"I have my ways," he answers, and I know if I was standing in front of him right now, he would be shrugging.

"And what ways are those? My number isn't public knowledge, Kalen. So, either someone I know gave you my number, or you paid someone to get it. So, which one is it?"

"When did you turn into a hard ass? You were never this assertive when we were kids," Kalen complains.

"Yeah, well, a lot has happened since we were kids," I say, rolling my eyes at the almost empty parking lot. "Now answer the question. How did you get this number?"

Kalen sighs but finally answers me. "I saw that you were working for the Quakes, so I called their front office and told them that I was trying to get in contact with you to get an interview. They handed it over."

What the actual hell?

The team wouldn't do something like that without telling me. Especially without asking for credentials. Kalen most likely had his agent or publicist call for it to be legit.

"What do you want?" I ask, getting into my car, angry.

"A man can't call his ex to catch up?"

"Said man cheated on his ex and tried to use her to get something he wanted. Besides, last I heard, said man was in a relationship and has no reason to be calling his ex at eleven o'clock at night," I say through my teeth, no longer feeling tired. Instead, I feel rage.

I should hang up, end the call right now, but a part of me wants to know what this asshole wants.

"Layla ended things," he says, and for a second, I almost feel sorry for him.

"Let me guess, you cheated on her, too." Wouldn't that be full circle? "Or did you use her too?"

"No," he says, sounding angry. "She called it off when she realized I wasn't going to propose."

An involuntary snort comes out of me.

Like his career, I've kept minimal tabs on Kalen and his personal life. Mostly because I was rooting for Layla and had hope that she would dump Kalen's ass and go find a man who was worthy of her. I didn't know anything about her or hadn't spoken to her outside of that day, but I still wanted the best for her, even if a part of me hated her. But after I ended things with Kalen, Layla decided to stay.

In the eyes of the public and the hockey world, they were the cute couple who have been together forever and would possibly be together for the rest of time. When Kalen got picked up by an NHL team, they made up this whole fake story about how they got together.

But I guess what they were telling the public and showing on social media isn't what was going on behind closed doors.

I'm surprised that word of Layla finally leaving Kalen hasn't made the news yet or made its way around the social sphere.

Of course, he wasn't going to propose. Kalen has to keep his options open for the next best thing.

"Good for her. I wouldn't have let you string me along this long. She deserves better," I say to him, a sadistic grin on my face. He might be hurt by his breakup, but I don't give a shit.

"Whatever," he asks, with even more bite. "Who's this guy you're seeing?"

"None of your fucking business," I say, not giving him any more information that what he already has. Vancouver and Chicago play each other, I don't need Kalen going after

Christian on the ice because I won't give him what he wants. "You have thirty seconds to tell me what the fuck you want. Otherwise, I'm going to hang up and block your number for good. Actually, that sounds like a good idea. Bye, Kalen."

"Wait!" he yells just as I pull the phone away from my ear.

"What?"

"There are rumors going around here in Vancouver that they are looking to trade me," he starts.

"Shocker," I deadpan.

"I need you to help make sure I get traded to a good team," he continues, as if I hadn't interrupted him.

I figured this was why he started contacting me all those months ago. I just didn't think that the asshole would actually have the balls to ask me. Color me surprised.

"And how am I supposed to help you? I'm just a photographer." I say, already knowing his answer.

"Talk to your dad. He can talk to the Knights GM, and they can trade for me." And there it is.

There is the request I've been waiting for.

"Not going to happen," I say about to hang up on him.

"Come on, Lia. Don't be like that. Do this for me, please." Oh, look at that, the asshole knows how to use the word please.

A single word is not enough to sway me, thank God.

"Fuck off. Get your agent to do your dirty work. I want nothing to do with you and your shit career."

"Do it," he says and I bet my paycheck that he said those two words through his teeth.

"Or what?" I hackle.

"Remember those pictures you sent me for my eighteenth birthday? One text message, and they will be out."

A chill runs through my body.

Like most people, I did some stupid shit when I was a teenager. One of them was dating Kalen, and another was sending the person who I thought I was going to be with for years nude pictures of myself.

At the time I was proud of them, but now I wish they would just disappear because this isn't the first time that Kalen has used them against me. The first time was when he first entered the draft. We had been broken up for a few months at this point, and he called me out of the blue. At first, being the naive girl that I was, I thought he was calling to get back together with me. He was flirty and even apologized for the cheating, and for a week or two, I believed every word that he said. Until he asked me to talk to my dad again. That's when I realized that everything he had told me was a lie. He was using me again. So when I told him no, he threatened to put my pictures online. I told him to shove it, but he continued to hold it over my head and continued to bring me down any chance he got. It lasted until he got drafted, but I never gave in.

"It didn't work the first time around, what makes you think it's going to happen now?" I say, feeling a lump forming in my throat from all the nights I went to sleep crying worried that he would do something damaging to me in that way.

"Because now you actually have something to lose."

I actually have something to lose.

The last time he had put me in this position, I had told him that the only people that he was going to hurt by releasing the photos was going to be my dad and possibly himself. I was nobody in the hockey world back then. I was just the daughter of a player. I didn't matter in the public eye or to hockey fans, but they did.

Now, starting in a few weeks I will no longer be a nobody. My position in the sport will actually matter and will be affected by something like this.

It would be easy to tell Kalen that I would go to my dad and ask him to consider acquiring him, but me doing so goes against everything I told myself I would never do.

Let someone use me to get to my father. Let someone use me in a way that's beneficial for them and throw me to the curb afterward.

No matter how much it will hurt me, how much it scares me with what will happen if those pictures come out, I can't do it. I can't give in and give Kalen something that he wants, no matter how much it destroys me.

"Release the pictures. I don't give a shit. I'm not going to let you use me to get what you want."

I end the call before he can say anything else and quickly block his number.

Kalen might be bluffing, he might not even have the pictures anymore, but I don't know for sure, and he is using that to his advantage. He knows that I'm going to battle with myself and stay awake every single night wondering if the next day will be the day those pictures make it to the Twitter accounts of hockey fans all over North America. He knows that I'm going to keep thinking about him and the pictures until they drive me so crazy, I finally decided to go to my dad.

He probably knew that I was going to tell him no and was banking on his back-up plan to get him what he wants.

"Fuck," I yell out, feeling frustrated beyond belief.

If I wasn't a stupid eighteen-year-old who wanted her boyfriend to see her as sexy, I wouldn't be in this mess. But I am, and the only thing I can do is blame myself.

The lump that was in my throat earlier is now fully formed and is the root cause of the tears are currently falling down my face.

I hate that I'm crying over something that Kalen will or will not do. I feel like I'm eighteen again, but the difference between then and now is when I cried over him and his stupid threats back then, I had my mom to lean on. Now, she's not here, and I can't go to her when I feel like I'm going to break.

I don't even want to go to my apartment. All I'm going to do there is let my mind play mind tricks on me about what Kalen is going to do.

So, the apartment is going to be a no go.

Christian's place is an option. Even if he's not there, I can go down to the beach and take in the sound of the waves and let the sound calm my mind and body like it has done so many times before.

And when Christian gets there, I can find calm another way.

Not even thinking twice about it, I start the car and start driving in the direction of the beach house. It's not what I had planned, but it's the one place at the moment that will have a calming effect on me and make me forget about Kalen and his threats of blackmail.

The whole way down the highway all the way until I get to the fishhook section of the road, I cry, and the tears continue to stream down my face as I drive through the neighborhood where the beach house is. The tears don't stop until I'm in the driveway already feeling the calm that the place brings me.

It's the proximity of the ocean, not the house itself.

As soon as I turn off the car, I'm getting out and heading to the front door. Thank God Christian gave me the code to his house a few weeks ago because no way would I be able to break into the house again in my current state of mind. No doubt the cops would be called this time if I did.

I'm going to dump all my stuff on the couch and go down to the beach, and then after I'm all calm and relaxed I'm going to hop in the shower and sleep. There is a slight chance I will miss Christian when he gets home, but I'm okay with that.

I punch in the code, and the second I push the door open, I let out a sigh of relief.

That relief is halted immediately, though. Because the second I step into the house, I hear music. Slow, romance-filled music. Definitely not the type of music that you would normally hear coming from this house. It makes me pause by the door.

Is Christian home?

He told me that his flight back from Chicago was going

to land in San Francisco at eleven fifty. Did it arrive earlier? Or did he catch an earlier flight? He would have told me if he had landed, he promised he would before he left.

Unless he didn't go to Chicago at all and planned a romantic night in. But if that was the case, wouldn't he have told me? Maybe that's why he kept telling me that I could spend the night here just in case he didn't make it back tonight. But if he had something planned, he would have at least texted me to come by the house a lot earlier than now. If I had known, I wouldn't have spent the last four hours at the stadium.

So many damn questions run through my head.

There's a shuffling sound coming from the living room, so I put my stuff down and slowly tiptop past the entryway.

I'm almost at the junction between the entryway and the living room when I hear what sounds like a woman's giggle come through above the music.

No.

No fucking way.

I have to be imagining things.

Someone must have broken into the house because there is no way that Christian lied about going to Chicago all so that he could bring another woman here. Where he was saying things about relationships and the possibility of more less than twenty-four hours ago.

No way is what I'm hearing what I think it is.

The tears from earlier start to flow again, and I just let them, not making any effort to wipe them away.

I take the last step to get to the living room, and something in me breaks.

The house is dark, the only light coming from the cloudless sky outside, but I'm still able to see everything. On the couch, with his back to me, is Christian, dark hair all over the place, shoulders pressed against the back of the couch and a woman on his lap, grinding on him while her hands roam his body.

I thought that a part of me had broken when I found out about Kalen and Layla, but that feeling doesn't even begin to compare to this one.

My eyes don't leave the couple in front of me, and I can't find it in me to say something to break them apart. I just continue to watch as they kiss and grind against each other as if the man wasn't in me this morning.

He's just like I thought he was. An egotistical asshole who only cares about himself and doesn't give two shits about who he hurts.

And here I am breaking for him. Crying over him.

I hate Christian Rodriguez so damn much.

CHAPTER FOURTEEN

CHRISTIAN

IF I EVER AGAIN THINK ABOUT taking two four-hour flights within the span of eighteen hours, across several time zones and back, someone should take my hockey stick and hit me across the back of the with it.

My body doesn't know whether to be tired or energized. My flight from Chicago arrived in San Francisco a little after eleven at night. After getting to my car and driving a whole hour home, it's after midnight, and all I want to do is crash for a good two days.

I should have stayed at my place in Chicago and caught the first flight out tomorrow morning. At the very least I would have been able to get a few hours of sleep. But no, I had to book my return flight for the same day. Apparently, I like to torture myself.

Grabbing my backpack from where I had thrown it on the passenger seat, I get out of the car and start walking up the street toward the house.

When I pulled up to the house, I noticed that Eliana's rental car was sitting in the driveway blocking the parking spot next to her.

As much as I wanted to be annoyed with her, I couldn't. The fact that she was even at my house, knowing that there was a chance I wasn't home, made up for it.

Maybe once I see her and have her in my arms, I will forget how tired I am and get lost in her in all the ways that I can.

A smile forms on my face at the thought of having her, and it stays there as I make it up to the house.

Once I make it to the driveway, though, the smile disappears because Eliana is currently speed walking out of the house as if it was set on fire or something.

Right away, I start to panic.

I look up at the house, and nothing seems wrong on that front, so whatever is happening is happening directly to her.

Seeing her running out of the house like that takes me by surprise. I become motionless and unable to speak. It's not until she starts to struggle to open her car door that I'm finally able to get out of my stupor.

"Eliana," I say, announcing myself in the calmest way possible. She already looks scared; I don't need her to get even more terrified.

At the sound of my voice, she jumps and frantically turns until she finds me at the end of the driveway.

She looks from me back to the house.

"Wha-what are you doing out here?" she asks, her voice shaking telling me that she's been crying.

"I just got here," I tell her.

I close the distance between us, seeing that she has in fact been crying when I'm about two feet away. The second I see tears rolling down her face, I close the distance even more and take her face between my hands, looking her over and trying to see if she's okay.

"What's wrong? Why are you crying?" I wipe at her tears trying to stop them, but they just keep on coming.

"You aren't supposed to be out here. I just saw you inside. You were just inside,' she says, shaking her head, all the while more tears fall from of her eyes, and her bottom lip starts to tremble.

"Baby, I just got here. I just got home," I say, bringing her closer to me and cradling her head against my chest.

"If you just got home, then who the hell is inside fucking some chick? My eyes didn't lie to me, Christian. You were inside with a woman on your lap and her hands on your body like she owned the damn thing," she yells, trying everything to push me away from her, but I don't budge.

What the fuck is going on here?

I run through Eliana's words as she tries to free herself from my hold.

Someone who looks like me is inside screwing someone. My guess is that Eliana probably just got here, walked in on whoever is in my house, and since she thought it was me, she ran out, hurt, that I was with another woman when I told her I would only be with her for the duration of our time together.

"Are you sure whoever is inside looks like me?" I ask,

pulling back from her, my heart hurting at the sight of tears in her eyes.

She gives me a nod. "Yes, dark hair and muscles."

Sounds about right. I tear my eyes away from her face and look around the street in front of the house. Sure enough, the car that I'm looking for is parked in front of my neighbor's house. How I missed it when I pulled up is beyond me.

He's fucking dead.

I untangle myself from Eliana ready to storm inside the house and rip my brother in half.

"It wasn't me inside the house," I say to her as I walk to the front door. Thankfully, she follows me.

"Then who is it?"

"My idiot brother who is about to meet a slow painful death," I say, pushing the front door open and instantly get met with a slow song and the smell of sex.

Oh, he's dead.

I storm through the entryway and slam my hand against the light switch to light up the living room.

Just like Eliana said, the person who looks like me is on the couch with a half-naked woman on his lap.

"Oh my god!" the woman shrieks, scrambling off my brother and grabbing her clothes from the floor.

My brother starts to collect himself but he's not as frantic as his friend is.

"What the hell, Christian?" Adrian, my brother yells out.

"Are you serious right now?!" I shout, trying really hard not to lose my shit. "What the fuck are you doing here?"

"What?" he asks like I walked into his place and not the

other way around. "Mom said that you were going to Chicago. What are *you* doing here?"

"Es mi casa!" I yell, failing at keeping my emotions intact. I take a deep breath and try to speak to my brother as calmly as I can. "So, because Mom told you that I was going to be out of town, you decided to break in and fuck your girlfriend on my couch?"

"It's not breaking in if I know the code to the front door and to your alarm." The asshole just shrugs. It's like Eliana all over again.

It's not breaking in if the door was wide open.

"And I'm not his girlfriend," the blonde announces, now fully dressed. "We actually just met. He told me this was his house."

"Fucking hell," I'm about to pull all my hair out. Not only do I have my girlfriend crying because she caught my brother having sex and thought I was cheating on her, now I have a strange woman in my house who my brother doesn't even know.

Adrian must see my frustration because he finally gets up from the couch and walks over to the strange woman.

"Meet me outside, yeah? I'll take you home. I just need to talk to my brother for a minute or two."

This woman must really be interested in my brother if she is giving him a nod and walking out to wait for him outside because she should be telling him to fuck off and calling a car.

As soon as the girl is out of the house, and the door is closed behind her, my brother turns to me.

"Why aren't you in Chicago?"

"Why the fuck are you in my house?" I ask, my anger somewhat controlled. The only reason I'm not fully losing it is because I know Eliana is in the room.

Adrian looks behind me before giving me a shrug. "I sometimes use the place when you're out of town. Women love the beachfront property."

"Ew," I hear Eliana whisper.

Ew is fucking right. Where else has my brother screwed some strange chick in my house without me knowing? Visuals start to form in my head, and I come up with two options. I either have to burn everything and buy new furniture or just buy a new house. I'm going with burning everything. I like this house too much.

"Who are you?" Adrian asks, a smile spreading across his face as he moves around me and walks over to Eliana.

"Um," Eliana starts and looks over at me, silently asking if she should tell him who she is or keep it a secret given the job she is about to start.

She was not a fucking secret.

"Her name is Eliana, and she walked in on you screwing the blonde," I tell my brother.

Adrian nods. "And I'm going to take a wild guess that you saw us and thought that I was Christian and freaked out. That's why you look like you have been crying."

My brother can be a prick sometimes, but he does have a heart when he wants to.

Eliana nods. "You two look really alike from the back," she whispers.

"Good genes," my brother announces proudly.

This night has taken a weird ass turn, and I'm fucking done with it. I just want to get to sleep.

"Adrian, go take the girl home, and don't bring anyone else back here."

"But the house sits empty for six months, if not more, so at least let me use it. Besides, I always plan it around the cleaning schedule. So, the house would be nice and clean just in case you pop out of nowhere like tonight."

No shame, this asshole has no fucking shame whatsoever.

"Leave, and I'm changing the codes to everything. Next time take the girl back to your place."

"Have you seen my place? It's disgusting half the time," he complains, thinking I'm going to give him some sympathy. I'm not.

"That's what you get when you live with five other guys. Get a hotel for all I care, but stop bringing women back here when I'm not home."

"Fine, but don't tell Mom about it. I'll probably get a chancla to the head," he whines out, already cringing at the thought.

"I'm not promising anything," I say, pointing toward the front door.

"Okay, okay. I'm out," he says, holding his hands up in defense. "It was nice to meet you, Eliana. Sorry about freaking you out. Hopefully, you can forgive my brother for whatever thoughts were running through your head."

Eliana gives him a small smile. "It was nice meeting you."

Without another word, my brother leaves the house, leaving me and Eliana to deal with the mess that he made.

"I'm sorry," I say, breaking the distance between us and taking her hands between mine.

"It's not your fault. Maybe if I had interrupted them and saw it was your brother, I wouldn't have reacted as strongly as I did," she says, pulling a hand from mine and wiping her face.

"Why didn't you interrupt them? I've only known you for two months, but I know that you wouldn't stand to be disrespected like that. The Eliana I know would have run over and ripped me a new one, calling me every single name in the book, and threatened to cut my dick off."

She shrugs. "I don't know. I thought I would have reacted like that, too, and I have before, but the second I saw them, I just froze. My head automatically said it was you, and it felt like something in me started to break. The thought of you lying to me about going to Chicago and being with someone else just started to hurt, and I couldn't understand it. It made me hate you so much and instead of confronting you, all I wanted to do was get out of here. In my head, what I was seeing was just confirmation that you were just another hockey player who was using me, and now that you had what you wanted, you were throwing me to the side like I didn't matter."

Another hockey player.

I hate that she lumps me together with another player who I assume hurt her and hurt her badly. Whoever that was is a fucking asshole, and she should know by now that I would never do something like that to her. No matter how we started, I would never hurt her as badly as the asshole who made her hate hockey did.

"An asshole cheated on you," I say, interlacing my fingers with hers and bringing her hand up to my lips.

She nods. "He did, and when it happened, I swore to myself that I would never put myself in that type of position again. I didn't give a shit if he turned out to be a professional athlete."

"I'm guessing the bastard was a hockey player?"

She nods, confirming my theory.

"And he's the other ninety percent why you hate the sport?"

She gives me another nod. "Yes. He's the reason."

"Is he in the league now?" I have to ask.

I see her throat bob as she answers. "Yes."

"Who?" Whoever it is, if I ever come across him on the ice, he is going to pay for hurting this woman.

Eliana looks up at me, her eyes filled with uncertainty as she bites down on her lip, holding the name on her tongue.

"Ellie, tell me who it is," I urge her softly.

"You've never called me Ellie before," she says, the sadness in her eyes disappearing a bit.

"And you never call me Chris," I say like it matters.

"Because it doesn't suit you. I like your full name better," she says with a smile forming on her face.

She's deflecting, I know she is. She knows the second she tells me the bastard's name I will try to hunt him down and make playing hockey impossible for him.

As much as I want to drop it, I can't. What that asshole did to her made her lose her trust in me, even if it was a misunderstanding.

"Who is it, Eliana?"

She takes a hard swallow, and after what feels like forever, she answers me.

"Kalen Bradford."

Bradford.

I don't know the name of every player in the league, but the name sounds familiar.

My mind goes to a game we played two seasons ago. It was the last game of the season with no hopes of heading to the playoffs, so no fucks were given during that game. We were playing against Vancouver, and one of their defenseman clocked me in the chin after intercepting a pass and going for a breakaway. We both got kicked out of the game and got a fine for fighting.

The dude's name was...

"The Canuck?" I ask because there is no fucking way. There has to be a different Bradford somewhere in the league.

But Eliana nods. "The very one. Except he wasn't a Canuck at the time. He was my boyfriend senior year in high school."

"I thought that he and his current girlfriend have been together since high school?" I ask. I looked into the guy after that game. He'd been all over the country before landing in Vancouver two years ago. Aside from the articles that I found about his playing style, the internet is flowing with cutesy shit of him and his girlfriend and how they were some match made in heaven or some bullshit like that.

"They were," Eliana says, letting go of my hand and heading into the kitchen.

I follow behind her and watch as she goes to the fridge and takes out the bottle of wine that I buy for her on every grocery run.

"They got together while I was still with him, and I found out during one of his tournament games. His parents knew because they were sitting right next to me while their son was making out with another girl right in front of me and weren't the least bit surprised." She takes a drink of wine straight from the bottle, not even bothering to grab a glass. "I went to every single one of his games, and I even asked my dad to go watch him play to better his chances at possibly getting scouted, and the asshole still found time to fucking cheat."

Damn. I guess I shouldn't ask if the prick still pisses her off. The way she is slamming back the wine tells me everything I need to know.

"I broke up with him right then and there, and the bastard still had the fucking audacity to ask me if I could still put in a good word for him with my dad. That's when I realized that I wasn't important to him. He was only with me to get something he wanted. He wanted an in with the NHL, and I had the ability to give it to him because of who my dad was. That was the first catalyst of my hate for all things hockey. The second was that same day with my dad. The tournament was hours away from home, and Mom wasn't feeling all that great, so I didn't want to bother her while she rested, so I called my dad, even if it wasn't his weekend. I knew he would come and pick me up. I called him a handful of times and sent him so many damn messages to come and pick me up, explaining what had happened between me and Kalen, but he didn't answer until two hours later and made me wait another four hours from home before he came to pick me up.

"And you want to know why he didn't pick up? Because he was out with his old hockey buddies celebrating the fact that he had just signed his coaching contract with the Knights. He cared more about hockey and his new position than he did about his daughter. In a span of a few minutes two men who I thought would never hurt me silently told me that I would never be as important or as worthy of their time as hockey is."

"That's not true. At least not with your dad," I interject.

Sure, Anderson has his issues, I'm not going to deny that, but he wouldn't put hockey in front of his daughter. Would he?

Eliana rolls her eyes at my comment and takes another drink of wine before she says anything.

"Did you know that my dad didn't fight my mom when she asked him for a divorce? She was tired of him never being home or helping her raise me, so she thought the only way he would get his head out of his ass was to ask for a divorce. But instead of fighting for the love of his life, he gave it to her because hockey was more important. Then she got sick, and I thought he would realize the mistake that he made and be by her side. That he would ask the Knights for leave so he could be with her during her treatments, but he didn't. He wasn't around. Sure, he paid for every bill, every hospital stay, and every single test, but he wasn't there. No matter how much I begged him, or my mom asked for him. Then she died and was he around then? No. He was at the funeral, was the grieving husband for a few hours, and then the next morning he jumped on a plane to coach a game. I had lost my mom, and I was a fucking mess, and he wasn't there. He put hockey before me, before her! Hockey has always come first! Not me! Not my dead mother! Hockey!

"You want to know why I hate it so much? Why I hate players and coaches alike? That's why. Because in the hockey world, I don't fucking matter. Every single person will always love the sport more than they love me. They will put the sport before me or anyone else. People will continue to use me because of who my father is, and my father will always put the sport first. It doesn't matter how much I love the sport, it and the people in that world, will always hurt me and disappoint me every chance it gets."

Tears continue to run down her face, the wine completely forgotten, and her body is shaking as if it's trying to release all the emotions that are currently swimming in her body, and she won't let it.

She's breaking.

I close the distance between us, and even though she tries to push me away, I don't let her and wrap my arms around her and hold her as tightly as I can.

A sob breaks through her, and she melts into my hold and lets everything that she was holding in out. She holds onto me as if I were her lifeline, and if she were to let go, she would drown.

But I won't let her. I will continue to hold until she no longer wants me to. I will keep her in my arms and tell her that no sport will ever be more important than her or worth more love than she is. As much as I want to tell her all of that now, I don't know if she will believe the words that come out of my mouth. At least not right now. I have to tell her those words when I know she will believe every single word I say.

For now, I will give her all the comfort that I can.

And hopefully soon, I will be able to tell her everything I want to.

We just have to get there first.

CHAPTER FIFTEEN

ELIANA

LAST NIGHT WAS an emotional roller coaster.

First with Kalen's phone call and his stupid threat, then walking in on Christian's brother and thinking it was Christian himself, followed by the trauma dump in the kitchen.

I don't think I've cried that much since my mom passed away. I needed it, though. I needed to air out my grievances, and Christian was the right person to do it with. I may not have told him everything, like the fact that I was already an emotional wreck all thanks to Kalen's call or even what he did before he got drafted, but I still told him enough to let the emotional weight that I didn't know I was holding lift.

It felt good to cry and to have someone hold me.

And he held me all night.

After all the tears stopped, Christian got me some water. After a quick shower, one that was not as eventful as the one we had the morning before, we got into bed, and I fell asleep with my head resting against his chest and his arms around me.

As we were lying there waiting for sleep to take over, it felt like we were doing something that we had never done before. Something a lot more intimate than what we are used to. Yes, we've had sex and have moved our insult-filled relationship to something that feels like a relationship of the real kind with labels and small romantic moments. It felt so good and every single part of me wanted to stay in that small bubble forever.

Eventually sleep did take over, and now I'm waking up and rolling over, feeling for Christian, but he's not there.

For a second, I start to panic, thinking that the bubble we were in had popped, but then I hear the shower running and relax into the bed and cuddle deeper into the mattress and the covers.

When Christian comes out of the attached bathroom, wrapped in only a towel and glistening wet, my brain and body start thinking of ways he can wake my body up.

"You could have woken me up, and I would have joined you in the shower," I say as soon as he sees that I'm awake.

"I wanted to let you sleep for a little longer, since you have plans today," he says, giving me a smirk and coming to sit next to me and placing a kiss against my lips.

The first time that I saw him in a towel he was shooting daggers at me through his eyes, and now he's kissing me like he can't get enough of me. It's strange how a few weeks with a person can change so much.

"What kind of plans do I have today?" I ask curiously when he pulls away.

"Not telling you. It's a surprise," he answers, getting up from the bed and walking over to his closet to grab some clothes.

I guess said plans don't involve him staying naked. Bummer.

"I don't do surprises, Rodriguez," I tell him, sitting up and leaning against the headboard.

"You'll do this one," he states, his tone telling me that there's no wiggle room. I think I like firm Christian better than grumpy Christian; I haven't made up my mind yet.

"Fine but does this surprise include a bed? Because yesterday was a little long and draining."

"At some point in the day, yes. But right now, no." He comes back into the room fully dressed, affirmatively putting any type of sexual activity on hold.

Even though he's fully clothed, I still take a second to admire this man's body.

There is something effortless about him. Right now, he's in jeans and a white t-shirt and is pulling on some Vans that you would never expect from a guy like him. But he pulls it off, and it makes him all that much hotter.

"Do these said plans include me looking for a place to live in Chicago? Because I'm supposed to report in a few weeks, and I still don't have a permanent address, and I very much would rather not stay at a hotel or at my dad's."

Christian turns to look at me. "You still don't have a place to live?" he asks like it's the wildest thing in the world.

I shake my head. "Not yet. In my head, I thought I had more time."

He gives me a head shake and goes back to putting on his shoes. "Just move in with me."

I think if I wasn't in bed currently, I would have fallen back and hit my head at what he just said to me.

He can't be serious.

But he doesn't take the comment back. He just sits there as if he didn't just suggest we move in together after only knowing each other for two months. We're not even in a full-blown relationship!

"Haha. Funny. Grumpy has jokes. So, are we going to look for a place for me or not?"

"I wasn't joking," Christian says, getting up from the bed and sliding on a button-up shirt that looks like it belongs in the nineties with the blocks of color.

I can't even concentrate on the shirt for long. All my head is trying to wrap around is the fact that he said he wasn't joking in the most serious way possible.

"Why the hell would I move in with you?" I ask, sounding a little more unhinged than I wanted to.

Christian gives me a shrug as he goes and sprays on his cologne. "You need a place to stay. I just renewed my lease yesterday, and it's not like we aren't somewhat living together already. It makes sense."

"No, no it doesn't make sense. I can't live with you."

"Give me one good reason." He stands at the end of the bed with his arms crossed, looking very much like the intimidating hockey player that he is.

I don't let that stop me, though. "For one, we're not technically together. As of this moment we are still very much summertime fuck buddies."

"I'm changing that today. Next."

He's changing that today? Is that the surprise?

I don't ask. I just continue. "We both work for a company that has a no fraternization rule. So, if we do become official, we can't keep our relationship secret at work and live together at the same time."

"I'll set up a meeting with HR. It's not like we'll be the first individuals to get together within a hockey team. We might have to keep it a secret for a little while, but we'll make it work."

I narrow my eyes at him.

He has a solution for everything, doesn't he?

"That easy, huh?"

"That easy. Come on, hermosa. Give me a good reason," he throws out with a smirk starting to form on his face.

He knows I got nothing, and he's taunting me. The asshole.

"I have a lot of camera equipment that needs to be properly stored," I throw it out knowing it's not a true reason.

He lets out a scoff. "Good thing I have three bedrooms back in Chicago."

"Of course you do." I roll my eyes at him.

Christian lets out a small chuckle and walks over to my side of the bed and takes a seat, caging me in with his body on one side and his arm on the other.

"Why don't you want to move in with me, Ellie?" he asks

in the most caring way possible. Maybe this is my favorite Christian.

Now it's me shrugging. Fighting over being truthful or if I should just make up another excuse that he will see right through.

I decide to go with the former.

"Because if things don't work out with us, I won't have any place to go. I have already fallen in love with this house. What makes you think I won't fall in love with that one, too? And I can be a lot. If you can't tell, I can be a little annoying when I want to be. Who knows how long you'll be able to handle me."

"Trust me, I know. Why do you think you almost had the cops called on you or almost landed in the ocean? You annoyed the living shit out of me," he says, a grin on his face. "Still do sometimes, but that's one of the things that I would never change about you. Same goes with your attitude. Most of the time I'm right there with you." He closes the distance between us even more, this time placing a finger under my chin and making me look up at him. "I'll be able to handle you as long as you are able to handle me. If we don't work out, we don't work out, but we won't know unless we try. And if that ever comes to that, which it won't, by the way, then you can kick me in the balls and make me help you find a place. I will even pay for the first year. All you have to do is move in with me when we get to Chicago."

"What about expenses?" Because no way am I going to let a man pay for every single thing in my life.

"I make more money than you," he starts to say, and I

shove him. "Damn, there was a but coming," he tells me right before leaning in and giving me a kiss. "I was going to say I make more money than you, so I would take care of the big expenses, and if you wanted, you don't have to, but if you wanted, you could take care of the Wi-Fi or groceries or any other bills you want. Again, if you want to. It's not a requirement to live with me."

It's enticing. Not only will I have a place to live, that's not my dad's, but I will also have Christian close by. After only a few short weeks, he has become my constant, something I haven't had for a very long time, not since my mom.

It's not only sex between us, but also laughter and building memories and so much more. And we can do that if we were living together and in the offseason we could come back here and enjoy a few months next to the beach. It's a win-win.

Crap, I'm actually considering this.

"Fine," I say the word and I see his eyes brighten up. "I will take your offer into consideration, and I will tell you what I decide once you tell me what this whole surprise is."

"I'll show you, but I won't tell you." He slaps a kiss against my lips and gets up from the bed. "Get your ass up and in the shower, Solis. We have places to be, and decisions to make."

I like that he uses the Solis last name and not Anderson.

"I hate you, Rodriguez." I throw out as he walks out of the room.

"Right back at you, hermosa. Ahora, apurate."

CHAPTER SIXTEEN

CHRISTIAN

"CAN I ASK YOU A QUESTION?" Eliana asks as I make the last turn toward my surprise.

"You can ask anything you want," I say, turning into the empty parking lot, surprised that she hasn't noticed where we're going yet. Or maybe she has and isn't questioning it yet. At the very least, I thought she would notice that there aren't any cars around.

"If your wife or your child were to ask you to stop playing, would you?" she asks, her voice a lot smaller than it was a few minutes ago.

I know why she is asking me this question; it's stemming from everything she told me last night, but it's still a little shocking to hear it.

Never did I have to think of an answer to that question. Did I ever think about getting married and having kids? Yeah, but I honestly thought I would be retired before settling down. Possibly have a kid or two if life went that way. I started thinking more about it when Liam and Chloe had Emma, but it wasn't like an eye-opening experience for me.

It takes me a second to think of an answer to give her. A hard yes is on the tip of my tongue.

If asked by a loved one, wife, child, parent, life partner, to give up the game, I would. No second thought about it.

The word starts to form on my lips, but Eliana stops me from saying anything.

"You know what, don't answer that. Of course, the answer is going to be no. I wouldn't want to give it up either. Especially if it was something that molded you. I wouldn't want to give up photography." She starts shaking her head, and right as I'm about to refute her answer, she changes the subject, finally realizing where we are. "Why are we at the boardwalk? And why is it so empty?"

As she looks around, I contemplate going back to the conversation at hand, but I don't know if me telling her will bring back some of the emotions that she was feeling last night. And I want her to have fun today, so I hold back.

"I rented it out," I say, turning off the car.

"You rented it out? You can do that during the summer?" she asks, her eyes wide.

"Apparently when you offer a big chunk of money, you can," I say, getting out of the car and walking over to the passenger side.

"Why would you do that? You know how many kids were probably looking forward to coming today and having fun?" she throws out, but still takes my hand to get out of the car.

"Calm down, I'm not that cruel. There are still kids

coming today. It's only ours for a few hours this morning. And for the rest of the day all tickets will be free."

"Why would you do that?" she asks again, lacing her fingers with mine.

"Because I wanted to do something for you that made you smile at least a little bit. I had it planned for a while, but then last night happened, and I thought it would be the perfect opportunity. I always had fun here as a kid. It was one of my favorite places, when it wasn't packed, so I thought it would be something fun for us, too, even though we might not be able to get on all the kiddie rides."

I wanted to make her feel happiness instead of the sorrow she was so vocal about last night. And if things don't work out for us, and she doesn't move in with me, then maybe she'll have a fun memory of our summer together.

"You're doing this for me?" she asks, bewildered that I would even think of something like this.

I'm not that much of an asshole.

I drop her hand and go to cradle her face. "Yes," I say, placing a kiss against her lips. "For you."

"Who knew you could be so sweet?" she says, kissing me back.

"Don't tell anyone. It's only for you because you wiggled yourself deep under my skin and if I don't keep you happy, then there's a possibility that you might cut my hands off."

"Not your hands, that's where the money is. It would be something a lot more precious," she says, throwing her arms around my neck and bringing her body closer to mine.

The grin on her face is a sadistic one, and I love it. "I wouldn't put it past you."

Wanting to feel more of her against my body, I lean down and burrow my face into her neck. Taking in her smell and smiling at how good she feels against me. All her delicious curves fill my hands so damn perfectly.

"We didn't get a chance to talk about the possibility of turning our relationship into more last night like you promised," she voices, letting out a giggle when I nip at her neck.

"No, we didn't," I say against her neck, peppering it with kisses.

"I say we do it. I say we turn it into more," she tells me, grabbing me by the hair and pulling my face away from her.

"Is that what you want? You hate what I do for a living, and for a good reason."

She nods. "It's what I want. I may feel a certain way about the sport that you play, but you have made me see that there are players out there who care more about other things besides the sport. You could have gone to get some ice time this morning, but instead you rented out a whole damn amusement park for me because you want to make me smile. I would say that's boyfriend material, don't you think?"

I let my hands slide down from her waist to her ass and give her a good grip.

"I would say so, but if we make it official, I have two conditions." I grin at her, knowing she's going to be mine either way.

She narrows her eyes at me. "What?"

"You cook me mofongo at least once a month as my cheat meal," I offer as my first condition.

She lets out a laugh. "Me cooking it for you last week wasn't enough?"

"Never. If I didn't have to carbo-load, I would have you make it every single day."

She shakes her head knowing that the days of eating pasta all day every day are upon us.

"Fine. What's your second condition?"

"You move in with me."

I wasn't talking out of my ass when I said the same thing earlier this morning. She needs a place, and I have a big enough condo for the both of us. Yeah, I like living alone, but I've liked having her close by day in and day out, and a part of me, a big part, wants her in my space forever.

"What if you get traded?" she asks after a few seconds of silence.

"Then I'll transfer the lease to you, or you'll go with me wherever I land."

Yeah, I'm planning ahead. We're just stepping into a relationship. I shouldn't be planning, but I don't give a shit. This woman is worth it, and I'm not going to let her go, now or ever, without a fight. Even if I'm fighting her demons.

"You make everything sound so damn easy."

"It is so damn easy. You just have to agree," I tell her, meaning every single word.

"And what if I have conditions of my own?" she throws back my way, telling me that she is so close to agreeing.

"What are your conditions?" I smirk at her. I'll give her anything she wants, possibly even giving up the game.

"We come to the beach house whenever we can during the season and stay here all offseason."

"Deal."

"We get through my first month with the team and then go to HR with our relationship. Together. And tell my dad at the same time."

"Done."

"Me and only me, nobody else. No sharing. No cheating. You want a side piece, you walk away."

"It's only been you since the day you broke into my house." I haven't spoken truer words.

That gets me an eye roll. "For the thousandth time, I didn't break in. The door was wide open. Are you ready for the final condition?"

I give her a curt nod. "Give it to me."

"No matter how much I get on your nerves, you will not throw me in the ocean. Ever."

Now it's my turn to narrow my eyes at her. "I will agree to every other condition but the last one."

We have a stare down for what feels like forever, but I come out the winner when she can't keep her eyes from blinking anymore.

"Fine," she finally concedes. "At least do it while we're at a warm beach or something. Not the Pacific."

"I'll see what I can do," I say, throwing her a wink. "So, is that it? Did we officially move to the next step in our relationship and agree that you are moving in with me?"

"We did, and to celebrate gaining a girlfriend, we're going to ride on some rides, you're going to win me a few prizes and buy me a corn dog and after the fact, you will take me back to your house and get on your knees so you can show me how good of a boyfriend you are."

I like how this woman thinks. "Deal, and after I get on my knees and make you come so hard you forget your own name, you'll get on yours and swallow my cock like the perfect girlfriend that you are." I press my body to hers so that she can feel just how hard for her I already am.

"Deal."

We lasted until two in the afternoon. The second the time on our phones hit two, we were racing away from the boardwalk and the rides and straight to the car to get home and get naked.

The whole day was filled with laughs and creating fun memories but also filled with suggestive comments, over the top flirting, sensual glances, and a very inappropriate way to eat a corn dog. Everything started becoming too fucking much around three hours ago. I even tried to sneak in a quick orgasm for Eliana in the haunted house, but she wouldn't let me. Something about cameras. As if I wouldn't be able to buy the security footage, but whatever.

We spent the last hour on the beach taking pictures.

Well, Eliana taking pictures and me posing my body in whatever way she told me. At some point, because I wanted a picture with her, I grabbed her camera and set it up on a lifeguard shack and took a handful of pictures of the two of us.

After that, my balls couldn't take it anymore, so I suggested we get out of there. Thank fuck she agreed.

As soon as we got to the car, though, she forbade me from touching her and told me to wait until we got to the house. Which only made me want to get to the house faster.

Which is why I'm currently speeding up my street and making my way up my driveway a lot faster than five miles an hour.

"I swear, you have issues with speed," Eliana grumbles from the passenger seat as soon as I come to a stop and turn off the car.

"No issues, baby. It's just pure adrenaline running through my veins, both on the ice and off." I quickly get out of the car and go to open her door.

"That makes no sense whatsoever," she throws out while getting out of the car.

"It does in my head. Are you going to walk into the house so I can eat your pussy, or am I going to have to drag you in?"

A pretty blush creeps up her face. "What does dragging me entail? My hand or hair? Or is it you throwing me over your shoulder like a starved man?"

"The latter. You want your hair pulled, I'll do that inside," I growl out as I close the distance between us, already imagining the feel of her silky locks in my fist as I pound into her from behind.

"Then I'll take the getting thrown over the shoulder, please."

"Thank fuck."

I don't waste any time bending down and throwing my woman over my shoulder. My hands instantly grip onto her thighs, and I hold her tightly as we walk toward the front door.

No time is wasted punching in the door code, a new one thanks to my idiot brother, and heading inside, straight to the bedroom.

The second I step over the threshold to the room, I feel my shirt lift up and a mouth meeting the skin right on top of my ass.

"Don't you fucking dare," I order, but the second that the words come out of my mouth, Eliana opens her mouth and bites down on the muscle.

"Fuck," I let out, which is quickly drowned out by a giggle.

"You're going to pay for that," I tell her as I bend down and let her fall in the bed.

"I thought you liked a little pain during sex," she says with the sexiest smile I have ever seen on her lips.

Fuck, this woman does things to me.

"During sex. Not while I'm walking."

"Oops," she says, leaning back on her elbows. "Then you should punish me. I'm a very bad listener." The way she flutters her eyelashes at me goes straight to my dick.

"Keep that up, and I will." I quickly take my shirt off.

"Hmm, is that a promise? And if I call you *Papi,* what

will you do? Will you fuck me until the only name I'm screaming is yours?"

"Fuck." Not being able to take it anymore, I climb on the bed and get on top of her, letting my body press against hers without putting all of my weight on her. I suck her tongue into my mouth and groan at the taste of her.

Never will I get tired of my mouth on hers. Kissing her and having her body under mine is what dreams are fucking made of. I want every single inch of this woman to be mine.

"Such a perfect beauty, with the perfect body," I say, grinding myself against her.

"Christian," she moans.

I pull my mouth away from her fully and place kisses against the corner of her lips, then her jaw and then down to her neck. She arches back to give me more room.

"Someone is needy today," I say against her skin.

"You've made me needy," she is able to say right before she lets out a moan as my hand travels the length of her body and settles right where she wants it. Right above her mound.

"Do you want what I promised you?" I continue to make my way down her body, biting her breast through her shirt and bra on the way down until I'm on my knees in front of her ready for my meal.

"Oh my god, yes!" Eliana answers, bucking her hips once I'm fully off her, bringing her core closer to my face.

"Then let's get you undressed." I pull away from her, and

from my position on my knees, I start working on sliding her pants off.

I take my time, wanting to savor every single second with this woman, savor every single damn inch.

She watches me as I pop open the button at her waistband, and she lets out a sigh when my hands slide under the material to start sliding her pants down with her panties.

Both my mouth and my dick love the sight before me. My mouth starts to water at what's about to come, and my dick starts to twitch wanting in on the action.

Eliana make quick work of taking off her shirt, followed by her bra. Her body glows in the afternoon sunlight, and all I want to do is capture this moment so that I can look back on it anytime that I want.

Maybe one day we'll do something with her camera, not today because right now I'm too hungry for her to think about leaving this room.

"¿Dónde quieres mi boca?" I ask her where she wants my mouth, as I slide a finger along her pussy, gently teasing her clit and her entrance along the way.

"En todo mi cuerpo," she says with a relaxed sigh leaving her lips.

All of her body.

"I'm going to need you to tell me exactly where you want it. Then you can have it," I say, leaning forward and gliding my nose from her hip all the way to the junction of her knee.

"You always make this difficult. Why can't you just put your mouth wherever you want and just make me come?"

"Where's the fun in that?" I say, dragging my tongue all

the way from her lower inner thigh to her apex. "I want to hear you beg for my tongue, fingers, mouth, and cock. I can't just give to you. So, tell me where you want my mouth."

Eliana huffs but does what I asked her to do. "I want your mouth on my pussy."

She places a hand on her breast and slides it along her body until she reaches her pussy.

I look up from where I'm concentrating on her inner thigh and watch as she plays with herself.

"This is where I want your mouth. You think you can figure it out from there?" she says, and I look up just in time to see a smirk form on her lips.

"Hermosa, you know that I can. I haven't failed at making you come with my mouth now, have I?" I grab the hand that she has on her pussy and bring it up to my mouth and sucking her fingers clean. "My favorite taste in the world."

"Put your mouth where your words are, Rodriguez."

"Who's the bossy one now?" I throw her a wink before hungrily placing my mouth against her core.

A gasp rolls through the room as I slide my tongue along her folds and circle her clit. I eat her out as if she really were my last meal, and I need her to survive. Every single one of my actions has her gasping and moaning out and gripping the comforter on the bed as if it's her only saving grace.

I lap at her before taking her clit into my mouth and sucking on her until she lets go of the sheets, and her hands land in my hair.

"Oh my god, Christian," she pants out, gripping my hair almost to the point of pain, but like I told her, I enjoy the occasional pain during sex, and this pain is exactly what I need to drive me fucking wild.

My hands travel up her body from where they were gripping her thighs, all the way until I have both of her tits in my hands. I grip her tits as if they were stress balls, my nails probably making indentations in her skin. Slowly, I loosen my hold on her and move my hand just a bit until I have her nipples between my fingers and give them a good tug.

That just drives her wilder.

"Do that, again. Please," she orders, arching her back some more, filling my hands with more of her.

"I'm not the only one that likes a little pain," I say against her, sliding my nose through her fold and letting her scent embed itself into my brain.

"I only like it when you do it," she lets out almost breathless.

"You like it when I do this?" I ask, and I twist her right nipple and squeeze at it at the same time.

"Yes." The moans that she releases are like music to my ears.

"How about when I do this?" I ask, pulling my face away from her and moving one of my hands down her body until I reach her pussy and give her a gentle slap followed by a slightly harder one that won't hurt her.

"Oh my god, yes." She grinds against me, liking the pleasurable pain.

"My kind of girl," I say, sliding my hand against her folds until my fingers are teasing her entrance. "Now, come for me, so I can fuck you and officially mark you as mine with cock."

"I'm already yours. I've been yours since that first night," she says, her legs opening wider.

"You have, but now it's official. Now, come on my fingers because my cock is throbbing to slide into your tight pussy."

I slide my fingers in and out of her, my other hand finally letting go of her breast and moving down her body until it's resting on her stomach and pressing down. I work her until her legs are shaking, and her moans are turning into screams.

"Come for me, baby. Cover my fingers with everything that you have."

"I'm so close," she pants out in almost a cry. "Christian, please. I need to come so badly."

I feel her tighten around my fingers, knowing she's as close as she says, so I lean down and take her clit in my mouth again and suck on her bud of nerves to get her as close to the edge as I can.

She tightens around my fingers even more and when her legs tighten against my head, I know she's exactly where I want her to be. One more suck on her clit and she explodes around my fingers.

"Fuck. Christian. Yes, oh my god, yes," she pants out and she continues to float through her climax, I slide my fingers out of her, and I stand up to full height.

My cock bobs and is already leaking pre-cum, even more so when I take my fingers in my mouth and suck her release off my fingers.

It makes me want to bend down again to lick her clean, but instead, I slide my cock along her wet fold, coating it in her release before grabbing her by the hips and flipping her over.

"On all fours," I order, and even though she hasn't recovered from her orgasm, she does it.

The second that she's in the position that I want her in on the bed, I stand behind her, marveling at how fucking gorgeous she looks like this. Her ass up in the air, waiting for me to lean down and take a bite. I love this woman's ass so damn much, it can turn into a very unhealthy addiction, but a welcomed one.

Since she gave me a bite, it seems only fitting for me to give her one in return. I caress the skin of her cheek, and she bucks into my touch. I lean down and take a bite of her, and when she lets out a yelp, I chuckle, caressing the bite and soothing it.

"See, I told you biting is better during sex." I place my hands on each one of her cheeks and spread her open so I can lick her from hole to hole.

"Christian," she moans, letting her upper body fall onto the bed. "I need you inside of me."

"Don't worry, hermosa. I'm getting there."

I give her pussy one last kiss before straightening up and lining up the tip of my cock with her entrance. Without warning, I slide into her tight pussy and slide right out only to slide back in until she is taking every single inch of me.

"This pussy is mine," I tell her, gripping her body and slamming into her over and over.

"It's yours. I'm yours," she moans into the comforter. "Holy fuck."

"I bet nobody has made you feel this good, this full, have they?"

"No, only you."

"Good," I groan, loving the sight of her ass slamming into me as her pussy takes every single inch of me. "Look at how good you take me. It's fucking perfect. The perfect view. Though everything about you is perfect. Your mouth, your pussy, your whole damn body, and this ass. Fuck, this ass. That's my favorite part about you, right next to your attitude."

I sink into her, feeling my release at the edge of exploding, but I need her to come before I do. I need to feel her tighten around me, then I can fill her up with every last drop that I have.

"I need you there with me. Tell me that you're close because I don't know how much longer I can hold on."

She lets out a groan as she tries to push her upper body up. "I'm close. I just came for you, and I'm already close again. Oh my god, Christian. I don't know how much more I can take. You feel so good."

"So do you. You fucking ruin me."

"Keep fucking me like that, baby," she says, moving her ass to meet each one of my movements. "I'm so close. I can't..." She goes silent and convulses around me again.

Not wasting a single second, I grab her hair and give her a pull like I told her outside I would and pound into her. I pound into her pussy, until our bodies are slicked with sweat and the only sound that is filling my ears is our bodies slapping against each other.

Eliana lets out one more moan, and that is all I need to come inside of her and fill her with everything that I have.

A growl escapes me as I feel the ropes of come leave me. I hold myself to her, slowly moving in and out of her, until I pull out fully and look down at the mess we just made.

"I lied," I say as I slide a finger against her pussy and wide my release all over it. Marking every single inch of her core. "You taking my cock isn't the most perfect view. No, the perfect view is seeing you full of my cum, and it dripping out of your pussy like this."

I coat my finger in both our releases and lean over her until my finger meets her mouth and I have her suck it clean.

She hums as she takes my finger in her mouth, and once there isn't a drop left, she falls to the bed, with the most content look on her face.

"I think that's the best sex we've had," she says, closing her eyes, still catching her breath.

I let out a small chuckle and throw my body against hers, leaving no space between us and taking her face between my hands. "That was nothing. We're just getting started. You're officially mine, and I'm going to take advantage of it every single chance that I get," I say against her lips.

"You won't hear me complain."

"Good. Now what do you say about fucking all over the house until we have to head to Chicago?" I shift until I'm hovering over her.

"I say, you better fuck me good, because I want to enjoy what is left of my summer."

CHAPTER SEVENTEEN

IT BECAME IMPOSSIBLE.

In the two months since we met, it has become nearly impossible for me to hate Christian. He bulldozed into my life in the most unexpected way, and as more days pass by, I can't help but be glad that he did.

At the end of June, I thought I was living my best life. I had signed with the Dark Knights as the team photographer, I had a summer assignment that would keep me out of Chicago until I absolutely had to be there, and I was taking in as much sun as I could while enjoying my time by the beach.

I didn't expect that I would cross paths with a hockey player, get on his bad side, and then end up in his bed only a week or two later. I was supposed to hate him, I was supposed to hate every single thing about the man, and since I already hated his profession, I shouldn't have been that hard.

But it was.

Christian showed me a side to him that I didn't expect. A side that sang to my body and soul. He made me laugh, showed me he cared with his comfort, and made me feel worthy of everything that life has to offer. He has made me feel special in a way that nobody else has.

He's made me feel beautiful like nobody else has, too. It's in the way he looks at me, in how he smiles at me, at how he kisses me and touches me. Every little thing that he does, makes me feel like the most beautiful woman in the world.

That's why he's made it nearly impossible for me to garner any hate toward him. He made it that way. He made it nearly impossible for me not to start developing feelings for him. He made it impossible to not start falling for him. To not want to spend every single waking moment with him.

And now that we are in Chicago, about to move in together, it's going to be even harder.

I'm going to be around him all the time. At home, at work. He will be everywhere I am, and I know how I feel toward him will just continue to grow stronger, until I fall so deep there will be no way out.

I should hate him for that alone, but I don't. I love it too much.

We made our way to Chicago, leaving the beach house properly fucked as Christian put it, two days ago. Christian came to the city with a single duffel bag and left everything else in California. Me, on the other hand, I came to Chicago with my whole life in suitcases. Since I travel so much for work, or at least keep myself traveling, I tend to move with everything that I own. And only stay in places that let me rent out an apartment or a house month to month.

I have some stuff at my dad's house, minimal but some, and some at the childhood home that my mom left me after she died. That stuff, though, is mostly things that have sentimental value or equipment that I don't gravitate towards very often.

Now that I'm moving in with Christian, all of my things are going to be in one location, which will be nice. It will also be nice to have an actual home for once and not have to move everything every few months every time I get a new assignment, or the travel bug hits me.

Who knew that breaking into a hockey player's house would be a blessing in disguise.

Right, I'm currently trying to organize all my gear in the spare room that Christian told me that I can take over. And well, it's not going well.

I have so much shit. Who knew camera equipment that could look organized in suitcases and camera bags, but out of them, it's a chaotic mess. I even found a lens that I thought I had lost months ago at the bottom of a duffel bag.

I've been at it for three hours while Christian is at Liam's house fulfilling some bet, and I honestly don't see an end in sight.

Looking around, I'm now thinking I should have accepted my boyfriend's invitation and gone with him.

"No, I have to do this. Once I'm done, I will be officially moved in," I say to myself, trying to convince myself to continue with putting things on the shelves and racks Christian put up for me yesterday.

But there is so much stuff.

I should really downsize all my equipment. Especially since the Knights will be supplying more. I didn't know it was part of my contract, but I learned last week that the team will be providing all new equipment on top of a team of photographers that will work under me to bring everything the team does to life.

Maybe I should do that instead of putting things in a certain spot. I might be able to find a program that accepts donations like this. Maybe an at-risk youth program that has kids interested in photography.

Deciding to see what things I can donate instead, I grab a box from the piles and start to fill it. I get about two things into the box before I'm getting pulled away by my phone ringing.

Dread starts to fill my body.

Ever since that night a few weeks ago, I've been panicking every time my phone rings. I keep thinking that it will be Kalen calling to tell me that he released the pictures.

His number is still blocked, but because I haven't been answering unknown calls ever since I last spoke to him, I have no idea if he has called. But I'm waiting for the day that I don't answer my phone, and there is a voicemail from him waiting for me where he tells me what he did.

I'm already dreading that day if it ever even comes.

Shaking my head, telling myself that it isn't Kalen, I grab my phone from where it sits on a box.

I slowly turn it over and let out a somewhat sigh of relief when I see it's my dad calling and not a disgruntled ex-boyfriend. But my dad isn't all that much better.

Our relationship has been better-ish ever since I signed on to work for the Knights. We've talked more these last few months, been less angry with each other, but things still aren't perfect. There are things that both of us definitely need to work on. We're trying, so that's something.

We may have talked these past months, but conversations were still few and far in between. The last time I talked to him was almost a month ago when I called to see if I could stay at his house while I got situated. He had told me yes, but I was still going to look at my options. His house was going to be my last resort, but I still had wanted to secure it.

There hasn't been any type of conversation since then, so I'm guessing he's calling to see if I'm still thinking about staying with him.

As much as I don't want to answer, not knowing how the conversation is going to go, I do. He's my dad, and I'm trying to be a better daughter.

"Hey, Sad," I say, answering the call at the last possible second.

"Hey, honey. How are you? I haven't heard from you in a while," he says from the other side.

I smile at the sound of his voice. As a kid, hearing his voice was my favorite thing in the world because it meant that he was either home or called because he was thinking about me or Mom.

"Yeah, I'm sorry. These last few weeks have been a little

crazy. The Quakes didn't have another photographer lined up, so I had to help them look for one, and that was a bit of a headache. But I'm good. Just getting ready for my first day at my new job. How are you? Are you ready for the season?"

"Better than I will ever be. I've never come into a season with a championship on my back, so I don't know if I should keep everything the same coaching-wise or if I should change things up to see if we better our chances of winning another Cup," he says, and I can picture him in his office pacing back and forth just contemplating this very question.

"Sounds reasonable. I would try to possibly change a few things and see how the team responds, and if it doesn't work, go back to the old ways." I offer.

"You think so?" he asks, most likely thinking of ways he can make my opinion come to life.

I nod even if I'm in the room alone. "Yeah. You have a solid team. One that I'm sure is just as hungry to win another championship as you are. There isn't much change you can make, but it's worth a try."

My dad is silent for a minute, probably thinking everything through. As he contemplates, I put him on speaker and start to pick things out again that can go in the donation pile.

Eventually, he speaks. "The Knights are a solid team. It's worth a try to change a few things. Maybe they will help," he muses.

"Maybe, but you won't know until you try," I say, from across the room.

"Thank you, honey," he says, sounding sincere.

I can't remember the last time I gave my dad advice, and he thanked me for it. It takes me by surprise a little bit.

"You're welcome, Dad." I answer, actually meaning it.

I'm not going to lie, but giving my dad advice, even if it was minimal, and him accepting it, felt nice. I may still hold some hate toward his sport, but it feels nice to step back into that space with him again.

"Listen, there's a reason for my call," he says, after another bout of silence.

My stomach churns a little bit at his statement.

Is he going to tell me that I should quit my job with the Knights before I officially start?

"What's up?" I ask, trying not to let my mind go into panic mode with overthinking.

"I want to apologize to you," he says, taking me by surprise yet again.

Now I'm the one going silent.

"What exactly do you want to apologize for?" I ask cautiously.

I put the lens I currently have in my hand down for fear of dropping it at what he's about to say next.

"Well, there's a lot I need to and want to apologize for, but the first thing I truly wanted to say I am sorry for is was the way I acted when your mom died. I should have been there. I should have been there from the very beginning. I should have left the team and gone to be with the two of you. You both needed me, and I was too stuck in my own head to realize it. If I could go back, I would. I would be there for your mom and tell her how much she meant to me, and I would be there for you when you needed someone to be by your side through all the hard stuff. There are so many things that I would change, and I know how badly I messed up and for that, I wanted to say that I'm so damn sorry, Eliana. I can never apologize enough to you, or to your mother, for not being there and all the heartache that I put both of you through. It might not be today, but I really hope that one day, you can forgive me even if it's only a little bit. I'm so fucking sorry, sweetheart. Please know that."

Something wet lands against my chest, and it takes me a long minute for me to realize that I'm crying.

For years, I had hoped that I would hear all of these words come out of my dad's mouth. I wanted to hear them so damn badly, but as time went on, and I never heard them, I eventually gave up on him ever admitting his actions back then were wrong.

I even thought there was going to be a chance I would have to drag the apology out of him.

Yet here he is giving me what I silently asked for all of these years. He's apologizing, and I'm too stunned to speak.

I take a minute to collect myself, wiping away at my face to get rid of the tears.

I clear my throat before I try to speak. "What brought this on?" After all these years, why now, and why not back then?

There are so many questions I want to ask him, but I don't know if I can.

My dad clears his throat as if his apology made him emotional, too.

"I don't know if you remember this, you were young and I

wasn't around a lot when you were older, so she might have talked to you about this; I'm not sure, but your mom always talked about dreams and how they all have double meaning?" he says, forming a question at the end.

My head starts to nod as if it was an automatic action. "I remember," I whisper into the phone.

My mom was big on dreams. She always said that your dreams are trying to tell you something or possibly provide a path that can be used as a way for someone who has passed to communicate with you.

"A few weeks ago, I had a dream, one where your mom was there. It had been a while since I've dreamed about her. Usually, dreams with her in them have always felt as if they were distant memories that my mind didn't want me to forget. This dream, though, felt as if it wasn't a memory but very much real. As if she was in the same room as me and was speaking to me as clearly if she was still here. As if she were right next to me." My dad chokes up at the end.

It makes me choke up too, but I try to keep my emotions in check as best I can. I can't start losing it right now.

"What did she say?" I ask, closing my eyes and trying to picture my mom in any way that I can.

"That I've already lost you once, and that I should repair our relationship before I lose you again."

Even more questions start to swing through my head. My dad was never one to believe my mom and all her dream talk and theories. Why is it that he's doing it now?

"When I woke up, I realized that she was right. I need to repair what is going on between us because if I don't, I'll miss every other future chance of being in your life and being the father you deserve. So, I decided to start by apologizing for one of my worst mistakes. One that affected you deeply."

For the second time during this phone call, I'm left surprised and speechless.

What should I do? What should I say?

I've wanted this for so long, yet I never came up with a plan as to what I would say or do if it ever happened.

I decide to give him the truth.

"I don't know what to say, Dad." I try to push my emotions down fully, but I fail.

"You don't have to say anything. You don't have to accept my apology right now or ever if that's what you want. I hurt you too much for you to forgive me after one apology. I owe you more than that. You deserve a lot more than what I have given you, and if you let me, I want to try my hardest to repair it."

More tears escape my eyes, and I don't know if they are from anger because it took him this long to get to this point, or tears of happiness because there is a chance I can get back the father I lost a long time ago.

"I want to try, too," I say, my voice so small that it makes me feel as if I were a little girl again.

My dad sniffles a bit on the other end before he speaks. "Maybe we can both start trying when you come and stay with me? We can have dinner together a few times a week and talk. I would really love to get to know my daughter a lot better and make sure I find ways to better be there for her in the future."

I smile.

That is something I've wanted for a very long time, but I think we both are just so stubborn that we needed an outside source to intervene and help us take our heads out of our asses.

Gracias, Mami.

As I stand there silently thanking my mom, what my dad just said, clicks in my head.

Crap. As much as I want to give my dad what he is asking for, it's going to be a little hard to do given that I won't be staying with him anymore.

"Actually, I found a place to live, so I won't be staying there anymore. I'm sorry, but the dinner part a few times a week can still happen. My new place isn't far from you. I can pop in whenever you want," I add, trying not to disappoint him in any way.

"You found a place?" he asks, more out of curiosity and not anger.

"Yeah, I--" I'm about to tell him that I moved in with Christian, but that might be a bad idea, so I stop. "An opportunity came up with a friend, so I took it."

My heart does something funny at the word friend, but it had to be said. My dad doesn't need to know I'm living and sharing a bed with one of his players. So where my dad is concerned, Christian Rodriguez is my *friend.*

"A permanent opportunity?" I can hear hope in his question.

I can't help but smile at the thought of me and Christian being permanent. "Yeah, a very permanent one."

"Good, I'm glad," my dad says through the speaker.

"Me, too," I say, looking down at the phone, part of me wishing that we were having this conversation in person.

"I guess we should have a dinner officially welcoming you to Chicago."

I nod at the phone. "I would like that. When do you want to do it?"

My dad starts answering the question, but it's quickly cut off by a door opening somewhere in the house and then Christian's voice ringing through.

"Babe, please tell me you're home! I have a poop situation I need help with!"

Poop situation? What the fuck is a poop situation, and why do I have to help?

"*Babe?*" My dad's question fills the room. The confusion in his voice makes me cringe. He definitely is not going to believe the whole *friend* thing now.

"Eliana, where are you? I seriously need help," Christian yells out, and I have to severely hope that my dad doesn't recognize his voice.

"I'm coming!" I yell in the direction of the hallway, before taking my phone off speaker and try to end the call with my dad before Christian comes in here and outs us. "Dad, I have to go, but I will take you up on that dinner. Set it up and send me the information, and I will be there." He starts saying something, but I quickly cut him off. "Okay, bye!"

I quickly end the call and cross my fingers my dad was

not able to tell that my boyfriend's voice sounds exactly like one of his players.

Pocketing my phone, I abandon all the camera gear, compose myself a bit so that Christian doesn't notice I've been crying, and head out to the living area of the condo. I'm still getting used to the layout, but it's a really nice place. Apparently Christian knows how to pick out real estate.

I walk into the living room, and the second that I do, I have to do a few double takes.

Christian is standing by the front door with a stroller in front of him and a baby in his arms. When a bark sounds out, I become even more confused about the scene playing out in front of me.

"I'm sorry, but why do you have a baby?" I ask, my eyes moving from him to the baby who is in his arms. The bundle of joy is thrashing against him, and if I had to guess from the whimpers I'm hearing, the baby is about to cry.

"Liam and Chloe put me on Emma duty until otherwise specified," he grunts out, beads of sweat forming on his forehead as Emma starts to whimper even more. "I think she exploded in her diaper. She smells so bad. It's the second time she's done it to me today. I'm starting to think she hates me."

I'm about to say something to him, but I'm interrupted by a bark that is coming from the stroller.

"Um, is there a reason why the stroller is barking?"

"Because I'm also on puppy duty," he informs me, turning the stroller so that it faces me. Sure enough there is a golden retriever puppy in the stroller. "You got a choice. Dirty diaper or watching the puppy and making sure that it doesn't eat anything in the condo. Please choose dirty diaper."

I close the distance between us and give him a smile and flutter of my eyelashes all before giving him my answer. "Puppy."

He's narrowing his eyes at me. "I hate you."

I smile. I'm usually the one who tells him that.

"Too bad. You're stuck with me," I say, giving him a pat on the shoulder. "Now go take care of Emma before Liam kicks your ass because you didn't change his daughter's diaper in time."

He rolls his eyes but pushes the puppy in the baby stroller over to me and grumbles as he walks over to the couch about how he is done taking bets that involve diapers.

I just laugh as I play with the puppy, occasionally looking over at Christian to make sure he's got a handle on the diaper situation. I can't help but to smile at the image before me, and for a split second, a different scene pops into my head.

One where instead of the baby being Emma, it's a little boy with dark hair and caramel-colored eyes. A little boy named Christian after his father and has the attitude like his mother.

The image is quick ,but it's not one that I will never easily forget.

Maybe one day, that scene will actually become reality.

For right now, I'm content with us playing pretend.

CHAPTER EIGHTEEN

CHRISTIAN

THE SHUTTER of the camera continues to sound throughout the small room, and every time it does, a hint of pride hits my chest.

Today, all the Knights are on site for what I like to call picture day. It's the second day of training camp, and the marketing team has everyone in full gear to get promotional videos and pictures to use throughout the season.

Every single year, I usually hate this day. Mostly because I could be spending my time on the ice instead of snapping pictures, but this year is different. This year, I actually don't mind taking time out of my day to take pictures or do promo shit. This year, I'm perfectly happy with slapping a smile on my face and saying cheese to the camera if I'm told to.

And that's because this year, Eliana is at the helm of it all, taking charge of every photo taken and every video that is shot.

The woman looks so in her element, so at ease, taking

charge and ordering everyone around just to get the perfect shot, and doing it all while having a smile on her face.

I don't know if this is how she is with all her jobs. I know I saw a glimpse of this during her last few weeks of her assignment with the Quakes, but even then, it didn't compare to the excitement and happiness that she is radiating now.

The second I walked into the room for my photo time slot, I saw that she was made for this job. Everyone in the room saw it.

And that shit right there is what continues to make my pride in this woman grow.

"He's doing it again," Blake whispers from next to me as he, Liam, and I line up for a shot.

"Who's doing what?" Liam whispers at the kid, looking over at him like he has a third head or something.

"Rodriguez is smiling again," Blake answers, nodding his head toward me.

"Am not," I refute.

I should make a mental note to shave the dude's head the next time we share a hotel room. Just to see if that will keep his mouth from saying shit.

"Are, too. Where's the grumpy asshole who we all know and hate?"

"He's not allowed to be grumpy," Eliana throws out, inserting herself into the conversation. "Now shut up, and stay still, Jacobi, or I swear I will have a banner printed of you with your mouth wide open and have it hung everywhere I can."

Damn. I didn't know I could develop even deeper feelings for this woman, but she proved me wrong with one single threat toward Blake.

"Shit. I can see why you two are an item. She's like a female version of you, just a whole lot prettier," Blake whispers just for me and Liam to hear, but that doesn't stop me from reaching over and slapping a hand along the back of his head. "Ow!"

"Shut the fuck up," I whisper yell through my teeth and try to give him my most menacing look so that he remembers to not mention anything about me an Eliana being together while within the walls of the arena or doing anything work-related.

We haven't gone to HR yet with our relationship, so we still have to keep it a secret and professional while we do anything related to hockey. We're also keeping the news that we are together on a need-to-know basis. I told Liam, Blake, and Logan because I knew two of the assholes were going to ask questions as if their lives depended on it. Logan didn't give a shit, but I told him anyway.

When I told them, I specifically told them to not mention anything about me and Eliana even liking each other while we were in the arena, the locker room, a plane, a bus, or anywhere where a Dark Knights logo was visible.

I knew Blake was going to be the one to not be able to follow orders.

"Sorry," he says, holding his hands up in defense. "I forgot. Won't happen again."

"Better not. If it does, you're going to be changing Emma's diaper for a day."

That day fucking traumatized me. Who knew that something so small and so adorable could release such nasty ass smelling poop and make sure it gets into every single crevice and article of clothing.

Whatever Liam and Chloe are feeding the kid has to be thrown away and burned.

I would be more than okay not experiencing that again for another fifty years, but even then, that is too soon.

"That's up to Liam, not you," Blake throws out, like we're in elementary school.

"I'm actually good with that arrangement," he says, giving our teammate a shrug. "So, talk away, Jacobi."

I shake my head. "I can still smell the second dirty diaper. It's like ingrained into my brain and now every time I see my couch, I smell it."

I shudder at the memory. I'm not used to changing diapers, so one little slip and everything I touched had green goop on it.

"That was your fault. You should have made sure that the diaper was properly secure before you left the apartment." Now Liam is giving me a shrug.

"You're the one who kicked me out with your kid and dog because you wanted to screw your girlfriend's brains out." I'm not babysitting again until both are potty trained. There was shit everywhere.

"That was a good day, though," my best friend throws back with a stupid smile on his face, probably remembering how the two of them screwed around until about seven in the evening.

"Boys, can we stop talking about baby poop and screwing and let me take my pictures?" Eliana says, sounding frustrated, but when I turn to look at her, I catch her smiling.

"Yes, ma'am," we all say at the same time.

For the next ten minutes, the three of us don't say a word and let Eliana take every single picture that she needs. When she is finally happy, she gives us the okay to leave.

"Did you guys hear we will be seeing who the new owners are?" Blake asks as we walk into the locker room to change out of our gear.

At the start of last year, there were rumors floating around all through the hockey world that the Dark Knights were going to be getting a new owner. Apparently, the one that we had was looking at selling because none of his kids wanted to take over. A lot of us didn't really care. As long as it didn't hurt the team and our chances of winning it all, we were okay with it.

The rumors went on for months, and finally around April, it was announced that the team had been sold to a private company. One that has a fake-sounding name, I might add. But since then, there haven't been any major changes to the team, since then and nobody has even seen the new owner in the building or knows who they are.

Locker room rumors as of this morning are saying that these new owners, whoever they might be, will be coming around in the next few days to introduce themselves.

Whether or not those rumors are true, I have no idea.

"Doubt that they'll come. We haven't seen them since

they bought the team. Why come around now?" I voice, pulling off my jersey.

"My thing is, why keep it a secret? Why buy the team under a private company and only show up when the new season is about to start? If I were them, I would have said who I was the second the contract was signed and took credit for us winning the Cup," Liam says, which has both Blake and me nodding in agreement.

"I say it's a woman. Someone who has rich people money and loved the sport so much that she bought herself the team to spite her parents or something. Or maybe to get revenge on one of her exes," Blake says, leaving both me and Liam speechless.

Liam turns to look at me and silently asks me with his eyes if Blake is okay, and I just give him a shrug. I've been asking myself the same question since I met the kid.

Blake realizes that we haven't reacted to his little theory, so he turns to look at us, his eyebrows bunched up. "What?"

"Where the fuck did that theory come from?" Liam asks, looking at him like he has three heads again.

Our teammate shrugs. "I was video chatting with Jainie, my sister, last night, and she was telling me about one of her romance books that our sister-in-law, Lennie, gave her about some billionaire chick, and I guess the story got stuck in my head."

"How is your sister?" I ask, curious about the youngest Jacobi sibling. Blake has an older brother and a younger sister. His older brother, Hunter, is starting quarterback for the San Francisco Gold, who has a Super Bowl win on his back. The guy is good, and I find it crazy that both brothers ended up going pro in two different sports.

Their little sister, Jainie, doesn't come around very often, but the girl is hella smart. From what Blake tells us, she's finishing up her bachelor's degree in athletic training, and since the girl has two pro athletes for brothers, she will have no trouble getting a job. If I remember correctly, she also has someone on the inside in San Francisco for their major league baseball team. So, the girl has options.

"She's good. Finally left her prick of a shithead boyfriend. Fucking hated that guy," Blake grunts out.

Liam groans at Blake's comment. "I don't think I will ever be mentally prepared for when Emma starts dating. That shit sounds scary."

The two of them continue to talk about keeping guys away from Emma and Jainie, all the while my mind wanders to Eliana and her relationship with Bradford.

Dude is a prick *now*. I can't imagine the type of prick he was back then. From what Eliana was telling me, I can tell that he hurt her badly. There's probably more to the story, and I don't know if Eliana will ever tell me, but even if she doesn't, the next time I'm on the same ice as Bradford, I'm beating his face in.

For checking me last year and for hurting Eliana when they were teenagers.

"Rodriguez!" My name is called out, and right away, I look up to see Coach Anderson standing at the entrance to the locker room, looking straight at me. "My office."

Fuck.

I've been called to Anderson's office only twice in all my years with the Knights. Both times were because I had gotten ejected from a game, and I was going to be suspended. So much shit goes through my mind as to why he may be calling me in.

Am I getting traded? That would suck on so many damn levels.

Is it about Eliana? Does he know we're together?

I have no fucking clue.

"I'll be right there," I answer him, and he gives me a nod before walking away.

This honestly can't be good.

"When was the last time you got called in?" Liam asks when I stand up from my bench.

I nod toward Blake. "The kid's rookie year for my last suspension."

"You don't think there's a chance..." Blake starts but doesn't finish, leaving the unfinished sentence up in the air. I know what he's talking about.

I shrug. "There's one way to find out."

When I reach Coach's office, he's sitting behind his desk looking at some of the paperwork that litters his desk. The man is trying to look busy, but we both know that he's just trying to kill time as he waits for me.

I knock on the door. "You wanted to see me?"

He looks up and gives me a nod. "Yeah, close the door and have a seat."

I do as he says and take a seat in one of the chairs in front of him. I don't say anything, just wait for him to start the conversation.

"You're not getting traded, if that is what you were thinking," he says, taking off his ball cap and placing it on the desk.

"Good to know," I say, giving him a curt nod.

So, if I'm not getting traded, and this sure as hell isn't about my conduct on the ice since we haven't even had our first exhibition game, it must be about his daughter.

He found out about us somehow, because he sure as hell didn't hear it from me, and I know Eliana hasn't told him. I don't even know if she's talked to him at all outside of the arena.

"How was your time off?" he asks, sounding a bit awkward even asking.

"It was fine," I say, not giving him any details.

"You have a house in California, right? Close to the Bay Area?" he asks, his eyebrows raising in question.

I give him a nod. "Yeah, off the Santa Cruz coast."

He nods, looking down at the paperwork on his desk. "My daughter was in the area this summer," he states, like we have normal conversations like this on an everyday basis.

"That's nice," I say, trying not to give too much away. Thank fuck I mastered my disdain expression when I was a teenager.

Anderson looks up at me finally and looks me straight in the eye.

He wants me to admit that I'm with Eliana, but that isn't going to happen. He's not getting a single thing from me. For all he knows, I didn't even know he had a daughter.

He looks at me for about twenty seconds before he lets out a sigh and breaks the silence. "I know she is living with you," he admits.

Do I admit that he is right by asking him how he knows that? Or do I keep quiet?

I go with keeping quiet.

Eventually he lets out another sigh and continues on to give me the answer that I'm looking for.

"I called her last week. She had called me a few weeks ago asking if it was okay to stay with me for a few weeks while she found a place to live. I hadn't heard from her, so I called, and she told me that she had found a permanent place with a friend."

Friend.

She told her dad I was her friend. It's cute, and it makes me want to show her how much of a friend I'm not when we are in bed later tonight, even though I know why she told her dad I was her friend.

"She must have had me on speaker because right before we ended the call, I heard a male voice in the background. It took me a bit, but I finally was able to figure out that it was you."

He called her last week? She didn't tell me that. I did notice that she was a little off, but I just wrote it off as her being nervous about her new job officially starting soon.

"Are you trying to make me admit to living with your daughter so that you can get rid of me? Or are you just telling me that you know I'm living with your daughter for the sake of conversation?" I ask, because if it's the former, I'm going to walk out of here without saying a single thing.

Anderson looks at me with a stern look on his face until he finally nods. "The second one," he admits.

Now it's my turn to give him a nod. "Okay, then," I say, relaxing a bit. "Yes, I'm living with your daughter. Actually, she's living with me. She told me that she hadn't even looked for a place here in the city, and I asked her to come live with me."

"Are you two friends?"

"Am I going to get traded if I say something other than friends?"

Anderson shakes his head. "No. I'm not going to let them trade one of the best left wings in the league. No matter the price."

One of the best left wings, huh? And here I was thinking I was just average.

"Okay, then, we're in a relationship," I admit, watching his expression to see if it changes. When it doesn't, I continue. "We know about the no fraternization rule, so we decided to not even look at each other while we are in or on any Dark Knights property. That will go on for however long either of us wears a Knights logo. Outside of that, I won't hide her. I won't hide my relationship with her."

My head coach sits in his chair as if what I just told him was just mundane talk, and I just didn't admit that I am in a relationship with his daughter.

He lets out a sigh. "Okay, just go to HR and get it squared away. That way you won't have any problems."

That's all he is going to say?

I guess that's what you have to do when you don't have a great relationship with your daughter.

"Already have it planned. Have a meeting with them tomorrow morning."

"Good. That's good," he says, nodding his head as if he were a bobblehead.

The man made such a big-ass deal about calling me in here and all he has to say about this is to make sure we meet up with HR and good? We could have had this conversation in the hallway or something.

"Great. Can I go now?" I say, placing my hands on the armrest about to push myself up when he stops me.

"Did Eliana tell you about our rocky relationship?" he asks. There's something in his eyes that has me slightly confused.

I give him a curt nod. "She did."

"I'm trying to repair it. I don't know if she told you that."

"She said that your relationship is definitely better than it was a few months ago. And even though she didn't tell me this, I know that she hopes that her working with the team will help with that." It's true. Every time she brought up her new position, she mentioned something about being okay with spending more time with her dad. That she wouldn't mind it as much as she would have a few years ago.

"I hope that, too. I also hope that after learning all this new information about me, it won't cloud your judgment of who I am, off the ice and on it."

This is something I thought about. I saw how much pain

Eliana was when she told me about all the shit that her dad put her and her mom through, so a big part of me is inclined to hate the man, just as much as I hate Bradford. But Shawn Anderson is one of the reasons why I wanted to stay with the Knights. He's a legendary player, but he's even more legendary as a coach. He has been with our team through the good and the bad and has never talked down to any of us because of our performance. To a lot of guys, he's like a father figure, even though he wasn't able to give his own daughter that.

I give him an honest answer. "It won't. I may not like the type of father you've been to Eliana since her mom got sick and died. Nobody deserves that, but that doesn't stop me from respecting you and doing what you tell me to do. I'm still one of your players, and I will continue to be for however long I'm on this team."

He nods and gives me a wave of his hand, dismissing me.

I know there's more he wants to say, but I don't push it.

I'm not two feet away from the chair, though, when he stops me again.

"Some words of advice, Christian," he starts, causing me to turn and face him again.

"Sure," I tell him.

"Don't do what I did. Learn from my mistakes. Don't make hockey your top priority. No sport is more important than your wife or your daughter. I made a lot of wrong choices when I became a head coach, and if I could go back, I would. I would fight for my wife when she asked for a divorce. I would have asked for leave when she was diagnosed. I would have been there for my daughter as she lost one of the most important people in her life. I would do it all over again in a heartbeat, but I can't, and look where it's got me. Don't do what I did. Make Eliana your number one priority if you see a future with her. She is worth every inch of life and love that anyone can give her."

There are tears in his eyes as he tells me all of this.

"Have you told Eliana that?" I ask.

He nods. "When I talked to her last week. Now that she's here, I'm going to try and be a better father."

"She would appreciate that."

"I hope so," he says, letting out a sigh. "Don't let her bust your balls too much. Her mother was the same way. I honestly don't know how she put up with me for so long."

"Because she loved you. She didn't give a shit about anything else, she just cared about you," I answer, not knowing where the hell that even came from.

"And does my daughter feel the same about you?" he asks, raising an eyebrow.

"I don't know. Probably not yet, but if she ever does, then I would feel the same way about her." And it's the truth. If I didn't think it would be moving too fast, I would have told Eliana by now.

"Don't hurt her, Rodriguez," he states as I start walking toward the door again.

"Don't have any plans to."

And he better not have any plans to do so either.

CHAPTER NINETEEN

"STOP WORRYING," Christian says, from where he stands in front of the mirror in the bathroom. He's currently making sure that his tie is tied absolutely perfectly, all the while I'm in our walk-in closet, trying to figure out what to wear today.

"It's my first away game!" I yell as I pull a dress from its hanger and drop it on the floor after deeming it unworthy.

"It's an exhibition game," Christian says, coming to stand at the closet door, leaning against the door jam, looking all hot and sexy in his well-fitted suit. I absolutely love the hockey dress code even if I don't like anything else.

"So? It's still my first time traveling with the team. I have to be presentable," I say, grabbing a pair of gray-colored pants and trying to decide if they will work. I can pair them with a white top and a jacket that I can put on the ground to be able to take pictures as all the players arrive on the plane.

Perfect.

Like the players, I also have to abide by the business

professional dress code when getting on the team plane. This is my first time traveling in this capacity, so I'm slightly freaking out.

"Wear what you wore last game," Christian throws out, which gets him daggers shooting out of my eyes.

"I can't wear what I wore last game." He doesn't get it.

"Why not? The black pants fit your ass so perfectly," he says, coming into the closet, closing the distance between us, and pressing his body against mine.

"You're supposed to be concentrating on getting ready for the season, not how good my ass looks," I say, pushing him away. I don't have time to get distracted by his body. I have an outfit to choose and have to head to the airport so that I can arrive before the players do.

"I can concentrate on both," he says, giving my ass a slap as I walk away from him.

I ignore him and quickly change before going over to my carry-on and double checking that I have everything that I need. I don't want to be missing anything.

"Babe, it's just a one away game in Detroit. We will be back tonight, you don't have to worry what you pack or what you wear. All you need to worry about is taking pictures," he says, coming up behind me and wrapping his arms around my body and dropping his face to my neck and giving me kisses on the exposed skin.

"Says you. For all I know, my pictures can suck tonight, and then tomorrow morning I will wake up with an email from the Knights telling me that I'm fired."

Christian hums. "Is there a reason why you are freaking

out about this game, but you didn't even say a peep about the one two days ago?"

I think about it. There's no real reason.

I shrug against him. "I think because there's a lot more at stake with traveling. I can forget my laptop charger, my camera charger, a lens, anything that could prevent me from doing my job. With the first exhibition game, I knew that if I had forgotten something, or needed a new battery, then I could just run up to go get it. Here it is different, plus I won't have the whole social media team with me, so I have to capture double the pictures."

"You'll be fine. You won't forget anything, and you will capture all the pictures you need, and when we get home tonight, I will show you just how well you did today," he says, letting his hand travel to the front of my pants and sliding under the waistband until he is cupping my pussy.

"Oh yeah, and how will you show me?" I ask, trying not to melt into him.

"With my cock, of course," he says as he slides his hand under my panties and starts drawing lazy circles against my clit.

"Of course," I say, a little breathless. I want to get lost in him, I do, but I can't be late. "So, save whatever your hand is doing for then," I say, stepping out of his embrace, and pulling his hand out of my panties.

"You're no fun," he whines, grabbing me by the hand and pulling me back and placing a kiss against my lips.

"You won't be saying that tonight," I say kissing him back, but then my alarm goes off, and I pull away. "Okay, I have to go," I say, grabbing my carry-on and my camera bag. "Do not be late to the tarmac!"

I run out of the condo without a second look and headed down to the car I had scheduled to arrive at the same time that my alarm went off. Perfect timing.

The car makes it to the tarmac in record time, and I'm able to get all my stuff on the plane and get myself situated down by the stairs to wait for the players to arrive all arrive within ten minutes.

For a good five minutes, I'm able to catch a breath and calm myself down as much as I possibly can. If we were at the beach house right now, I would be going down to the water and dipping my toes in.

Unfortunately, we won't be heading there until November, so I will just have to think about it until then.

Ten minutes after I get situated on the ground with my camera in hand, the players and coaching staff start to arrive.

I haven't spent a whole lot of time with these men yet, but some do wave and smile when they see me point the camera at them, which I greatly appreciate. It makes the job a whole lot easier.

One by one, they all start to arrive, and my little finger is clicking away trying to capture the most perfect candid pictures.

Blake, who I learned is one of Christian's friends, arrives with another player, Logan, and they both give me smiles and greet me by name as they walk up the stairs to the plane.

Liam and Christian are some of the last ones to arrive, both of them sending smiles my way, and my boyfriend sending me a wink that I'm able to capture. The wink was supposed to be for me, but I can see if the social media team can use it as a birthday post for him or something.

The last to arrive is my dad. I learned from Christian that my dad arrives last because he wants all the players to arrive before him. That way nobody is late.

He sees me on the ground, and he also sends me a wave and a smile before going up.

Things have shifted between me and my dad since preseason started. It partly has to do with us working together, but it also has to do with the fact that he knows about me and Christian.

After we got home from picture day, Christian told me that my dad called him into his office to tell him that he knew that I was living with him. For a second, I got scared that my dad was going to either trade Christian or get me fired. But thankfully, neither happened.

I was also told everything that my dad said during this little meeting, and the second that I heard what he said, I felt happy. He was trying, and that's all I needed.

When everyone from the team is on the plane, I head up, too, so that we can take off.

As soon as I step onto the plane, I see a sea of players, and as much as I want to find Christian and sit next to him, I take a seat with the social media team, so that we can get pictures edited and schedule social media posts while we fly over to Detroit.

I'm so enthralled by my work, that I don't notice that my dad has approached my seat until he's right next to me.

I slide my headphones off and look up at him. "What's up?"

He has a weird look on his face that I can't pinpoint. Does he look nervous? What is there to be nervous about?

"Walk with me to the back of the plane, yeah?" he says, nodding his head to his right and walking away before I can even say yes.

Instantly I start to worry, but I push it down as I get up from my seat and follow my dad. On the way back, I catch Christian's gaze from where he sits next to Liam, and he raises his eyebrow at me after seeing my dad walking in front of me.

I just give him a shrug and continue walking until I'm with my dad at the back of the plane.

"What's going on?" I ask my dad as soon as we are alone and away from prying ears. "Am I getting fired?" I ask, not being able to hold in the question any longer.

"Why would you get fired?" he asks, his face going from worried to confused.

"I don't know, why else would you bring me to the back of the plane?" I say, looking up at the man.

"You're not getting fired. You've been on the job not even two weeks, and everyone is loving you. That's not why I brought you back here."

"Are you going to tell me that HR changed their minds on my relationship, and we have to end it?" I knew it was a possibility that they would backtrack. They don't want a lawsuit on their hands.

"No, that's not it either," he tells me, shaking his head at all my crazy ideas.

"Then why are you looking at me like you are about to tell me that someone died? It's freaking me out, Dad. What is going on?"

My dad looks down at me for a minute before he lets out a long sigh. "The social media team is going to be asked to make a post about a new acquisition. One player for the sixth-round pick at next year's draft.

"Okay, why are you telling me this? Tell the social media team." I'm sure they can get a post done before we even land.

"I'm telling you because of who the player is," he answers, his eyebrows furrow.

"Why would I care what player the team acquires?" I ask him, not understanding why this is all so important.

"Because you know this player."

That's when it all clicks.

The new player acquisition is from Vancouver, and if my dad is telling me before it goes public, it's because he was trying to prepare me.

It's Kalen. I know deep in my bones that it's him.

I want to ask if he's joking, but by the look on my dad's face, I know he is telling the truth.

Kalen Bradford is officially a Dark Knight.

"H-how?" I stammer out, my mind going fifty miles a second. All I can think of is that he released the pictures. I didn't go to my dad, and now my body is on the internet for the whole world to see, and somehow Kalen is a Knight.

"His agent knows how to play dirty. Apparently, Kalen

has something incriminating against someone on the team, and in exchange for not releasing whatever it is that he has, he asked to be traded to the Knights. The owner and GM talked about it for a few days and finally agreed to his terms and contacted the Canucks yesterday morning, and the deal went through ten minutes ago."

He got what he wanted.

He used what he had against me and got what he wanted. Now the Knights, and my dad, are now paying for my mistakes from when I was eighteen, with a player who will possibly destroy the team connection they currently have.

This can't be happening.

"I don't want him on my team any more than you do, but I don't have a say. Are you going to be okay with it?"

Never. I will never be okay with it. Yet, I find myself nodding yes to my dad.

"Okay, then start getting ready. Because he arrives at the arena tomorrow morning."

I hear my dad's words, and all I'm able to do is nod and hope that this is the end of Kalen blackmailing me with those pictures.

He's already a Knight, what more can he possibly want?

I'm too scared to ask.

CHAPTER TWENTY

CHRISTIAN

SOMETHING IS UP WITH ELIANA. She's been off since we got off the plane in Detroit last night, and it continued well after we got home at three in the morning.

I noticed it when we got on the bus to head to the Detroit arena, but I didn't question it. I just thought that she was just keeping everything professional.

But when we got back to Chicago, I started to question her quietness, especially when she got into my car, even though there were still team employees around us.

When we got to the house, she said she was tired and went straight into the shower and was in there for a good twenty minutes. By the time that I went to the bedroom, she was lying on her side of the bed, pretending to be asleep.

So, I got into bed and just laid there, listening as her breathing evened out, and she truly fell asleep.

When I got up at five to get a workout in before the

morning skate, I debated waking her up but decided against it and let her sleep in.

Now morning skate is here, and I see her walking around the rink taking pictures, and I want to stop what I'm doing and go to her, but I can't. And because all I want to do is go to my girlfriend, my skating has been absolute shit.

"You're extra grumpy today," Blake says to me as he skates by, stealing the puck that was just resting against my stick.

I don't even argue with him because he's right. I am extra grumpy today, and it's all because I have no idea what is happening with Eliana.

I'm not the only one who is acting as if they don't want to be here, Coach Anderson is acting the same way. So, something has to be going with the both of them for them to be acting this way. I need fucking answers, and I need them soon.

Thankfully, Coach calls it about twenty minutes later and the second I step off the ice, I'm both relieved and frustrated. Relieved because I get to go home and possibly corner Eliana in hopes that she would tell me what the hell is going on and frustrated, because even though the season hasn't officially started, I still was shit on the ice.

We all head to the locker room in our practice facility, and the second that we are all in and situated in our designated areas, the doors close, and Anderson stands in the middle of the room getting ready to say something.

I swear, if he gives us a speech about how we aren't performing like we were a few months ago during the playoffs, I'm going to strangle him. It's preseason training camp, this is where we are supposed to weed out all the bad vibes.

"We are doing good out there. There are a few tweaks that we can make before the season opener, but that's all. Every single one of you is on top of your game, and if everything goes well and how we want it, we can get the repeat," Anderson says to the room, and everyone nods at his statement.

Anderson takes a pause as he looks around the room, as if he is looking for something. He must not find it because eventually he lets out a sigh and continues talking.

"This offseason wasn't very eventful for the Knights. We didn't lose players and we gained a few, but we also had an injury during our first exhibition game of the season. Stalinski is out on LTIR until cleared by the team doc."

Damn. Long term injured reserve is not what a player wants to hear, especially if you are just coming off a winning season.

"Because we are down a player, the front of the house has decided to trade for a new defenseman. Today, I would like to welcome Kalen Bradford to the Chicago Dark Knights."

As soon as I hear the name, everything clicks.

No fucking way.

Everyone in the room looks over to the door, and it's like that shit in the movies. As soon as Anderson says Bradford's name, the locker room doors open, and the asshole appears as if he is royalty or some shit.

The second I see the fucker's smirk, I'm fucking pissed

and feel like wringing his neck. This fucker doesn't belong here.

Anderson goes into the spiel about our new addition, not sounding so happy about this trade himself.

The little ceremony to welcome Kalen to the Knights lasted a whole five minutes. The asshole even goes around the room to introduce himself to all of his new teammates, a smile always on his face.

He comes over to my side, shaking Logan's hand and then coming over to me with a hand extended. I ignore it.

"Hey, man. I'm Kalen. It's nice to meet you," he says as if he doesn't remember that he slammed his fist into my chin last year. Two games. Two fucking games I was suspended because of this asshole.

"I know who you are, and I don't give a shit," I say, turning my back toward him and starting to take off my practice gear.

"What the fuck is your problem? I'm just being friendly," he throws out.

I don't have to turn around to know that the guy is probably pissed at my refusal to shake his hand. He probably isn't used to people not kissing his ass every time he walks into the room. He isn't hot shit enough to warrant that attention. Dude is second tier at best.

"I don't have a problem. You just don't belong here," I say to him without turning around. The bastard isn't worth my time, like Eliana wasn't his.

"Your front office seems to think so," he says, and I turn in time to see a sneer on his face.

"Yeah, well, front offices can make mistakes." There is so much shit that I can tell him, but I don't. Instead I just get my practice gear off and head to the shower.

The second that I'm dressed and ready to head home, I walk out of the locker room but instead of heading to the parking lot, I head to Anderson's office for some answers.

Unlike the last time I was in his office, I don't knock. Instead, I just storm in and shut the door behind me and have a stare down with the man in front of me.

He lets out a sigh and breaks the silence enveloping his office. "I'm not happy about it either," he finally says, bowing his head in the process.

"Not only did he fucking cheat on your daughter, but he also slammed his fist into my face and got me suspended for two games. How the fuck is he even here?" I ask, trying to figure all of this out, but I can't. I feel like I'm missing part of the bigger picture.

"Don't you think I know that? Bradford has been trying to get on this team since before he got drafted, but I've somehow convinced the front office that it wasn't a great idea. This time around, my hands were tied. The team had no other choice than to acquire him."

"There's always a fucking choice. It's not like Bradford is holding something over the team's head," I meant the last part to be a joke, but the way Anderson tenses up I figure out that Bradford is indeed holding something over the team's head.

"Just deal with it, Rodriguez. There is nothing that we can do. The contract is signed, and Bradford is with the Knights for at least two years."

Fucking hell.

"He is holding something over the team's head, isn't he? The Knights are calculating with every single fucking thing they do, including who they bring on as a player. There is nothing calculating about all of this." I'm getting angrier and angrier by the second.

Anderson looks up at me from where he is sitting behind his desk and is debating with himself if he should tell me what he knows or not. I can see it in the eyes that he passed on to his daughter.

He bows his head and starts nodding. "According to Bradford and his agent, he has some incriminating files pertaining to someone on the team. He had his agent reach out and tell the Knights that their options were to either sign him, or he will release this incriminating information that nobody knows anything about."

"Why the fuck would the team do something like that? I seriously thought that our front office had more balls than that."

"Why do you think?" Anderson stands up from his chair and stabs one of his fingers against the wood. "The kid only has one connection to this team, and that connection is me through my daughter."

He's not suggesting what I think he is, is he?

"Are you saying that whatever incriminating files Bradford has involves Eliana?" If I wasn't pissed off earlier, I sure as hell am now.

"It might be. When I told Eliana last night that we signed Bradford, she looked fucking terrified. Like one of her worst nightmares had come true." Coach says, answering my question as to why Eliana was acting weird last night.

I try to think of what Bradford may have on her, but I keep coming up blank.

While I'm thinking, Coach continues. "The kid has been wanting to become a part of this organization since I signed to be head coach. When they were dating, he kept telling her to butter me up about him. To have me go to his games, so I could see for myself what a good player he was. He had an in with her, and he wanted to use everything he could get. At the beginning, I did what my kid asked me to do. I looked at her boyfriend, went to a few games, but he wasn't NHL material. At most, he would possibly be able to make it work in the AHL. He didn't like that, so what did he do? He broke her heart, and even then, he still asked her to put in a good word for him with me.

"How the fuck he was able to get drafted is beyond me, but he did, and since he stepped into the league, he's wanted to be a Knight. So, what a coincidence that the season that Eliana gets hired by the team, Kalen magically has something that can hurt someone and his only request to not release it, is to get signed?"

Anderson is right.

As much as I don't want him to be, Anderson is right. Bradford has to have something on Eliana and is using whatever it is to get what he wants. The asshole probably went to her first and told her to put in a good word for him with the team, or he would release whatever information he has on her.

"He had to have gone to her. Told her to talk to the team on his behalf and help him get traded here. Knowing Eliana, though, she probably told him to fuck off, and so he went straight to the team himself. And because no team wants bad press, they agreed," I muse, feeling like we are in some type of spy movie, and we are trying to figure out what the bad guy is up to.

"Has Eliana mentioned anything to you?" Coach asks, starting to pace the length of his office.

I try to think.

The only thing that I can come up with is the night that she walked in on Adrian and the strange woman. She told me about her relationship with Kalen that night, but I had felt like there was still more to it. You don't just hate someone that deeply because they cheated, they had to have done more.

There is no doubt in my mind that Kalen has done more to her than both her dad and I know about.

"Not directly, but when she told me about their breakup, I definitely felt like there was more to the story, but I didn't press her on it," I tell him, feeling anger toward myself for not doing so.

Coach stops pacing and comes over to me and places a hand on my shoulder. The man looks fucking pissed, and he has every single right to be. Someone is using his daughter. Or at the very least is trying to.

I feel the same way. Someone is trying to use my girl, and my blood is fucking boiling. She doesn't need that shit in her life, and she sure as hell doesn't need it from someone like Bradford.

"Maybe you *should* press her on it. It might be the only way we will find out what the fuck Bradford has. And the sooner we do, the sooner I get him off my fucking team."

"I'm not going to make any promises about getting that fucker off this team, but I will try with Eliana."

"That's all I ask."

CHAPTER TWENTY-ONE

ELIANA

I SHOULD HAVE TAKEN a mental health day.

Ever since my dad told me about the Knights signing Kalen, it feels like my mind and body have been working overtime.

Last night at the Detroit game, I could barely concentrate on work, but I was able to power through and get the best pictures I could in the state that I was in. But then we landed back in Chicago, and it felt like my concentration had depleted completely, and the only thing that I wanted to do was beat myself up for letting an ex, who I haven't even seen in ten years, control my life so damn much.

And that's what I did.

I did it in the car as Christian drove us to his condo. I did it in the way-too-long shower that I took when we got home, and I did it again when I pretended to be asleep so that Christian wouldn't ask me any questions the second that he got into bed. I hated doing the last part, but I knew he was going to ask questions. I knew that he was going to want to know more, but I wasn't ready to give him that. I should, though.

Christian and I may have only been together for a short period of time, but he deserves to know every single thing about me, including this. He deserves to know about those pictures and the weight that they still place on me, even if I don't even remember what the hell I was wearing in them or if I had my hair up or down.

I thought about doing it last night when he got into bed, but I couldn't make myself say the words. I got scared. For a split second I thought that if I told Christian about these pictures, he would judge me for it.

He hasn't judged me yet in all the time we have known each other, at least not like this. He has teased me, but I was scared that this was the time he would judge. So, I didn't tell him a single thing.

And now I regret it.

I needed someone to talk to, and he was the perfect person. Yet I'm keeping everything inside and just trying to make it through the workday without having a breakdown.

I was able to make it through the morning skate and take a few pictures from different parts of the rink, but ninety percent of the time, my mind kept finding number ninety-three on the ice.

From where I was standing, he looked angry, and I could say with confidence that he was angry because of me and because I haven't told him anything.

I just need to get through today, and I will tell him everything. From the pictures to the blackmail to the call I received all those weeks ago as I was leaving the Quakes' arena—absolutely everything. I want things to go back to normal, and that is the only way to do it.

After the morning skate finished up, I head to the media space we have on the lower level to get ready for a photoshoot with the newest Knight. I tried to see if I could pawn off this shoot to someone else on my team, but unfortunately no one was available, so now I'm in charge of Kalen's welcome-to-Chicago photoshoot, and I'm going to hate every single second of it.

But it is still my job, so I have to actually go through with the shoot without thinking of ways to make it as torturous as possible.

It's going to be hard, but it's very much possible.

After walking into the media room, the team has here in their practice facility and making sure that it was clean enough, I spend the next twenty minutes prepping the room and having the equipment assistance bring in Kalen's jersey.

Eventually, everything is all set to go. All I need is for Kalen to show up so that we can get the show on the road.

It takes another half hour after everything is done for Kalen to finally walk into the room.

The second I see him for the first time in ten years, I have the strongest urge to strangle him and make sure that nobody is able to find the body.

He still looks the same as he did when we were eighteen. The only difference is that his dirty blond hair is longer, and he has more muscle on his body.

But he still very much looks like the self-centered, didn't-care-who-he-hurt, cheating bastard that he was all those years ago.

"Hi, Lia," Kalen says to me as soon as he steps into the room as if we are old friends about to catch up. The fact that he still calls me Lia just irks me and makes me grind my teeth.

"Kalen," I say, my tone sounding very much annoyed.

"Long time no see. You look good," he says, letting his eyes travel up and down my body as if I were a prize for him to win.

I'm not. I never was, and I will never be.

"I wish I could say the same about you," I say before moving the conversation to the topic at hand. "Go ahead and get your jersey on. This is a quick process, and it will not take more than ten minutes."

"Do you mind if I just change here?" he asks, already making the move to lift his shirt off, but I stop him before he gets any further.

I try to resist the urge to roll my eyes. "Yes, I do mind. There's a changing room down the hall. Use that."

"But you've already seen everything before. Where is the harm in that?"

Is he serious right now?

"For one, this is a professional setting. You are more than welcome to get undressed here, but know that if you do, I will be calling HR. You wouldn't want to be released from your brand-new contract and lose everything now, would you?"

I can tell by Kalen's expression that he knows I'm not bluffing. He wants to test my limits; well, I'll test his.

With a grunt, Kalen grabs his jersey from where it hangs on the small clothes rack and walks out of the room.

I take the time alone to collect myself. It's been ten whole years since I was last in a room with the man, and the anger and hatred that I felt all those years ago is still there. The only difference between then and now is that the anger and hatred are twofold and a lot more prominent. So prominent that just hearing him breath is pissing me off. Knowing that he is even in the same building as me, working for the same team, pisses me off beyond belief that I'm seeing red everywhere I turn.

Instead of enduring Kalen on my own, I call in the social media team into the photoshoot. That way they don't have to wait for the photos. They can transfer them as we go and not wait for me to send anything over. Not only is having them there faster, but it also helps keep my anger at bay and Kalen quiet.

For the whole photoshoot, he doesn't say a word. I don't know if it's because he doesn't want me to follow through and call HR if he steps out of line. or he's quiet because there are other people around, and he doesn't want them to hear anything that he might say to me.

My guess is that it's the second one, but I don't give a shit. I'm not going to put myself in a position where I will be uncomfortable. Especially while doing something that I love.

"Alright, I got everything. If we are in need of anything else, someone from my team will set something up after the morning skate," I announce, wanting Kalen out of my space as fast as possible.

"You won't be doing it?" the fucker asks, and as soon as I turn to look at him to tell him no, I will not take any pictures of his willingly, the asshole decides it's the perfect time to pull his jersey off, leaving him shirtless and in a pair sweatpants that I'm sure has some of the other girls here with me blushing.

What the fuck is he trying to play here?

I don't bother asking him. I just roll my eyes at him.

"I'm pretty confident that I told you that there is a dressing room for you. This is very much a professional setting, and if you can't respect that I will have to go to the higher-ups. This is your one and only warning. You disrespect me or someone on my team again, I will make sure that the front office hears about it."

I'm being a hard ass, but I don't care. After everything he has put me through, he doesn't deserve my kindness or even my respect.

Kalen stares me down as if I will become a puddle just by having his blue eyes on me. Maybe when I was eighteen, but no way in hell is it happening now.

When he sees that I'm not backing down from my stance, he gives me a smirk and raises his hands up in mock defeat.

"Okay," he says right before he closes the distance between us and leans down until his mouth is close to my ear. I try to push him away, but he doesn't budge. "You better be nice to me, Lia. You don't want those pictures getting out, do you?"

His question causes a shiver to run down my body.

I guess I have my answer to the question I asked myself last night. This is what Kalen is going to do. If things don't go his way, he's going to pull out the picture card and go about his day.

"You wouldn't fucking dare," I say through my teeth, keeping my voice low so that the other girls that are packing up the space don't hear.

"Maybe I would. That way people would get the chance to see the body you had before. You know, the body that gave its virginity to me. The nice little body that men drooled over and was nothing like the one you currently have."

Tears start to prick at the back of my eyes, and a lump starts to form in my throat.

The Kalen I first met when I was seventeen was sweet and kind. That person is so far away from the one who is standing in front of me. The one in front of me is vicious with his words and his actions.

I thought the worst he would do was release the pictures. That a few people will see them and then forget about them within minutes. I never thought about what people might say, especially if they start comparing the me of ten years ago to me now.

The way I look and the body that I have is something that I have always been proud of. I embrace every single curve, lump, and bump that my body has to offer. I have never been self-conscious about it. Never wanting to hide it. Never in the last ten years have I seen a picture of myself as a teenager and wished that I was that weight again. I've never seen anything wrong with having a bigger butt, more meat on my thighs, or even a bigger stomach. And I absolutely love the fact that there is a man like Christian who appreciates every single inch of me. He treats my body as a temple and doesn't make me question a single thing about myself. I have always been confident and strong in who I am.

But right now, the confidence and strength are waning. And I hate it so much. All it took was Kalen saying a few little words, and I'm doubting my beauty.

Somehow, I'm able to find my voice, even if all I want to do is just crawl into a hole to escape Kalen and his threats.

"Do it," I say, the prickling behind my eyes intensifying. "See what happens."

I'm saying these words trying to show that I'm stronger than he thinks I am, but I'm breaking on the inside.

Kalen lets out a laugh. "Maybe I will. I got traded to the Knights. I wonder what else I can get?"

He gives me a sadistic smirk before turning his back to me and leaving the room.

The second I no longer see him I feel like I'm able to breathe again.

Last week I was excited about what this season was going to bring to me, but right now I'm dreading it, and it's all Kalen's fault.

Feeling the need to get out of here, so I don't have to see him again today, I dismiss the girls who are still in the room, telling them to head back to the office and I pack up my things.

I'm not prone to panic attacks, but I feel like I'm about to have one. I frantically throw everything in my bag and close up the room before I start running toward the first exit I can find.

As I run, I try to tell myself that Kalen is just talking out of his ass. That he is just trying to rile me up and will never do anything. But he got traded, he's here, and he did that by using the photos in an indirect way. What is my life going to look like if he does it directly?

I don't want to think about it or even know.

I run through the tunnels of the arena until I'm in the players area. I thought I was running to an arena exit, but for some reason my brain brought me here for some unknown reason.

You know why.

I was telling my body to run as far away from this place as possible, but my brain was saying to run toward the one person who would make everything better. The person who would hold me but also go after Kalen and make him pay for what he is doing.

The one person who has made me feel safe and loved in a way that nobody else has since my mom died.

I look for him in the open locker room, in the kitchen, and gym, but he's not in any of those.

Did he go home?

Maybe he did, and I should head that way, too, but I don't. I just keep frantically looking for him.

The ice.

He could still be here and on the ice. He mentioned a few

days ago how he likes staying after morning workouts are over and enjoying the ice all by himself a little bit before coming back the next morning and working.

So I run in that direction.

Thankfully, the arena is almost empty, except for a few lone equipment assistants, so I'm not bumping into anyone.

By the time I reach the door to the ice, I'm out of breath, but I don't care. I power through as I push open the doors and step into the rink.

I let out a sigh of relief when I see a figure at the other end of the rink, shooting pucks into a net.

Just as he was doing all those weeks ago back in California. And just like it did back then, my heart soars. Who knew that this man would turn into my everything in such a short amount of time.

"Christian!" I yell out, hoping that he doesn't have earbuds in.

Right away, he turns and finds me standing at the edge of the ice. I don't know if he can tell, but I'm shaking. I also feel like I can't catch my breath. I was right about feeling a panic attack coming on.

Christian abandons his stick on the ice and skates over to me right away.

"What's wrong?" he asks as he gets closer to me, frantically looking me over. The second that he sees the tears in my eyes, his face and whole body turning into stone.

I don't even have to tell him who might be the cause of my crying. He already knows.

"What the fuck did he do?"

I push down the lump in my throat and tell him what I should have told him last night. "He's blackmailing me with nude pictures I sent to him when I was eighteen."

IF I DIDN'T HAVE an exhibition game tomorrow or the season opener two weeks from now, I would be taking Eliana to California, to the beach house, to the place that calms her, right now.

But of course, timing isn't on our side right now.

We got home about an hour ago.

After she told me what Bradford had against her, she told me everything else that has come along with it.

With tears in her eyes, she told me about the threats that came her way right before Bradford was drafted. About how when she got the job with the Knights, he reached out to her, and then he reached out to her again a few weeks ago and threatened to use the photos again if she didn't do what he said.

Apparently, this was all the night that she walked in on Adrian. Not only was she a mess because she thought I was cheating on her, but she also had Kalen contacting her and trying to use her position and his blackmail to his benefit.

Thankfully, she told him to fuck off, just like I figured she did.

She apologized for not telling me. She also blamed herself for everything that Kalen had done including how he facilitated his trade. She said the team is now paying for her mistakes.

That pissed me off. Whatever Kalen is doing now is not her fault. She decided to do something for her boyfriend when she was eighteen. Nobody could have known that he would go this far with it. This falls on Kalen and Kalen only.

As she was telling me, all I wanted to do was go find the motherfucker and beat the shit out of him.

But my girl needed me more, so after her tear-filled confession, I brought her home. We had lunch, and I was planning on distracting her for the rest of the day, but she ended up falling asleep about fifteen minutes ago.

Me on the other hand, I'm wired. I have way too much information that I shouldn't be keeping to myself. There are other people that need to know.

Is it going to be enough to get Kalen traded a day into his contract with the Knights? I highly doubt it. The fucker probably put in a no-trade clause and no other team would be able to touch him for a while. But at the very least, key individuals in all of this would know, and we can protect her a little better.

As soon as Eliana was asleep, I texted Liam, Blake, and

Logan to meet me at the arena. I also texted Anderson, and they all agreed to meet me there.

I don't want to leave Eliana when she needs me, but this shit is too much for her to handle on her own.

If she gets mad at me for getting involved, then so be it. I can handle her being pissed off. What I can't handle is her being hurt or some asshole wiggling nude photos of her over her head all of her life.

I don't wake her when I leave to head to the arena. I didn't see the need.

The whole way there, Eliana is not far from my mind. When we first met, it bothered me that she would lump me in with the hockey players who had wronged her. But now that I know the huge asshole her ex-boyfriend is and how her dad basically abandoned her during some of her moments of need, I understand.

I would hate hockey players and hockey in general, too. Especially if it has only hurt me or didn't give me a whole lot of good memories.

Pulling into the player parking lot, I spot Liam, Logan, and Blake standing by the entrance. I pull into an empty spot, and I walk over to meet them.

All three of them give me confused looks as I approach them. When I texted them, I didn't tell them what was going on, I just told them to meet me here.

Not a single one of them has to be here for this, but they are my family away from home. And since this involves one of our teammates, they should know.

"Thanks for meeting me here," I say to each of them.

"Sounded urgent," Liam voices, and our other two team-mates nod in agreement.

"Kind of is," I say, opening the door to the arena and waving them inside.

They follow behind me, and the four of us head down to the locker room area. When I texted Anderson, I thought that he was still at the practice facility, but he said to meet him here.

I direct my teammates down the hall to the team's meeting room.

When we walk in, I see that Anderson is already there with some young guy who looks oddly familiar.

"You have to be fucking kidding me," Logan grumbles behind me which takes me by surprise.

Logan doesn't say much. Hell, the guy is grumpier than I am. So, him giving any type of reaction is a big deal.

Who the hell is this guy?

I look over at Liam and Blake, and they just give me a shrug. They don't know either.

"Gentlemen, meet the new team owner," Anderson says, probably seeing the confusion in our faces. "Grayson Lane."

We all introduce ourselves to our new team owner, all but Logan. If I cared, I would question him for acting like a super asshole, but what Logan does or doesn't do, isn't my issue.

"I thought the Lane family wasn't going to buy the team?" Liam asks.

"They didn't. I bought it of my own accord. Well, I

bought it back. Nightwing International, the company that bought the team, is my own."

"How old are you?" I find myself asking because no way is this guy even old enough to drink, let alone to buy a hockey team.

"Twenty-six," he answers.

Damn. I don't think I know of an owner who is younger than forty.

"I got to ask, does your family have a thing for *Batman* or something? Because Nightwing, the Dark Knights, all Batman related," Blake muses.

I've never been much into comics. Sure, I watch the movies, but would have never guessed those names were associated with a guy who dresses up as a bat.

"You can say that," Grayson answers.

Great. I would rather be talking about how to keep Bradford away from Eliana, not learning why the Knights have the name that they have.

"Is there a reason you're here besides the impromptu introduction?" I ask, wanting to get the point of all of this.

Grayson looks over at Anderson before he looks at me. "Shawn tells me that you may know what Kalen Bradford has, that is supposedly incriminating to an individual on the team?"

I give him a nod. "I do. I just didn't think that it would require ownership to be involved."

Grayson gives me a curt nod. "Normally they wouldn't, but given the circumstances, I'm the one that approved Bradford's trade. Our GM was against it, but I was the one who pulled the trigger. Whatever he does while wearing the Knights' logo, it's on me."

"Wait, incriminating? Given the circumstances? What the fuck are you all talking about?" Liam asks.

I forgot that I didn't tell my teammates how Kalen Bradford came to be a Dark Knight. It has only been a few hours since I found out, and everything has just gotten crazier since then, so I forgot that nobody else knew.

I turn to look at my teammates. "Bradford was traded to the Knights by using blackmail." "You can do that?" Blake asks, his eyebrows shooting up.

I shrug. "Apparently."

"Bradford's agent approached the team at the beginning of the week. At first, because it wasn't coming straight from the Vancouver front office, we weren't entertaining it," Grayson starts letting the rest of the guys in on what's going on, filling in the pieces of information that I was missing. "Eventually, his agent came to us and essentially gave us an ultimatum. Trade for Bradford, giving Vancouver a draft pick, or he releases something that could possibly hurt someone who works or plays for the Knights."

Hearing it all out loud, this all sounds like something you see in movies, not in real life. Not in the true reality of the NHL.

It's all so freaking wild honestly.

"Who does he have information on?" Liam asks, sounding as bewildered about all of this as I feel.

Both Shawn and Grayson look over at me.

"Eliana. She told me about an hour ago."

"Why Eliana?" Logan asks, and with his question as an opening, I tell them everything that Eliana told me concerning Kalen. From how they dated in high school and how he would use her to get her dad to notice him to her taking pictures to how he is currently using them against her. I tell them how he called her a few weeks ago and told her what he would do if she didn't use her position on the team to get him what he wants. And when I tell them about what she said she endured today, every single person in the room is red with anger. Even Grayson, and he doesn't even know her.

"Please tell me there's a fucking way to trade this asshole. He's been here a day, and he's already causing problems," Liam throws out from where he is sitting across the room.

We all look to Grayson for an answer to our captain's plea.

The second that he shakes his head, I know that we are screwed when it comes to Kalen.

"His agent was smart. They added a no-trade clause. He's not going anywhere unless he wants to. If he doesn't get injured, he will be a Knight for a while."

Injured.

Logan and I look at each other at the word. We both know how to fight on the ice. They call us enforcers for a reason. We can probably make something happen during practice or something.

"Don't even think about it," Anderson reprimands us, noticing how Logan and I are looking at each other. "I already have one problematic player on my team. I don't need two more starting shit and getting suspended. We're just coming off a Cup year, let's keep it fucking civil and with no national headlines."

"We didn't even say anything," I argue.

Anderson just shakes his head. "I saw it in your eyes. So, whatever you two idiots were thinking, put it away."

"I'm trying to protect my girlfriend," I throw back, frustrated that there isn't much that I can do, but sit back and continue to watch Kalen as he skates on my ice and torments my woman with threat and blackmail. I'm so damn frustrated that I don't even care if the team owner knows I'm in a relationship with one of his employees.

"And I'm trying to protect my daughter. You going after this asshole, and possibly landing in jail for beating the shit out of him, is just going to hurt her, and she's endured enough of that. From Bradford, from me. No fucking way are you going to do it, too." The fire that Eliana sometimes has in her eyes when she is angry, is the same fire that fills Coach Anderson's eyes right now.

He told me that she was a lot like her mom earlier, but I can see bits of him in her, too.

"Fine," I sigh. "I won't beat the shit out of him. But what do you suggest we do? Like Liam said, he's been here for a day, and he's already fucking shit up."

Now Anderson is the one letting out a sigh. "I don't know. Asking her to quit is out of the question."

That's a stupid idea. "She likes this job too much to do that."

"She doesn't have to quit," Grayson adds, placing his hand on the back of the chair next to Blake. "We can keep her away from Kalen as much as we possibly can. If we need him for a photoshoot, we can have one of Eliana's assistants do it. When we travel, we put as many people between them as we can. When we're here or at the practice facility, we do the same. I'll make some calls too, and get her a new phone and number, give her a little more distance from him. And who knows, maybe he'll decide that he wants to go somewhere else before his two years are up, and he will ask for a trade."

Every single person in the room lets out a huff.

We all know that if Kalen has wanted to be a Knight since he was a teenager, he's not going anywhere.

"We can make his time here miserable," Logan throws out, looking down at something on his phone.

"We can try, but I doubt it will work. If we have a good season, he will stick it out until the very end," Liam adds, shaking his head at Logan's suggestion.

"So, our options are to keep Eliana away from the asshole and nothing else?" I ask, feeling more defeated than I felt when I walked in here.

The whole room goes quiet at my question. They know I'm right. We're not the Rosetti family. We're not the Mafia. We can't make people disappear like magic whenever they piss us off. We're just a hockey team that doesn't have a whole lot of options.

Eliana can file a police report against him, but that won't go anywhere. He hasn't committed an actual crime.

Our only option is to keep her away from him, and that's it.

"I think it is," Anderson says, shaking his head. "I know

you hate it, Christian. I hate it, too. But there isn't much that we can do."

There isn't much that we can do.

I hear the words, but they aren't good enough, even if I know that they are true.

We all sit there a little bit, feeling defeated that we weren't able to fix the problem or at least come up with a decent solution. For me, I'm just pissed off.

I feel like I'm failing Eliana in some way.

After sitting in the quiet room for God knows how long, we finally decide to go home.

When I walk into the house, I find Eliana in the kitchen making dinner. I don't have to ask what she is making. Just by the smell of it I know what it is. Mofongo, tostones and some enchiladas de mole.

She gives me a small smile when she sees me.

"Here I thought that I was going to have to bail you out of jail," she says, sounding like herself and as if she wasn't having a panic attack earlier.

"And why would you think that?" I ask, coming up behind her and wrapping my arms around her body.

"Because I woke up, and I found a note that said something about going to the arena for a meeting. I took a wild guess and figured that the meeting was about Kalen," she says shrugging against me.

There's no point in lying to her. "It was."

Her head bobbles a bit as she concentrates on the pan in front of her. "And what was concluded in this meeting?"

"That as long as Kalen is here, we're not letting him near you." I place a kiss against her neck, her scent calming me.

She nods and doesn't say anything for almost two minutes.

"I can take care of myself, you know," she says as she starts plating the food.

Moving my hands to her hips, and I turn her until she is facing me. As soon as I can, I take her face between my hands and make sure she is looking me in the eyes.

"I know you can. That mouth is like a weapon on its own." She smiles up at me, "But with something like this, you shouldn't take care of it on your own. You have me, let me do what I can to make sure that you are okay. Let me make sure that you are taken care of, and that the stupid motherfucker who you once called boyfriend, knows that he can't hurt you. Not as long as I'm around. Not that you need me."

Her arms make it around my waist, and she gets on her tiptoes to place a kiss against my lips. "I need you. I've needed you for a while now, and I'm going to need you for a while more."

"Good, because I'm not going anywhere. No matter how much you say you might hate me." I lean down and give her another kiss.

"Times like these? The hate is minimal, non-existent."

That's all a man needs to hear.

CHAPTER TWENTY-THREE

ELIANA

"YOU SUCK, Rodriguez. Maybe if you got your head out of your ass, you actually might be able to score one for your team!"

"Keep talking woman, and I swear you're going to end up in the ocean this time. That pretty mouth of yours will freeze right off."

"All I hear is words and no action!"

It's currently November. The season officially started a few weeks ago, and so far, it's looking like it's going to be another good season for the Knights. They have a game against San Jose tomorrow night, and the team traveled to California a day early to get some ice time in. Because we haven't been to the beach house since September, we decided to come here and spend the rest of the day after the team's morning skating session.

The weather isn't all that bad either, especially given that fall is in full swing. The sun is out and there's a bit of wind, but nothing that would have us inside bundled up.

Christian, Liam, Logan, Blake, and Sophia are all playing volleyball, or at least trying to play, while Chloe, Emma, and I are a few feet away watching our men get destroyed. I'm pretty sure Christian's face has met the sand more times than the ball has.

"Jesus," Chloe, Liam's girlfriend says, shaking her head. "And I thought Sophia and Blake were bad. You and Christian are on a whole different level with the insults."

I let out a laugh at Chloe's comment. Usually when we're around other people, Christian and I tend to keep the banter to a minimum. Well, at least we try to. There are definitely times where it slips out, and one of us says something that makes the other roll their eyes, but there is always a smile close by. To some people, it can be a little too much, but for Christian and me it's who we are, and we see it as an extension of our relationship.

I've seen how Sophia is when she's at games cheering on Blake, and the girl is definitely something else, but it doesn't compare to half the shit I say to my boyfriend.

"We've been at each other's throats since the day we met. It seems fitting to let it continue," I answer her with a shrug.

"Liam told me something a few months ago about Christian texting him that you bit his ass?" she asks, raising an eyebrow as if she is asking me if the ass biting is code for something sexual. In this case, it wasn't. Last night, though, was a whole different story.

"That was warranted," I tell her. "He was going to throw

me in the water, I had to do something to stop him and ass biting was the only thing I could think of."

"Yeah, and something she does often," Christian grumbles, leaving the game he was playing with his teammates and coming to sit next to me on the sand.

"Only when you are a caveman, and you are flinging me all over the place."

"I'm not *flinging* you. You take fucking forever to do things, like getting into the house when we have important things to attend to," he eyes me in a way that has me crossing my legs, "and me carrying you over my shoulder is me just speeding up the process."

"I don't take forever to do things," I say, smacking a hand against his arm.

"Sure, you do," he says as he waves at Emma who's in Chloe's arms trying to get loose to play in the sand instead of the blanket we are currently sitting on.

"Name one thing," I order, narrowing my eyes at him.

"Washing dishes. Putting your camera equipment away. Cleaning the closet at the condo."

I said one thing, and this asshole gives me three.

"I do those things." And I do, neither house he owns is a pigsty.

"You do, I'm just saying that it takes you forever to do so."

"She's also always late and flakes a lot," Liam chimes in as he sits next to Chloe and reaches for their daughter. The second the little girl is in her dads arms, she lets out the sweetest laugh that makes us all smile.

"What are you talking about? I'm not a flake. Who even asked you, anyway?" The late part I can't refute. I have to set alarms to make sure I make it to places on time or a few minutes early. I've been doing it since the season started, and so far, it's working out perfectly. Not a single day have I been late.

"You flaked on me the night of the ballet," Liam says, giving me a knowing eyebrow raise. "You're the reason we have Emma."

"Your dick is the reason you have Emma. And I didn't flake. I canceled at the last minute because I had to go to dinner with my dad."

"How about two weeks ago when I told you to meet me at that Italian place, but you went home?" Christian throws out, slinging an arm over my shoulders and bringing me closer to his body.

I pinch his side.

The team had put on an event at a rec center, and I was there getting as many pictures as I could of some of the players who had attended and the kids. Because Christian had an appointment with the team doctor for a hand issue, he didn't go and messaged me that we should have Italian from this one restaurant.

"You never specified that we were meeting there. You just said let's have Italian, so I thought you were going to go get it and head back to the house. It's not my fault you didn't communicate well."

"I know how to communicate just fine, hermosa," he says leaning in and placing a chaste kiss on my lips.

"Whatever. You knew I was a chaotic mess when you met me. Now you have to deal with it."

"I'll deal with it for as long as you let me," he whispers, and I melt into him.

Would it be wrong if we told our friends to leave so that I can have some fun with him in the beach house?

"I missed this place," I say a few hours later as Christian and I sit out on the balcony and listen as the waves crash in the darkness.

"Thanksgiving week is a little crazy, but we can come back here for Christmas and spend it with my parents, if you want. My mom cooks up a feast. Tamales, buñuelos, pozole verde, everything you can think of, she makes. It's the one time during the season, I let myself eat all that I want."

Yeah because the one thing that they don't tell you about hockey players is that all they eat is pasta, so damn much pasta. Breakfast, lunch, dinner, and every single snack in between. Pasta, pasta, pasta. And because of the good girlfriend that I am, I eat it, too, but I don't know how much more pasta I can take.

I honestly don't know how my mom did it if she ever did. I don't remember eating mountains of pasta as a kid.

I lean up and place a kiss right at the edge of his jaw. "I would love to come to Christmas here."

"You and your dad don't do anything?" he asks and I give him a shrug.

"We get together, have dinner, but that's it. We haven't made it into a big thing since my mom died."

A part of me wishes that we would. It would be nice to have one day a year where we act like an actual family.

"You want to invite him for Christmas?"

"Can I? I think your mom's food would remind him of my mom."

The first time that I went over to Christian's parents' house and ate his mom's food, I about cried. Mexican food is definitely different from Puerto Rican, but it still reminded me of my mom's cooking. I couldn't remember the last time it was that I had a meal like that. Graciela, Christian's mom, even offered to look up Puerto Rican recipes so that she could make them for me the next time I was over. I did cry that time.

Christian nods. "Yeah, I think it would be nice."

I smile up at him. "I'll talk to him tomorrow. Thank you."

"Anything to get you to smile at me like that."

Things have been better, a lot better, between my dad and me. We talk almost every day, we grab lunch or even breakfast when neither one of us is busy, and he has apologized a lot more for all the stuff he did these last few years and when I was growing up. He has also been trying a lot harder since the team signed Kalen, and he found out what Kalen has.

On the ex-boyfriend forefront, things have calmed down somewhat. Kalen is still on the team, but he hasn't brought up the pictures, at least to me he hasn't, but it could be that I haven't been anywhere near him since the day of his photoshoot.

According to the new team owner, Grayson Lane, who pulled me into his office a few weeks ago, he and Kalen had a meeting. Grayson told me that he didn't mention that he knew about the pictures to Kalen, but that I put in a complaint, and that it was best that he kept his distance.

No complaint was put in, mostly because a small part of me thinks that Kalen is all talk and will never do anything, but I'm not one hundred percent sure. I'm still waiting for the other shoe to drop if it ever does.

The season still has a ways to go.

I'm not afraid of him, not after the panic attack he induced. If he does something, I know I can take it, and that I will be okay. There is a team of people standing behind me who will make sure of it. Christian will be behind me and that is all I need.

In the five months that we have known each other, Christian has become something to me that I never expected. At the beginning, he was just a hockey player who I wanted to annoy, and in a very short time, he became someone who I want in my life forever. He became someone that I want to spend my life with and possibly grow a family together.

We're alike in a lot of ways and different in others. We argue and butt heads a lot of the time, but that's who we are, and we make it work.

One of the things that helps us is the fact we have the same work schedules. Working for the same team is a blessing in disguise because I have no idea how we would be able to handle him traveling with the Knights and me all over the place jumping from assignment to assignment.

We've kept our relationship hush hush for the most part. Only select people know, and HR has instructed us to not show any form of affection while we are working or representing the team in any capacity. We were also instructed that sneaking around isn't allowed either while in any team facilities. Whether we are traveling or at home. So far, we've been able to follow the rules, well for the most part. There have been a few stolen kisses here and there, flirtatious glances, but nothing major.

The major stuff comes when we're home, and it's one of my favorite parts of my day.

We moved fast, really fast, and we are still moving with no end in sight.

"Hey," I say, poking a finger into his side.

"Hmm?" he says, looking down at me.

"Have I told you that I'm glad that the house I broke into was yours?" I ask, shifting so that I can swing my legs over his thigh and straddle him.

"So, you are admitting that you broke in?" he asks, placing his hands on my hips and dragging me closer to him.

"Only this once. Ask me any other time, and I will say that you left the door open, and I walked in. Which is what happened." I say, wrapping my arms around his neck.

Christian chuckles, and my heart sings hearing it. Before I walked into his house, I thought he was a hard ass, a grumpy, anger-filled man who didn't smile or laugh. Turns out that he does, and it's the best thing in the world. I absolutely love hearing him laugh.

"No, you haven't told me," he finally answers, his hands sliding down until they are on my ass. I'm still in my bikini from earlier, since I felt too lazy to change.

"Well, I am because if I hadn't, then I wouldn't be here right now. I wouldn't have had you by my side when Kalen came to the Knights, and I wouldn't be thinking about spending Christmas with my dad. We would have still met, but it wouldn't have been the same. Accepting the job offer with the Knights was one of the best career choices I've made, and walking into your house that day was the best choice I've made for me. That choice gave me you and a future with someone when I thought I wasn't going to get that until I was at least forty. Now I'm falling in love with the grumpy hockey player who threatened to call the cops on me that day."

I see when the look in Christian's eyes shifts at the word love.

It's something that I've felt for a while, maybe even going back to the day we went to the boardwalk, and it has intensified a lot more since we've been in Chicago. Up to this point, though, I haven't said it.

I've wanted to. I've wanted to tell him those words more often than not.

They've been on the tip of my tongue almost every single day, but I can never find the courage to say them.

Mostly out of fear that Christian won't feel the same way since we've technically only been together for a little over two months, or that he will say them but won't mean them and will walk away a few months later. It has happened before, and it has traumatized me beyond belief.

He has shown me more times than I can count how much he cares about me; in the way he talks to me and the way he takes care of my body when we're having sex. I see it and hear it, but caring for someone isn't the same as falling in love with them.

"You've said that you don't do hockey players, yet here you are falling in love with one," he muses, gliding his thumb along my hip.

"I guess I just needed the right player to come into my life and show me that not everyone involved in the sport is one and the same."

Christian nods, keeping eyes down at where his hands are on my body.

"On the way to the boardwalk, you asked me if I would quit if a loved one had asked me to. The question surprised me. Up to that point, I hadn't thought about it. But when I went to answer, you stopped me." He looks up at me, and there is this fire in his eyes I have only seen on the ice, while there's a stick in his hand.

"I knew what you were going to say," I say, my voice low as I drop my chin slightly.

"You don't," he says, placing a finger under my chin and making me look up at him. "I would do it."

His words take me by surprise, and I have to take a few seconds to run through what he just said to be able to answer.

"Wh-what?"

"I would do it. If you'd ask me, if you ask me right this very second to quit, to give up hockey and the team, I wouldn't hesitate. I would quit."

Tears start to form in my eyes. "Why would you do that? Hockey is your life."

"That's the thing. Hockey isn't my life. It's only a part of it. I can quit right now and be okay. Because you are more important. You are my life. Not some sport. You are the most important thing to me, and later down the line if we have kids, they will be, too. I would quit for you. I would quit for our hypothetical children. I would do it and not regret a single thing. Because I love you more than anything else. You are more important than any stick, game, or even the Stanley Cup. You matter. You matter to me, and I will never put hockey before you because I love you."

Not being able to hold it much longer. I lean down and place my lips against his.

For so long this is what I looked for. I wanted someone to put me first, to love me and to be there when I needed them. Christian is giving me that, and I couldn't be any more grateful for him and everything that has yet to come.

I pull back from him, and he starts wiping away my tears.

"I would never ask you to quit," I say, rubbing at my eyes to make the tears stop.

"I know, but you have that option. If shit gets tough, or I lose myself in the game, forget a kid's birthday or our anniversary; you have the ability to ask, and we will go from there."

"Kids, huh?" I ask, sliding my hands into his hair.

"Yup. I'm willing to negotiate how many."

I smile at him, liking the sound of kids running in and out of the beach house during the offseason and then cheering on their dad while he's on the ice making us proud.

"Let's leave the negotiation for another day. Maybe on our anniversary, we can talk about it."

"And what anniversary is that?" he asks, sliding his hands to my ass again and sliding me forward until there is no space between us. "We have three."

"Three?" I ask, trying to rack my brain for what the three dates could be. I know two, but what is the third one?

"The day you broke in, the day we became official, and the first night you were in my bed." His eyebrows jump up and down, and a smile grows on his face.

"That last one is not an anniversary." I say, rolling my eyes at him.

"I'm counting it as one," he says, digging his fingers into my skin. I love it when he grabs my butt and doesn't hold back.

"Fine, but I'm holding the negotiation until our official anniversary."

"Fine by me." He slams my body into his, which makes me giggle, and he kisses me, but his kiss is slow and sweet, and it stays that way for a few minutes until he pulls away. "I love you, hermosa."

"I love you, too."

We go back to kissing, but this time there is nothing slow and sweet about it. It's hungry and desperate.

Christian pulls away, but only to move his mouth from mine down to my neck and continues to move until I'm on my back, and he's on his knees in front of me, his face inches away from my pussy.

"I've been fantasizing about you in this bikini since the last time you wore it. That away game two weeks ago where you shared a room with someone else? I jerked off at the thought of you in this while I was in the shower. I came so hard. I think it's time to make the fantasy come true. What do you say?" He licks me through the bikini fabric, and I let out a small moan.

"Oh my god, yes," I say, arching my back wanting more.

"Then get ready to scream out my name."

CHAPTER TWENTY-FOUR

CHRISTIAN

THE SEASON IS in full swing and from the looks of things, it's going to be a good season, on that might end with us heading to the playoffs again.

We've had our ups and downs this season like any other team, but the difference between them and us is that we are hungrier than ever to keep the Cup here in Chicago. We will fight through any injury or trade that may hit us and make sure that when the end of the season comes, we will be one of the top teams moving on to the next round.

Tonight, we have a home game against Las Vegas, the number one team in the western conference right now, and everyone is on their fucking toes. Winning tonight is the top priority, and we are ready to do everything we can to make it happen.

And because we need all the help that we can get, superstitions are in full swing.

Mine included. When you have a good thing going, you

do the same thing the next game too and hope you get the same result. If you don't, you change things up.

Like a lot of guys on the team, I have my set of superstitions and quirks I do before every game.

Nothing over the top like wearing the same underwear or socks. But it's still something that I do before every single game.

A few years ago, I noticed that I had a lot of noise moving through my head before every game. Noise that would distract me and stay with me well into the game.

One day for some weird reason, I went into the meeting room and just sat there, trying to calm my mind a bit before everything became chaotic. Someone had left a book, so I picked it up and started reading. For fifteen minutes, I didn't think about hockey. I didn't think about winning or if someone on the other team was going to do something to piss me off, and I was going to spend time in the penalty box again.

I didn't think about anything but the story I was reading.

When the fifteen minutes were up, and I went back to the locker room to get dressed, I thought I was going to feel frustrated because instead of reading for fifteen minutes, I could have gotten game ready, but I didn't. There was no frustration, and for once, since I first started playing, I was able to concentrate on what was going on the ice and not let the noise distract me.

So, I did it again the next game and the game after that until I finished the book, and now years later it is something that I do before each game, stashing a new book in the room every few weeks.

Liam asks me all the time where I disappear to for twenty minutes, but I never tell him. There's nothing wrong with what I do, but I still just keep it to myself. I don't need him or anyone else invading my quiet time. Every one of my teammates is loud as fuck.

Tonight, it feels like the noise is twice as loud as it usually is, and it's all thanks to the intensity of the game happening in less than an hour. Right away, I know that more than anything, I need my quiet time. I need my alone time, and I need to get my head on straight. So that I can get on the ice and help my team get the win tonight.

Forty minutes before we hit the ice, I grab my phone from the top shelf of my locker and head out to the meeting room where I stashed a book a few days ago that I'm excited about starting.

I don't make it even five feet out of the locker room before bumping into someone. And out of all the teammates that I could have run into, it had to be fucking Bradford.

"My bad," I say, doing my best to not instigate anything. The dude has been quiet these last two months, but I'm not risking it. Who knows what the hell would set him off and have him start blackmailing Eliana again.

"You should watch where you're going, Rodriguez," Bradford says, closing the distance between us, getting up close and personal. The dude is an inch or two shorter than me, it wouldn't take much for me to swing my arm back and check him on the chin like he did to me.

"And you should check the fucking attitude before I knock you to the ground. I said my bad, after all."

"I don't have an attitude, but even if I did, you should be used to it, shouldn't you?" The fucker gives me a smirk that I'm seconds away from punching.

"I have no idea what you're talking about," I say, shoving him out of my way, I get about a foot away from him when the asshole starts talking again.

"Of course, you do. You know since you're fucking Anderson's daughter. That chick has an attitude like no other. And that mouth? Fuck, don't even get me started on that." He lets out a whistle like we were buddies and exchanging stories over drinks, and he isn't talking about Eliana.

I'm about two inches away from ripping this guy's neck out, but I keep it contained as much as I possibly can. It's one thing to get in a fight on the ice, but it's another to do it in the locker room.

"If I were you, I would walk the fuck away. Right now," I growl out, getting in his face, hoping he says something else so I can beat the living shit out of him.

"Or what? You going to go to HR to file a complaint? Go for it. I'll still have the memories of her, and I'll be able to think about her whenever I want. I'll still be able to remember how she felt under me. How her lips felt around my cock. You know why she sucks dick so well? Because she learned on me. Next time you slide into her—"

My fist lands against his mouth. Listening to his words

made my blood boil, and the second he started talking, I saw red.

I don't give him time to react. I slam my body into his, crashing through the doors of the locker room, and I start pummeling his face in.

Bradford is able to get a hit in and then another, and before I know it, he is trying to slam into me, but I'm able to step out of the way at the very last second.

I throw a punch, and I'm able to drop Bradford to the ground. He tries to get up, but I push him back down with my punches.

I hear yelling around me. I feel people trying to pull me off of him, but I don't budge. A few more punches land on the asshole's face before someone is able to rip me away from him.

I'm vaguely aware that Logan and Liam are at my side, pulling me away from the asshole, like I'm the fucking problem.

When we're a few feet away, I see the damage. There's blood, but the asshole has a smirk on his face like all of this is some kind of sick joke, and he wasn't just insulting Eliana with the way he was talking.

"You're going to pay for that, motherfucker," Bradford says, getting up from the ground, not a single one of our team-mates helping him.

If the bastard needed any indication that he didn't belong here, this is it.

"Like I give a fuck. Come at me all you want, but you talk about her or even mention her name ever again, you're fucking dead. I don't give a shit what you have on her. You are fucking dead."

Bradford doesn't like my threat because the fucker decides that he can charge at me and not suffer of the fucking consequences. If he didn't notice none of our teammates took his side before, he definitely notices now, because Logan lets go of my arm and steps in Bradford's line of sight and throws a punch that causes him to fall to the ground instantly.

"Enough!" Anderson's voice roars through the room as Bradford spits out blood onto the locker room floor. Everyone who isn't the fucker on the floor turn to look over at Coach. "We hit the ice in thirty minutes, and you assholes are drawing blood? What the fuck is wrong with you?!"

Nobody answers.

"Crawford, let go of Rodriguez and step away." Liam follows order, begrudgingly, but he follows them. "If your last name isn't Rodriguez, Volkov, or Bradford, go get fucking dressed." He orders the team before turning back to the three who threw punches. "The three of you, medical room right fucking now. You're not playing tonight."

There goes us winning the game against Vegas.

"That's fucking unfair!" Bradford yells as he gets up from the floor. "Rodriguez charged me! I shouldn't be getting benched because of him."

Anderson, who is at a level ten of pissed off, approaches Bradford and stares him down. "You're fucking lucky that sitting out a game is all you're getting right now. If it were up to me, you would be halfway to another team right now." Anderson walks away, and a security guard is standing at the doors, waiting for us to start walking to the medical room.

"I'm sorry, man," I say to Logan as we walk down the hall to get treated. "You should be playing tonight."

Logan shrugs, assessing his hand from the punch he gave Bradford. "Don't sweat it. The fucker deserved it. I've been wanting to do that since it was announced he was coming here. Besides, you would have done the same for me."

"Without a second thought." And it's the truth. Whether it be Liam, Logan, Blake, or any other teammate, no matter the situation, I will have their back. There is no question about it.

We walk into the medical room, and our medical staff start checking us out. Thankfully they are wise to separate Kalen from me and Logan. I don't want to see the mother-fucker, let alone hear him breathe.

Logan gets told he's free to go after a quick scan of his hand. It might bruise, but there is no damage whatsoever.

Me, on the other hand, I do have damage. I sprained my wrist a few weeks ago, but I was able to tape it up and play through the pain. Turns out that punching Kalen just made the problem worse. The sprain went from mild to severe, and now I have to sit out more than one game. And if I get suspended because of this, it will be even longer before I'm able to hit the ice again.

Fucking perfect.

The only highlight to come from all of this is I hear our head athletic trainer say Kalen has a broken nose and has to head to the hospital so that they can set it.

About ten minutes later, Grayson Lane walks into the room looking like he was about to sit down and watch the game from the comfort of the owner's box.

The doctors fill him in on both me and Kalen, and not even two minutes later, Kalen is walked out to be taken to the hospital.

"How's the hand?" Lane asks as one of the trainers wraps it up.

"It's fine," I tell him.

"You know what you did was stupid, right?" he asks, raising an eyebrow at me.

I nod. "I know, and if he antagonizes me again, I will gladly break his nose a second time."

"Why? Why would you risk your career like that?"

He doesn't get it.

This has nothing to do with my career. All of this is solely about Eliana. I could lose my career for all I cared, just as long as Eliana was there at my side, I would be fine.

But I give Grayson the simplest answer.

"Because she's the most important thing in my life."

And she will always be. From now until my very last breath.

CHAPTER TWENTY-FIVE

I POINT my camera at the ice for the millionth time tonight. There is still no sign of number ninety-three. No sign of him during warm-ups, no sign of him during pregame. He's not on the ice or on the bench. We're well into the second period and I have yet to see him.

Last time I checked, he was playing.

Did something happen between when we arrived at the arena and when the game started? He seemed fine. He was actually excited about the game, going on about how they were going to beat Vegas and show everyone that the Knights have what it takes to have a repeat.

He had hand problems a few weeks ago, maybe the problem is back, and my dad decided to sit him out as a precaution.

That's my thought process as I get up to the glass and shoot a few more pictures from next to the penalty box. When my dad yells out a line change, I notice that ninety-three isn't the only one who isn't on the bench or on the ice. Logan and Kalen are missing too.

What the actual hell is going on?

Stepping into one of the tunnels, I check my phone quickly to see if there are any injury reports that were posted before the game started. There's nothing.

There isn't even a post stating who wouldn't be playing tonight.

Hurriedly, I type out a message to Christian asking where the hell he is and pocket my phone. The buzzer goes off, so I quickly step out of the tunnel and get back to work.

Looks like Vegas just scored another one and are now ahead by two.

Great. The Knights needed this game.

I make my way around the ice again, capturing all the pictures that I need. When I'm behind the Knights bench, I try to get someone's attention, but my attempts go unnoticed.

Letting out a frustrated sigh, I decide to go up to the WAG section to try and see if I can find Chloe or Sophia.

Thankfully, they are able to spot me right away, so they wave me over. As I close the distance between us, their smiles disappear.

"Are you okay?" Chloe asks through the roar of the crowd. Emma is on her lap, wearing ear protection headphones and jumping up and down like she is just as excited about the game as everyone else.

"Yeah, you look nervous," Sophia stares from where she sits next to Chloe.

"You can say that," I say, crouching in front of them. "By

any chance, do either of you know where Christian is? Or why he isn't on the ice or bench."

The second they look at each other I know that they do.

They both turn back to me, and Chloe lets out a sigh. "There was a fight in the locker room before warm-ups. It was between Christian and Kalen, that's all Liam told me."

A fight.

And it was a fight about me, no doubt.

Instantly, my whole body goes from worried to terrified.

There are so many questions, but the most important one is, is Christian hurt? That has to be why he's not out here. They must have sent him to the hospital or something.

"I'm sorry," Chloe continues. "Liam didn't say where he went."

I give her a small smile. "No, it's fine. You knew more than I did. I'm going to look for him. Catch up with you ladies later?" I ask, but I'm already halfway down the stands.

I should be working, but right now there are things that are more important. On my way down to head back to the team area, I pass by one of my assistants.

"Hey, I have to take care of something really quick. Do you mind grabbing some pictures by the glass?" I ask, already sliding off my camera.

"Yeah, of course. Go do what you have to do."

"Thank you."

I'm about to run toward the locker room when my phone starts to buzz in my pants pocket.

I take it out right away and see that it's Christian.

Please don't be in the hospital.

Sliding my thumb along the screen, I open the text message and let out a sigh of relief.

CHRISTIAN

Meeting room.

Relief washes over me, and I make my way down to where the Knights watch their game footage.

It only takes me five minutes to get to the room, and when I get there, it's completely dark. I'm about to question if I'm in the right room, when the light turns on.

My eyes adjust a bit, but I'm able to see Christian in one of the chairs at the front of the room.

He turns in the chair he is sitting in, and I see that his face is all bruised up.

If this was any other time, I would make a snide comment regarding the bruises, but this isn't any other time. There is no doubt in my mind that those bruises are there because of me, and knowing that makes me feel sick to my stomach.

"Hey," I say, giving him a small smile and closing the distance between us. "What happened?" I ask, crouching down next to him, and that's when I noticed the wrapped wrist.

If this is how Christian looks, I'm afraid to ask how Logan and Kalen look.

"Bradford was running his mouth," he answers, grabbing my hand and lacing his fingers with mine.

"And him running his mouth turned into having bruises

all over your face?" I ask, lifting my free hand and gliding a finger along the bruise forming just to the side of his nose.

"He was saying things about you, Eliana, and I just flipped." He takes the hand that is touching his face and brings it to his lips. His voice is low as he speaks. "I wasn't going to stand there and let him talk about how good you felt under him or how he was the one that showed you how to give a blow job. More than a few punches were thrown, and now I'm not playing against Vegas as punishment, and I'm out with a sprained wrist for at least a week."

I flinch at what he says. I thought that this was behind us. I thought that since Kalen hadn't so much as said a word to me since the day he arrived here, that he would have moved on.

But I guess I was wrong.

"I'm sorry," I tell him, feeling angry that he's injured and now can't play because of me.

"Why the hell are you apologizing? You weren't the one who punched me in the face."

"I know, but this still all happened because of me. You two fought because of me. Maybe taking this job was a bad idea. If I hadn't, he wouldn't be here right now, and you wouldn't be nursing a sprained wrist." I should have said no. If I knew that me being here was going to cause this many problems, I would have said no.

"Stop." Christian orders and starts pulling at my hand to make me stand up to full height. He pulls me into his lap, until I'm straddling him, and when I'm situated where he wants me, he leans in to give me a chaste kiss on the lips.

"This wasn't a bad idea. You deserve this job and so much more. That fucker would have used those pictures if you were here or not. You could have been across the world, and he still could have blackmailed you so that you would talk to your dad about him. Don't let him make you question your choices."

He's right. I know he is, but I'm still questioning everything.

"It's hard not to. I see your face all bruised up and I can't help but to think that it was my fault."

I let my finger glide along his jaw to just under his eye. He'll heal and in a few days, the bruises will no longer be there, and all of this will be a distant memory. That is if it doesn't happen again. All it will take is Kalen opening up his mouth, and we will be back here.

God, how I wish that he would let himself be traded.

"It wasn't." Another kiss lands against my lips. "My face is like this because of me. Because I want to protect you from all types of harm. It's this way because I want to show people that you have someone in your life who would risk it all for you. To show them that you have someone who loves you and can't stand around as people say things that would disrespect you or bring you down." Another kiss, this time just past the edge of my jaw. "And let's be honest, we both know that I have anger issues. I'm surprised that I haven't snapped at the asshole before tonight."

My heart soars for this man. He has shown me time and time again that he was different. That he wasn't like the player who came before him. Christian Rodriguez is a gorgeous man inside and out, who loves me, puts me first, and will protect me in every way that he can.

I love this man so much.

"Let's go home then. I want to thank you for sticking up for me, and I want to do it in our bed, in our home. Let me thank you," I say, sliding my body closer to his, but not any further.

I have a need for him. A hungry need, but I'm not going to risk us getting caught.

Thirty minutes. That's how long it takes us to get back to our condo after I got work situated and Christian grabbed his things.

The second we step over the front door threshold to the condo, we start to take off each other's clothes and start exploring each other as if we never have before.

As we kiss and let our hands roam, I'm mindful of Christian's wrist and do what I can to not hurt him more.

After letting our tongue dance together, Christian lifts me and walks us to the bedroom, where he places me on the bed and starts falling to his knees before me, but I stop him.

Tonight isn't about me, but about him.

He has always put me first. Has made me feel special and loved and worthy of everything under the sun. And tonight, I want to do the same for him.

I want to show him how much he means to me. I want to show him how much I love him.

Getting up from the bed, I move until I'm in front of Christian, and I am able to push him down on the mattress.

As soon as he is sitting down, I fall to my knees before him and waste no time taking him in my mouth.

The way he moans and pulls at my hair has me sucking harder and sliding him in further. He hits the back of my throat in the most delicious way. I continue to work him until he becomes desperate, and as much as I want him to come in my mouth so that I can swallow everything that he has, he pulls away and lifts me up. This time instead of laying me on the bed, he pulls me onto his lap so that I can straddle him just like I was doing back in the meeting room.

As I lift myself and slide down onto Christian's cock, I look into Christian's eyes and see everything that I didn't know I wanted. I see love and lust all wrapped into one.

This man loves me as much as he lusts for me and makes me feel beautiful in every possible way.

This thing between us started with some music and a break in. With hate and annoyance toward one another that I never thought would dissipate. But it did. We went from being a pain in each other's asses to friends to lovers and then to a place where neither one of us can see a future without the other.

A twist of fate let us meet and brought us to this very moment.

Christian's hands slide to my ass, and he grabs me as he pounds into me in the most delicious way. Our moans fill the room, and every inch of our bodies are covered in sweat.

It isn't long before we move into a different position, and Christian is hovering over me, telling me how much he loves me. How perfect I am. How I was made for just him.

I tell him the same.

We kiss as my legs start to shake, and when the man above me slides in me one more time, I lose it and explode.

An orgasm rips through me, and within seconds, Christian is following suit.

His groans are one of my favorite sounds, right next to his laugh.

After we clean up, we climb back into bed, and as we lay there, I can't help but to think about a few things.

Growing up, my life centered around hockey. Everything that there was to know about the sport, I learned. It was my favorite thing in the world until it wasn't. I've been hurt by the sport and the people in it. I thought it was something that I was going to hate for a long time, and then I stepped into Christian's house, and everything changed.

I fell in love with a hockey player, something that I vowed that I would never do ever again, but it became impossible.

Christian Rodriguez made it impossible for me not to fall for him.

He is everything.

And if I could go back to that day at the beach, I would do everything the same. I would break in, turn down the music and continue to get under this man's skin until it became unbearable for the both of us.

There is nothing that I would change.

"Hey," I say as my head lays against his chest.

"Hmm," he hums, almost asleep.

"Thank you for putting me first. Thank you for being

there and showing me that you care. Thank you for loving me."

Christian's eyes pop open, and he shifts slightly to look down at me. "You don't have to thank me for any of that."

"I know, but I wanted to. You gave me something that I always wanted. Something I needed, and I can't thank you enough for it."

He looks down at me and gives me a smile. "You're welcome, but I want you to know one thing."

"What?"

"For me, you will always be the most important thing in my life. No sport will ever come before you. You have my word."

"Promise?"

"I promise, hermosa. From now until my last breath."

EPILOGUE
CHRISTIAN

Two Months Later

BYE-WEEK.

The one week during the hockey season that I usually don't look forward to.

Almost every single player and coach that I know is counting down the days until we have more than a three-day break. Me on the other hand, for the past seven years, I've been counting down the days until the week ends and I'm back on the ice where I have a sense of belonging.

Every year has been the exact same thing. Every year except this year.

This year, I'm not looking forward to the week being over so that I can head to the rink on Monday morning. I'm not looking forward to leaving my place in California to hop on a plane and head to Chicago. This year, I want to make time stop just so that I can enjoy a few more days of this bye-week with Eliana with no damn interruptions and not think about anything but her.

But of course, shit doesn't work that way.

The week started five days ago and now in a little less than two days, we have to head back to Chicago. We'll still be in our bubble when we're home, but I have to share her with everyone else for the rest of the day.

"Is there a reason why you look like someone ran over your puppy?" Eliana asks as she comes out of the bedroom and into the living room where I'm currently sitting on the couch, trying to watch the NHL All-Star pregame coverage.

I wasn't chosen as an all-star this year, which I'm completely fine with. Gives me more time with my girl. Liam, on the other hand, did and now the poor bastard is freezing his ass off in Minnesota.

"Because I don't want to go back to Chicago," I grumble as I watch the team mascots try to play dodgeball.

Not going to lie, our Knight is the best-looking dude out of all of them. He's definitely better than the Tampa Bay one, that's for sure.

"You surprise me. I thought you would be chomping at the bit to head back home. You don't do well with days off, unless it's summer," she says, coming into view and the second I see what she is wearing, I forget about what the hell I was watching on TV.

Eliana is in one of those string bikinis that I fucking love. They leave absolutely nothing to the imagination and my mouth waters just by the sight of her. It's like every single one of her curves is begging me to grab her and have my way with her.

"Where are you going?" I ask, turning off the TV and sitting up on the couch, all my senses on high alert.

"Down to the sand," she says, picking up one of her cameras from where it sits on the coffee table, checking to see if it's charged.

We've been here five days and there is camera equipment everywhere. You would think this was a photography studio or something. That and the dishes that have been in the sink since last night.

"You're going to go down to the sand like that?" I ask, standing up from the couch, my voice going up a little bit.

I'm all for wearing that bikini. She can wear it every single damn day for the rest of our lives, but only for me. I don't need some dickwad staring at my woman and imagining the shit that he could do to her. That's my job.

Eliana rolls her eyes at me. "I wear this all the time."

She brings up the camera and snaps a picture of me. I'm not amused.

"Yeah, but usually you wear something that covers you a little bit more."

The way she purses her lips has my cock twitching. "Is there something wrong with what I'm wearing? I've never heard you complain before."

"Hermosa, this isn't me complaining," I tell her as I close the distance between us. "This is me, simply not wanting some asshat that is passing by to look at my woman and think things about her that should only be running through my head. So, if you're going to go down, put some clothes on."

My hands land on her shoulders and I slide them down her body until they rest against her hips and I'm bringing her closer to me.

"So now you're telling me what to do?" The way she crosses her arms across her chest and pops out her hips and me going to half chub.

"I am."

She rolls her eyes and stands up on her tiptoes to whisper in my ear. "I only take orders from you when they are of the sexual nature."

Fuck. This woman and her mouth.

Two can play this game.

"Is that so?" I ask, giving her a smirk, bringing her body closer to mine. She gives me a nod. "Then, how do you feel about this order? Get on the couch and lean your chest against the back cushions."

"And if I don't?" her smirk matches mine.

I let my hands slide further down her body, until they are on her ass and I'm palming her.

"Then you can get on your knees. Your choice. You come first or I do."

"Is this a punishment?"

"It is. You want to know why?" She nods, biting down on her lip as I lean down to whisper in her ear. "Because this bikini is for me and me only. This body is solely for me to fantasize about, solely for me to enjoy. I find anyone thinking about seeing you on your knees or having your ass in their hands, they're going to get a stick up their ass and a puck to the face."

She looks up at me for a long minute, challenging me as she narrows her eyes at me, all the while her body rubs against mine, telling me that she's second from giving in to me and my orders.

One of her hands lands on my bare chest and slides up and then back down and tweaks my nipple a little. "I think I will go with option number one."

"Good choice. Though, you're not escaping option two."

"You won't hear me complain," she says, giving my nipple one last tweak before leaning up to place a chaste kiss against my lips and sauntering over to the couch. The way her hips sway back and forth has my lower body screaming to be wrapped around her.

I watch her as she gets on the couch and gets in the position I told her to. Her tits press against the top of the couch cushions, and she arches her body back enough for her ass to stick out and give the most amazing view. I don't waste any time walking behind her.

"¿Haci, mi amor?" she asks, looks back at me, fluttering her eyelashes.

I can't help but lick my lips. My girl is the sexiest woman I have ever seen, and when she purrs out her words, even more.

"Fuck. Yes." I stand behind her, my hands landing back on her ass and caressing her smooth skin. "Let me show you what seeing you in this bikini does to me."

"I already know what it does to you." She wiggles her ass

against my hand, leaning back more until she is almost resting against my stomach.

"Then let me show you again. I don't want you to forget." I untie her bikini bottoms and let the piece covering her ass, fall back.

Eliana opens her legs just a bit, and the fabric that was covering her pussy, falls to the couch, leaving her bare from the waist up.

I slide a finger along her pussy and find her already wet simply by the anticipation of what is about to come.

"So wet already. I knew arguing with me got you all needy for me. Or were you thinking about my mouth on this pretty pussy? Or were you looking forward to getting on your knees and swallowing my cock?"

She lets out a sound that is almost a moan. "All of it."

"Hmm," I say as I lean forward and place my mouth on her pussy as I spread her open for me.

I don't waste any time fucking her with my tongue. I dive right in as if I were a starved man.

This is what I want for the rest of my life.

Me and her, losing our minds and bodies in each other until we both go crazy. This past week has been just that. There was no outside noise. There was no passing Bradford in the hallway, because even though I broke the asshole's nose, he still hasn't waived his spot on the team. There was no tiptoe around the arena, making sure that we don't get caught kissing or looking at each other for too long. There were no awkward moments with her dad. There was nothing, but the two of us. And that's all I fucking wanted. What I needed.

I have my girl and the Knights are close to possibly going to the playoffs again for a repeat. That is all I need. and I'm going to do my part to have our team stay at the top, but it doesn't matter as much as it did last year.

Last year I was hungry for the sport. I was hungry for the cup and was hungry to win. This year, that hunger is still there, I'm still going to try everything that I can to get my team to the top and to have a repeat year but now I'm hungry for something else.

Eliana.

I'm hungry for her and all the love that has and will give me.

I'm hungry for every single thing that she gives me and that includes every orgasm and every single moan.

"Come to my tongue, baby. Give me everything that you have," I say against her, sliding a finger into her and doing everything that I can to bring her closer to a release.

"I can't," she pants, lifting her upper body from the back of the couch.

"You can and you will." I order, sucking on her clit and sliding yet another finger in her, feeling her tighten around me.

"Christian, please," she begs, and I can't hold back anymore. My cock is begging for relief right along with her, and the only way I can get that is if I feel her wrapped around me all hot and tight.

I give her one last good lick, savoring her taste, before pulling away and out of her, to give us what we both want.

Standing up on the couch, I position myself right at her entrance and slide into her. Her moans sound in my ears and it's one of the sweetest sounds that I have heard.

I continue to thrust into her, and she continues to meet every single one of my movements, making all of this even more fucking amazing.

We continue our little dance until we are both breathless, she's screaming out my name and groaning our hers.

The second I release everything that I have into her, I make a mental note for myself.

Buy her all the damn bikinis she wants and tell she can't wear them.

The after-sex cloud that me and Eliana are in became too much. So instead of heading to the bedroom for round two or at the very least for a nap, we stayed in the living room watching some cop show she found while she was scrolling through social media.

Now, we are about three episodes in and have no plans to move.

Fuck, this feels good. If this is what we did for the rest of our lives, I would be a happy man.

I am trying to pay attention to the cops on TV chasing a

bad guy when my phone starts to ring. Without thinking, I shift Eliana's legs from where they rest on my lap and grab the phone from where it rests on the coffee table. I have every single intention to ignore whoever is on the other side, but I'm apparently fucking my girlfriend put me in too much of a good mood that I decide to answer.

"Hello?" I say into the phone.

"Please tell me you're in California." A male voice sounds through from the line. I look at the number, but it's not one that is saved on my phone. I recognize the voice and for a second I think it's my brother but then I realize it's Blake.

Why isn't he calling me from his phone?

"I am. Why? What's up, Jacobi?" I ask, debating if I want to be a good friend right now, or to just hang up on him. He probably has some weird ass request.

"Can you come to San Francisco, please? I need a favor."

Right on the money with the weird request.

"Aren't you supposed to be in Montana right now?" I'm pretty sure that I remember him saying that since his brother's team didn't make the Super Bowl this year, they were both going to spend some time with their mom and stepdad at home this week. Did I hear him wrong?

"Yes." His tone is clipped, telling me that I did in fact hear him correctly.

"Then why do you need a favor in San Francisco?"

"Because something came up with Sophia and now, I need you to come bail me out of jail."

"What the fuck are you doing in jail, Jacobi?!" I yell out.

"What?!" Eliana exclaims from next to me. She put on one of my shirts a bit ago, but her tits still bounce at the motion. I turn to look at her and see that she is sitting up and pulling out her phone. No doubt to text Sophia.

I get up from the couch and head to the bedroom to pull on some clothes. Such a fucking shit show.

"I got in a fight with Sophia's sad fucking excuse for a boyfriend and he called the cops. Can you bail me out or not?" He asks, sounding frustrated and scared at the same time. I'm probably his last resort right before Coach, since his brother is probably still in Montana and Sophia might be with her boyfriend given the circumstances.

Fuck.

A few weeks after the season started, Blake told us that Sophia started dating some guy. Both Liam and I noticed right away that Blake didn't like the guy whatsoever. But not liking the dude doesn't land you in jail. If Blake is behind bars, that means that things got nasty, and the cops had no other choice but to arrest him. Or it could be that the guy just hates Jacobi and after a small tap to the face, he called the cops and cried assault.

I want to put all my money on the second one. I want to believe that the guy that has gotten into one fight in all of his hockey career, didn't beat someone face in and isn't in jail for something more than a small punch to the face.

But it involves Sophia, and when it comes to her, Blake can go to hell and back. If she was in trouble, he would do everything and anything to keep her out of harm's way.

I quickly get dressed and head back to the living room

where I find Eliana already dressed and holding up my keys. How did she find clothes before I did?

I have no idea, but fuck, I love her.

"Yeah, give me an hour. I'll be right there," I say to my friend and teammate.

"I'll be here," he says, like he has so much shit on his shoulders "Thank you, Christian. I'll owe you one."

"Yeah, you will. Okay, we're heading out." I hang up the call and both me and Eliana walk out of the house. "What did Sophia say?" I ask as we get into the car.

Eliana shakes her head. "She didn't answer," she says before taking a pause. "This is bad, right? Like bad, bad?"

So many scenarios pop into my head, each one worse than the one before it.

"Fuck. I hope not." I start that car and back out of the driveway. "Let's go bail out, Jacobi and hope that he didn't ruin his relationship with Sophia.

THE END
WANT TO READ WHAT LED TO BLAKE LANDING IN JAIL AND WHY SOPHIA WASN'T HIS FIRST CALL?? FIND OUT IN HITTING THE GOAL LINE!

WANT MORE OF ELIANA AND CHRISTIAN CHECK OUT THE EXTENDED EPILOGUE!

EXTENDED EPILOGUE
TWO YEARS LATER

Two years later

I walk up to the water and let the coldness of the Pacific Ocean meet the skin of my feet like it has done a million times before.

The coldness makes me shiver but I don't care. I'm on my favorite beach in the whole world, a few feet away from the house that changed my whole life.

Two years ago today, I had finished a photo session with the Quakes and drove down the coast a bit until I found a beach that wasn't littered with people. I was relaxing until I wasn't and then everything changed.

I walked into a stranger's house, he threatened to throw me in the ocean, a few other things happened and then he became the love of my life.

In the two years since we first met, a lot of things have changed but a lot of things have stayed the same.

Christian still plays for the Dark Knights, he just signed a contract extension for another four years, and I'm still the team's head photographer, something I plan to do until I no longer can.

There have been disagreements, and plenty of make ups. There have been nights on the couch and days where we don't say a single word to each other, but we always are able to push through it. There has even been a pregnancy scare or two, where one of us was excited and the other was terrified. But everything that we have been through are going to continue to go through, just continues to make us all that much stronger. We may still annoy each other and throw insults at the other without holding back, but that's who we are, and it just makes us love the other person more.

And our love for each other will continue to grow as long as we don't let the little things get in the way.

Today, we are having one of those little things.

The season for the Knights ended a few weeks ago after they lost in the Stanley Cup finals against North Carolina. It hurt, I'm not going to lie, especially after seeing all the work they put in this season and last. But I just know that come the new season, they will be better than ever.

Because there wasn't any reason to stick around Chicago, since there weren't any celebrations that needed to be had, Christian and I had planned to come straight to California, to the beach house for a few weeks to destress. Well, I had planned. Apparently, my boyfriend had other plans.

Plans that I wasn't aware of until I was looking for flight. When I asked him if would prefer a morning flight instead of one later in the day for a specific day, he told me he had a guys' trip planned for the same day to New York.

I wasn't mad about the trip. He can go on any trip that he wants. With whoever he wants.

It was the fact that he didn't tell me that bothered me, and it bothered me even more when he told me to come to California without him and that he would join me a few days later.

Well, it's a few days later, and the grumpy asshole is still not here. Doesn't he know that I had plans from the first second we got here?

Last summer, we had decided to spend the off season traveling Latin America, so we didn't spend a whole lot of time at the beach house. This year, because we both wanted to decompress, we were going to spend all of the off season here. We were going to do everything that we did our first summer here and more and the asshole had to go and ruin it.

If he would have told me sooner, I would have pushed back coming here, but no, he had to tell me after I had put in my credit card information on a nonrefundable ticket.

When he gets here, if he ever does, I'm going to throw his ass in the ocean.

You can't even move the man.

So? I'm supposed to be moaning out his name right about now as we watched the waves crash into the sand. Instead, he's still in New York with his friends.

Assholes. All of them are absolute assholes.

I'm being salty for no reason. If Christian said he was

going to come in a few days, then he will. Maybe they decided to extend their trip or something.

Who knows, the man didn't tell me anything about this trip.

Maybe I should call Chloe or Sophia to see if they knew about this boy trip or if I was the only one left in the dark.

Just let it go. It's not a big deal.

My mind is right.

I take a calming breath and let myself feel the water on my feet and get lost in the way the sand feels as it pulls away. I look out onto the water and see a seal close to the shore but still far away for it not to be disturbed by any humans.

I raise up the camera that is currently secured around my neck and take a few pictures of the beautiful creature swimming around. I take pictures until the seal disappeared under the water and then decided that it would be a good idea to set up the camera on the lifeguard shack to get some nice stills.

I'm about to turn around when someone wraps their arms around my waist.

For a second, I contemplate screaming and hoping that one of the houses up on the cliff has someone in there that will hear me scream and come to my rescue, but then I smell it, his cologne, and I relax.

"I thought that you were going to meet me here in a few days," I say, melting into his hold but still have a bite to my tone.

I'm definitely salty about him being late.

Christian buries his face in my neck and slides his arms

around my waist pulling my body closer to his, as if we weren't nearly attached already.

"I'm sorry, hermosa," he says, placing kisses all along my exposed neck.

"Are you going to tell me why this guys' trip was so important?" I ask, sliding a hand over his and sliding it up my body.

I missed him and I'm not ashamed to get what I've been needing since we've been apart.

"I had to pick something up," he says, biting down on my earlobe.

A huff leaves my mouth. "You told me to come to California by myself because you had to pick something up?"

Look, I'm all for traveling on my own. I'm a strong, independent woman that doesn't need a man at her side at all times. Hell, I went to Paris by myself during the NHL bye-week this year for a clothing brand photoshoot. But there are times I want my man at my side, and this was one of those times.

Especially a day like today, where it's legit one of our anniversaries.

He hums against my neck. "I'll make it up to you, I swear."

"How? Because I'm ready to throw your ass in the ocean."

"You're not going to want to do that."

"Oh yeah? And why is that? Don't think that I could fling around your huge ass body? Because I'm strong. You being a hockey player doesn't scare me."

Christian laughs like he doesn't think I can take him. I can.

"That's not why." He pulls away from me, and instantly I want to pull him back and feel his body against mine.

I let out a sigh and start turning to face him, feeling annoyed. "Give me one good reason why I can't throw you in–"

My words stop when I turn around and see Christian down on one knee with a black velvet box in his hand.

A gasp escapes my lips and tears start to form in my eyes.

"Because if you throw me in the ocean, I might lose this." He opens the ring box and in between the black cushion sits a ring with a square yellow diamond in the middle. From what I can see it sits on a gold band, and I don't have to see it out of the box to know that it's perfect.

I'm absolutely speechless.

I mean, we've talked about the possibility of getting married, of having kids and being together until we are both old, but I didn't think he would propose anytime soon.

"Remember that away game in New York around Christmas?" he asks, his voice having a shake to it.

I nod, not being able to find my voice.

"Remember that morning before the game, me and you took a walk and passed by a Tiffany's, and you stopped to look at the window display they had? And you told me that when I propose to you, no if, but when I do it, I better do it with a yellow diamond?

Tears fall down my cheeks.

It was a throwaway comment. I didn't actually think that he would listen.

"I was going to get you that ring. I even went into the store in Chicago, and was going to buy it, but then I remembered who the ring was for. I remembered that the woman that was going to wear the ring didn't deserve a ring that someone else walking the street was also going to have. She needed a ring that was just as much of a spitfire than she was. She needed a ring that was hers and hers alone, that way she knows just how much she means to me. She needed a ring that told her how much I loved her every time she looked down at it. So, I left the store and went to find a place that would make a ring that was worthy to be on your finger. Because that's what you deserve, Eliana. You deserve the whole fucking world, and if you let me, I want to give it to you. So that's why I told you to come here without me. Because I needed to pick up the ring."

My voice still hasn't been able to come out, so I just stand there like a dum-dum and watch him as he takes the ring out of the box and reaches out for my hand.

There is no hesitation, my hand slides into his.

This is really happening.

Oh my god!

"Eliana, you are the most important thing in my life. Above hockey, above this beach house, above any contract that I can sign, you are the most important fucking thing in my life. Through all the banter. Through all the fights, through it all, you are it for me and I will take everything that you throw my way. I love you. I love you so damn much, even if you want to throw me in the ocean. So, with everything that I have, I want to ask you this. Will you marry me, Eliana? Marry me, hermosa because I need you more than you can ever know."

I'm nodding before he can even finish.

I fall to my knees and wrap my arms around his neck and place kisses on his mouth repeatedly as I answer his question.

"Yes. Yes. Yes. Yes. Yes!"

Christian laughs and pulls away from me just enough to slide the gorgeous ring on my finger and goes back to kissing me.

Our kisses are no longer little pecks of excitement, they are full of hunger and desire and so much love.

"I love you so much," I say to him.

And I do. I love him in ways that I cannot comprehend.

"I love you too, hermosa. You're mine forever now. You won't be able to get rid of me."

"Never."

Two years ago, I would have laughed in someone's face if they had told me that I would get my happily ever after with a hockey player. But now, I can't picture my life without him. I can't picture ever going to a beach and not having him at my side.

This man has shown me time and time again that I mean the world to him, and I can only hope that as we grow old together, I can do the same for him.

Christian Rodriguez is the man that made me love

hockey again and, in the process, made me love him with everything that I have.

He has shown me so much and I'm never going to let him go.

Not even if he throws me in the ocean.

I'll just throw him right back and we will freeze together.

THE END.

Read Blake and Sophia's story!

Grab Hitting The Goal Line today and start reading!
Read it today!

Are you wondering if Logan Volkov is getting his own book?
He is!
But before we get to Logan, we have to step into the darkness
a bit.
And why not start that by stepping into the world of the Lane
Family?
Book 1 of the Lane Family is coming Fall 2024! I hope you
are ready!
Pre-order now!

PLAYLIST

Players - Con Leroy
Here With Me - d4vd
Lipstick Lover - Janelle Monáe
Baby - Eslabon Armado
Alone -Jozzy
bad idea! - girl in red
Falling - Trevor Daniel
Noche De Sexo - Wins & Yandel, Romeo Santos
If I Ruled the World - Nas, Ms. Lauryn Hill
Lost - Frank Ocean
Angel Baby - Troye Sivan
I wanna Be Yours - Sofia Karlberg
Call Out My Name - The Weeknd
Falling for U - Peachy!, mxmtoon
I don't rly like u - Role Model
Baby I'm Yours - Arctic Monkey

Love - Keyshia Cole
Open Arms - SZA, Travis Scott
K-Pop - Travis Scott, Bad Bunny
All of the Girls You Loved Before - Taylor Swift

Powerful Deception

Fake Love

Salutis Meae

ABOUT THE AUTHOR

Jocelyne Soto is an independent author living in California. She loves reading romance and discovering new authors. She comes from a big Mexican family, and with it comes a love for all things family and food.

Jocelyne has a love for her mom's coffee and writing. In her free time, you can find her reading a romance novel on her kindle while writing heartwarming and chaotic romance stories in between. From sport romance to dark romance, there is no limit as to the type of stories that will come to Jocelyne's mind.

Check out her website for ways to connect with Jocelyne!
www.jocelynesoto.com

BB bookbub.com/authors/jocelyne-soto

g goodreads.com/jocelynesotobooks

O instagram.com/authorjocelynesoto

d tiktok.com/@authorjocelynesoto

f facebook.com/authorjocelynesoto

X x.com/authorjocelynes

P pinterest.com/authorjocelynesoto

Join my ever-growing Facebook Group. You get first looks, sneak peeks and giveaways!

NEWSLETTER

Sign up for my Newsletter!
You will get notified when there are new
releases to look out for, giveaways and more!